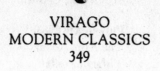

VIRAGO
MODERN CLASSICS
349

Kate O'Brien

Born in Limerick in 1897, Kate O'Brien lost her mother when she was only five, and was given a boarding education in a convent before studying at University College, Dublin. She worked as a journalist in London and Manchester, and for a year as a governess in Spain, whose landscape and people were to exert a profound influence on her thinking and writing. Her marriage, at twenty-six, to a Dutch journalist soon ended and she spent the rest of her life alone. Kate O'Brien's original success was as a playwright but the publication of *Without My Cloak* (1931) won her rapid acclaim as a novelist. This was followed by eight further novels, two of which, *Mary Lavelle* (1936) and *The Land of Spices* (1942) were condemned for their 'immorality' by the Irish Censorship Board. Kate O'Brien dramatised three of her novels, and *That Lady* (1946) was made into a film. Noted also for her travel books, a memoir and a study of St Teresa of Avila, Kate O'Brien was honoured by the Irish and British literary establishments. She died in 1974.

Novels by Kate O'Brien

Without My Cloak
The Ante-Room
Mary Lavelle
Pray for the Wanderer
The Land of Spices
The Last of Summer
That Lady
The Flower of May
As Music and Splendour

THE LAST
OF SUMMER

Kate O'Brien

With an Introduction by
Eavan Boland

A *Virago* Book

First published by Virago Press Limited 1990
Reprinted 1994, 1999

A CIP catalogue record for this book
is available from the British Library

ISBN 1 85381 165 3

Printed and bound in Great Britain by
Clays Ltd, St Ives plc

Virago
A Division of
Little, Brown and Company (UK)
Brettenham House
Lancaster Place
London WC2E 7EN

INTRODUCTION

I

We have to imagine the moment. The road curves away in iron heat; the air of the little town smells of roses and porter; a river is loud and seems familiar. A young woman is resting against a wall. She is looking into her handbag mirror. Defiantly, and with a sense of incongruity, she splashes her mouth with lipstick and continues her journey. The wall she leant on is covered with moss and is low at first, and then higher until it comes to an entrance gate. And then the drive is full of crackling undergrowth and bamboo and rhododendron, all unkempt. When the curve is complete and the house appears — its name is Waterpark — it is low and cream-washed and the story is about to begin.

Moments have something in common with musical statements. They can move fast or slow down; but the speed and delay are often different versions of the same melody. The Irish countryside of these opening pages appears ordinary and quiet. But as Angèle Kernahan approaches the house at the end of the drive, she brings — with her lipsticked mouth, her questing sensibility — the fragrance and danger of another cadence. She will evoke for the people who call this their home, who don't yet know of her existence, the headlong, brakeless speed of the European moment. This, after all, is the late summer of 1939. She will remind them, for good and ill, that the past is inescapable. She will bring into their consciousness the names of threatened cities and wasted loves. She will change everything before she leaves.

The Last of Summer is a book which mixes fictive theatre with argumentative magic. The dialogue can be cutting and funny; the description is a marvel of thrift. Again and again, on page after page, we will find ourselves in rooms which have a claustrophobic realness. Here, for example, is the north-facing dining-room in Waterpark. Surely, we say to ourselves, we recognize these crows making a racket outside the window; surely we miss the sound of the river here. Now we are in the snug in the hotel, all green baize and Victorian mahogany and caged canaries.

None of this should blind us to a central fact: in this book Kate O'Brien has designs on us. For all her economy of narrative and force of characterization she will, from time to time, invoke her privileges as an interventionist author; and, far from seeming intrusive, this will come to be one of the rewards and pleasures of the story. Now and again she will touch us on the shoulder, anxious that we should notice the fragile co-existence of these two moments. For a few days her characters will be together in this Irish country house. They will scheme and remember; they will quarrel and fall in love. Nothing else will change. The river will be as loud, the ilexes as solid. The geraniums on the front steps will be ready to take in before the first frost. The yew tree on the drive will still look blue in moonlight. Only the people, with their memories and secrets, are changed; only they play out a subtle dialogue between fatalism and free choice. "Woe to those", writes the Polish poet Czeslaw Milosz, "who suddenly discover historical time unprepared, as an illiterate would discover chemistry."

II

There is another moment, of course: the one outside the book — the one, that is, in which it is written and which it serves to disrupt and formalize. We need to ponder this one too if we are to understand certain things. Which is not to say that we need to understand these things in order to enjoy the novel; not at all. The current is swift and the enchantment pulls us in. But there are shadows and whispers here, echoes and pleadings. It will do no harm at all to trace them back into Kate O'Brien's life; to come on their outline in her development as a novelist.

In 1941 Kate O'Brien was forty-four. The thirties had been a good decade for her, settled and successful. Not so the twenties. They were as stressful and turbulent as the ten years after them were composed. In 1924, for a brief time, she was a wife. She married Gustav Renier — later well known for his polemical book *The English, Are They Human?* — in Hampstead Town Hall. For exactly eleven months she lived with him in two rooms in Belsize Avenue, Hampstead. Then the marriage broke apart. Contemporaries differ in their accounts. There are suggestions that she married Renier, who was then a thirty-year-old freelance journalist, after a good deal of importuning on his part. More likely, the villains of the piece are neither husband nor wife but those conventions of an age which a gifted, free-spirited woman must have found constraining.

Angèle Kernahan, the heroine of *The Last of Summer*, is twenty-five when she walks up the drive of Waterpark house; a year or so younger than her author when she took those vows in Hampstead Town Hall. There may well be shadows here; we may well be catching a glimpse of that early fracture between imaginative vocation and the shape of conformity. Certainly, *The Last of Summer* is more a tragedy of conscience than a comedy of manners. In the fifth chapter Angèle stands at the edge of the Moher cliffs with Martin, her cousin. Beneath them are rock and water and one black canoe; beside them the perilous survival of windflowers and orchids. Suddenly their oblique, parrying conversation takes a serious turn as Martin challenges her:

"Angèle, are you going to play old hell with me?"

"Oh no. I like you terribly, Martin. There's no 'old hell' — we're relations, after all. First cousins."

"I don't think we need pay much attention to that. If they

wanted the forbidden degrees observed they should have announced them in time! Not that this is a proposal of marriage, by God!"

"I don't want a proposal of marriage. I'd loathe to be married."

"But you like family life."

"Yes. I think it's a perfect thing. But it's not for me. I'm quite unsuitable."

This is one echo; and there are others. When we read about Angèle Kernahan arriving at Waterpark, bringing the surprise and danger of the unknown, I think we are entitled to see another inference there. This time the year is 1915 and the place is University College Dublin, where Kate O'Brien is a student. Like other first-year arts students, she attends Roger Chauvire's lectures on French literature. In 1962, in an essay called "UCD as I Forget It", she recalled that experience: "He took literature into cold daylight; he cut it out clearly as an exact and exacting skill. Listening to Chauvire upon French writing in the 17th and 18th century, I grew up." The exact daylight, the cold skill, continued to excite Kate O'Brien. But so also did human passion, inside and outside literature. The dichotomy between them is a constant motif in her work. *The Last of Summer* elaborates it.

The world Angèle Kernahan represents is a far cry from the settled customs of Waterpark. Her father may have belonged there but her mother, now dead, was an actress with the Comédie Française. On the distaff side, therefore, Angèle is heir to a complex of disciplined self-expression and deep vocation. These are possessions her creator values highly, and their cost and survival are powerful themes in this book.

Love and exile; choice and vocation. They are constant themes, consistent oppositions. By the time this book is finished Kate O'Brien has come a far way down the road of her own calling. This, after all, is her sixth novel. She has left behind the rooms in Belsize Avenue and the flat in Bloomsbury where she wrote her first novel, *Without My Cloak*. She no longer makes such frequent visits to Ireland and the big house in Strandhill, the property of her brother-in-law, where she wrote *The Ante-Room*. She has transmuted her experiences as a governess in Bilbao, where she minded her two charges, José and Hélène, into *Mary Lavelle*. She has purged her disappointment with de Valera's Ireland in *Pray For the Wanderer*. Her fifth novel, *The Land of Spices*, has been banned in her own country. Now, in a new flat in London, in 33 James Street, she takes on small wartime assignments for the Ministry of Information. And here, in *The Last of Summer*, she attempts once again to heal the past by examining flawed human love in a rigorous light.

III

The rigours are not in the plot. The sequence of narrative is simple and rapid, with an almost classical unity. Angèle Kernahan comes to Waterpark. She is unannounced and, in some quarters, unwelcome. More than a quarter century ago her father had left this house, gone to France and married a French actress. Now Angèle enters the house of her aunt-by-marriage, Hannah Kernahan, a resourceful widow who rules Waterpark with the help of her eldest son, Tom. This is the world Angèle Kernahan finds; this is the one she disrupts.

The character of Hannah Kernahan is one of the strengths of the book — indeed, one of the strongest portraits in all of Kate O'Brien's work. This is a characterization made up of insight and irony. Hannah is possessive and adroit. Much of the glitter of the novel comes from changing perspectives on her, as she is seen through the eyes of different characters. To her son Tom she is almost a saint; to her friend Dotey, a martyr. When Dr. O'Byrne comes to see her, to ask her help in arranging the union of his daughter and her son, his private musings during their conversation throw a harsh and important light on Hannah's manoeuvrings:

> Dr. O'Byrne almost nodded his head as he listened to this delicate little speech — so exactly did it tell him what he had

already told himself very often about this woman. She's certainly a great fly in the ointment, he reflected now with anxiety. I could hardly choose a worse mother-in-law for my girl. And she's only about fifty, so far as I recall, and she hasn't a thing wrong with her. Superb organic health. Nothing to stop her hanging on in vigour into the nineties. Upon my word, I think Norrie will need the heart of a lion to face it . . . But it's no joke — setting herself up for life against as selfish a case of mother-love as has ever come to my knowledge, so help me!

The true rigour of this book, and the unswerving moral intelligence of its writer, can best be seen in this characterization of Hannah, and in the clash between her and Angèle. The first is scrupulous and surprised by need; the second is a veteran of pride and its corruptions. Hannah knows how to hold and keep; she knows how to fend off and crush. In her dramatization of this contest between two women and two kinds of passion, Kate O'Brien shows her gift for the cold daylight and exact skill she had admired years before in Chauvire's lectures. Now she deploys those skills to achieve what the book sets out to be: an anatomy of love.

IV

A novel is closed between covers; a painting is confined within its frame. They are both, in one sense, artificial borders. All artists are at work on a continuous statement; the poem, the painting, the novel constitute just a fragment of it. In order to judge the statement we must look at the part. In order to understand the part we have to consider the whole statement.

Kate O'Brien is that kind of artist. There is a consistent — even a visionary — quality about her most assured work. It would be misleading to call *The Last of Summer* her best book, but it comes in the best phase of her work. It is marked by the same themes, the same struggles to heal and resolve, which are so luminous in *The Ante-Room, The Land of Spices* and *Mary Lavelle*. In its preoccupation with the fractures between sense and spirit *The Last of Summer* has more in common with these — her finest novels — than with the plangent and polemical *Pray for the Wanderer* or the Galsworthyian *Without My Cloak*.

In this book she returns to the class which fascinated her. The Kernahans are Catholic Irish and there is more than an echo, in her descriptions of the dash and risk and obstinacy of Ned Kernahan, of her own past. Her grandfather — also called Tom — had brought his family and the debris of an eviction into Limerick on an ass cart. He bought a horse, sold it at a profit, bought another. Soon Tom O'Brien was an acknowledged authority on horseflesh and in Ireland at that time it was an excellent thing to be. Horses were everything. The whole of a gentry class rode to hounds, harnessed their thoroughbreds and paid handsomely to have a good piece of horseflesh which would make them the envy of their neighbours. By the time Tom O'Brien died he was building a villa to go with his stud farm.

Kate O'Brien's father took on the business. By her own account he was an expensive and cheerful man: "He dressed well in tweed cutaways," she tells us in the autobiographical fragment *Presentation Parlour*, "his hands were freckled, expensive and well cared for; everything about him was of good taste and quality from cigar to boot to handkerchief."

But there are shadows here. This was a class which made a world at a price: a world of increasing wealth and uneasy conscience, where the women wore stays and rouged their cheeks, had their clothes made by Dublin dressmakers and tried to forget the hauntings of the past. This was Catholic Ireland; it was never nationalist Ireland. Steadily, obstinately, it had shut out the cacophony of the times: the Land War, the evictions, the disgrace of Parnell. As the nineteenth century wore on and the twentieth began, this prosperous class loaded its tables with food, its sideboards with silver, and stopped its ears to rumours of rebellion and self-determination. We get a glimpse of their insularity in the way Roseholm — the house of the Mulqueens in *The Ante-Room* — strikes the new visitor,

Nurse Canning:

> This big and quiet house, so excellently run, this spacious dining-room, full of mahogany, its roaring fire, its two long windows facing a smooth green garden, its heavy silver tea-service and silver dishes filled with food which no one ate, all this was of fascinating interest . . .

There are similarities between Roseholm and Waterpark. Both are actual places with a symbolic inference. The novelist Benedict Kiely has aptly said of the first:

> The Ante-Room of the title is not a place where the bourgeoisie suffer before they become poets, but the dread hall of silence and pain where body and soul kiss for the last time before the final parting in death: and death and departure, suffering and sin, exile, love satisfied and yet never satisfied, have been predominant themes in Kate O'Brien's novels.

'We can scarcely hate anyone we know,' says Hazlitt. And Kate O'Brien is determined we shall know these people. To do so we have to follow her as she exposes their self-deceits, their dreams, the corruption of their loves. *The Last of Summer* opens quietly. The hot road, the long drive; a diffident girl and an unknowing family. This could be a conventional story: a novel of passion and surprise such as the post-Victorian era is all too rich in. But after a while we see the glint of the scalpel. There is a rottenness at the centre of this quiet possession. Hannah Kernahan is emblematic of it, and her relation to her son Tom is all wrong. We know that. But we should also know that the emblem suggests something more. In her selfish desire to hold on she suggests the wider, historical class from which she comes: those who shut out the shadows and treasures of history; clutched at strength and despised weakness; harmed what they owned and were destroyed by what they shunned.

Yet Kate O'Brien — with the exception, perhaps, of *Without My Cloak* — has no real interest in being a social or historical novelist. She has a feel for action and event as background, but her foreground is an imaginative and mysterious place where events can quickly become shadows. Certainly, history is a presence in *The Last of Summer*. These people come from countries under threat. Angèle knows that people she loves are at risk in France. Martin realizes that he can have no part in Ireland's neutrality in the coming war; he will join a French regiment. Jo, his sister and Hannah's only daughter, is aware that the coming struggle casts a shadow on the contemplative life.

But the issue in this book is not history. It is the confrontation — played out in a private theatre of obsession and love — between doom and choice. One passage, towards the middle of the novel, canvasses the whole undersong. Angèle is sitting on the top step of a jetty. She has found her way there by following the path south through the trees, past the burnt-out house and up a lane leading from it. This has brought her to Brady's pier. And here she contemplates the difficult issues of love and self-love:

> But now she was committed. She had pledged her love and faith and if she was surprised by the peace that brimmed from a surrender so vast for her and so absurd, the surprise was only instinctive, for she was without experience. I love him enough. She did not know that this was almost never true, and that it was not became manifest to many lovers even within the very pleasure of their first embrace. Love can survive, a little or a long time, this lesson of its insufficiency — because it must, because self-love and self-respect insist; because pleasure is strong, and compromise is an understood necessity, and because lovers learn to understand love cynically and yet value it. Love is too frequent an event to be frequently complete; whether or not by direct experience it is probable that every living heart knows this and is resigned to it.

Kate O'Brien believed in love. Her novels, from *Without My Cloak* to *The Last of Summer*, are witnesses to that faith. But she also believed in what she called, in her study of Teresa of Avila, "this science of the spirit". In the best of her work there is a clear, painful sense of the conflict between love and this "science". In Angèle the unstated conflict is there from the start. Angèle, after all, is an actress. She feels within herself the power of a vocation; a calling to be solitary, single-minded, ruthless in the pursuit of a gift. Yet such gifts, in Kate O'Brien's work, are always mysterious and ambiguous. They imply necessity and they promise pain. They provide hints of the fracture between sense and spirit, ritual and rite, sexuality and intellect, which shadow and enrich her work.

IV

I met Kate O'Brien only once. She came to our house for dinner. I was newly married at the time and anxious to serve her the food she liked. It so happened that I knew what food she did not like. In a delightful, quirky travel essay called *My Ireland* she had written:

> I may be afraid of bossy waitresses but I am not at their mercy . . . I have asked, for instance, if I could have a minute steak, a plain green salad and a glass of wine. Always no . . . I have been so driven to experiment that I have asked for a linen napkin, instead of a paper one. (But that last may have been a bit unreasonable.)

I read her remarks with attention and anxiety. That October night she got a linen napkin, a minute steak and whatever green salad an Irish autumn could provide. She was elderly and frail, with an easy grace in conversation and recall. I could see her eyes glitter now and again with a joke, like Yeats's musicians on their steep hill of lapis. What stays with me, however, is nothing to do with food or a preference for linen. It is a remark she made which illuminated her poise of spirit and imagination. I was pressing the claims of some person, on the grounds — infirm, I am sure — that they had a great sense of humour. I can still see her features: aquiline survivors of a classical beauty. She regarded me thoughtfully. When she replied, her tone was a deft blend of mirth and menace. "I am entirely against", she said, "the promotion of a sense of humour as a philosophy of life."

I include that small, personal snapshot because even at the time it revealed and confirmed something which still, at this distance, seems important. Above all, Kate O'Brien was an artist of balance and proportion; a seeker after poise; a healer of divisions. What grace human life could afford happened, she proposed, at rare moments of truce: when the spirit and the senses put aside their quarrel. But in her search for equilibrium — and her novels, including this one, are a commentary on that search — she allowed herself no diminution of costly and subversive questioning. She tolerated neither evasion nor simplification. In her best fiction there are no palliatives: neither false comfort nor easy laughter.

The Last of Summer offers neither. It is a story of love and choice; of subtle and exacting surrenders to design. In Angèle and Tom we see star-crossed love. In Hannah we see the arts of peace twisted into the vindictive strength of a latter-day war goddess. For the rest of them — Martin, Jo, Corney — we may reserve the roles of victim or witness; it hardly matters. The great strength of the book is to make us see how these elements can be choreographed into an ironic and heartbreaking pattern. The past repeats itself; but in such a way that we understand it freshly. The future is in doubt, and present certainties prove illusory. As we read on, the enchantment grows: we know these are dangerous matters; we know we are in safe hands.

Eavan Boland, Dublin, 1989

CONTENTS

THE porter said he'd mind her bag.

"To be sure, Miss. Look, I'll put it inside here, the way the sun won't boil it on you."

"Is it far from here to Waterpark House?"

The old man looked at her with interest.

"Mrs. Kernahan's place you're wanting, Miss?"

Angèle nodded.

"Is it far?"

"Yerrah, no. Half a mile, maybe, and a bit. No walk at all, if it wasn't for the heat that's in it this evening, glory be to God! But sure, isn't it a wonder Mr. Tom and Mr. Martin wouldn't be here for you, or Miss Josie herself, in the Ford?"

Tom. Martin. Miss Josie.

"They aren't expecting me," Angèle said. "They don't know I'm in Ireland."

"Ah well, if that's the way! Will I give them a ring-up on the telephone, Miss, and maybe the Missus could send down for you?"

"No, thank you. I'd rather walk. I don't mind its being hot."

"Well, you're young and light, God bless you." They stood outside the station, under a lime tree. A cart loaded with corn brushed against them, leaving wisps on Angèle's hair.

"Move on there, Jimmy, like a good boy," the porter said to the child on top of the corn. When the cart had passed he pointed down the road.

"Turn to your right below McMahon's, Miss, and straight on down with you through the town until you come to where you'll turn sharp right again at the extremity of the street. Follow on then by the side of the water till you see a big ivy wall and a gate in it. And that'll be Mrs. Kernahan's place for you."

I

"Thank you very much," Angèle said.

"Not at all, Miss ; you're welcome."

She turned right at McMahon's. "The Town" lay before her—a wide, down-sloping street of white, pink, grey, and yellow houses. There was a church, there were some little shops ; children in doorways, a pony trap outside a public house. The village of her father's childhood.

The sky seemed very high, a space of pure blue ; trees threw banners of shadow across the brilliant little houses ; the air smelt of roses and of porter. There was hardly a sound in the street.

Angèle had always purposed to visit the place of her father's birth, but her intention was to come there later in life, when she was famous, when she was happy ; to come in deliberate search of the past. I am Tom Kernahan's daughter. Do you remember him ? He married Jeanne Maury, of the *Comédie Française*. Yes, I am Angèle Maury—how quick of you ! Ah, do my photos find their way to Drumaninch ?

She did not like to come as now, unready and unknown, and merely because to do so was a refuge, a pretext. But perhaps she would not have set out at all on this absurd tour with Rhoda and those others had she not known that in fact somewhere in the strange little country they visited there was this bolthole she could use. When would she learn to stand and debate with life ? When would she face the customary uses of "yes" and "no" ? Rhoda would have had her note at tea-time ; so would Bob have had his. They would all have sworn at her casually, had tea in the stuffy Mellick hotel, and gone on their way towards Galway—hardly wondering what she would make of her unknown relatives ; forgetting her entirely as they looked for cocktails in Ennis. Except Bob. But he would forget her too—he had the wish to do so, and Joan would sit beside him in the car. She ought to have understood, without trial, her own incompatibility with such a holiday party. Not that way. Not that way, if ever.

If the relations were inhospitable she could perhaps sleep

one night in this closed-seeming hotel. The Royal Anglers' some fading gold letters said on the blue stucco. She remembered some talk of her father's—Mrs. Cusack's seed cake at the Royal Anglers' and the fishermen in the bar eating it hot with their whisky, and the great salmon lying at their feet. Yes, opposite was Paddy Cusack's tackle shop—just as father said. Shut and dead now, with a queer old face peering out of an empty, dusty window.

The most quiet village she had ever been in. If the relations were inhospitable she would go to Dublin to-morrow, cross the sea to-morrow night, and be in her own room on Primrose Hill on Thursday morning.

She heard the sound of the river now—that sound which had run through all her father's talk of Ireland. She came to what the porter had called the extremity of the street and turned and saw wide, broken, islanded water and open land to the west.

She leant on the low wall. She thought of how her father had constantly dreamt of return to this place, and suddenly felt in a pang of admiration the perfect rightness of living away from it, being its exile. Mother always said that Father was the ideal exile. She smiled. Memories of her mother, who had died two years ago, were close to her. What would Mother have made of this dead-still Drumaninch, on that brilliant return visit which all three were one day to have made? That lovely, intelligent voice, those serious eyes; the incessant, uncompromising French, the little feet of Paris; the industry, the probity, the urbane good sense. The artistic failure that never in fact failed; the success that never took fire.

Angèle opened her bag and looked at her face in her mirror. She didn't suppose it would matter to the Kernahans if she looked shabby—anyway, if she was shabby in this old linen suit it couldn't be helped—but she might as well look properly made up. They seemed to hate make-up in Ireland, but really she had overdone the caution with her lipstick. She unscrewed it now and reddened again her wide, red mouth. She shook

3

her hair back from her brow. I wonder what they'll think of me. I wonder what I'll think of them.

She turned from the water and looked back towards the village. Mother dead ; Mother married to a man from this little place. Two surprising things—more surprising the longer you accepted them. From far away, from babyhood, she heard the lovely voice ; she lay in bed, in a cot with bars, and heard her mother studying a part she would never play. *Athènes me montra mon superbe ennemi.* She had known all the great parts of the French theatre—indeed, all the great plays. She was a rock in any company. *Athènes me montra mon superbe ennemi.* Perhaps she had not understood that line. But it was a pity she had not played what she desired to play. Always Cléone, always Oenone. Never Hermione, never Iphigénie, never Phèdre.

The girl winced in fear before such a fate, which she had seen accomplished. Better stay here, I'd say. Better endure this lonely place and be good. But Mother *was* good.

A few children climbed up from the rocks of the river. They sat on the wall and stared at Angèle. They were very poor, but they looked happy.

I suppose I had better go on, as I've begun this thing. Mrs. Kernahan's place—which of the family is she ? Mr. Tom. Mr. Martin. Miss Josie. I've forgotten, or else I never knew who they are. Mrs. Kernahan must be married to Uncle Corney—but then it should be Uncle Corney's place, surely ? No. Uncle Corney never married, as far as Father knew. Uncle Ned is the eldest—Waterpark House belongs to him. So why is it "Mrs. Kernahan's place" ? Oh well, I'll know soon. I suppose all those Mr. Toms and so on must be my cousins ! Well, now I'm here I might as well face them. After all, they can't eat me. And I'll go back to London to-morrow. Anyway, nothing could be worse than what I was doing.

She smiled. How very much better Bob would enjoy himself now. He was all right if he didn't see what he couldn't

4

have. Lovely to be alone ! Perhaps she'd just stay at the Royal Anglers', and not face the relatives at all .

The children edged a little nearer, watching her. Angèle smiled at them ingratiatingly. The girl was big and bright-eyed. She stared at Angèle with animosity.

" What happened your lips ? " she asked suddenly, with a powerful sneer.

The other children looked alarmed, but they giggled.

Angèle hurried past them, along the empty road. She was shaking, dared not speak or look back. She felt tears of fury in her eyes. What a fool she was ! Surely she knew yokeldom by now, in many countries, and was accustomed to being a stranger, looking a stranger, in places where strangers are targets ? But in this shaft sped by a rude little girl—no novelty —she felt without reason a greater force than could have been intended ; she felt an accidental expression of something which had vaguely oppressed and surprised her, these ten days, in the Irish air—an arrogance of austerity, contempt for personal feeling, coldness and perhaps fear of idiosyncrasy. In this most voluptuously beautiful and unusual land. She could not help the tears in her eyes. She hated the rudeness and she heard the insult to her reddened mouth symbolically—so self-conscious was she. She heard it as an ignoble warning from the people of her father. If I could only stop being so idiotically self-conscious ! If I could give up responding to every dotty little nothingness that blows my way !

The tears did not fall. She laughed outright. At herself and at the rude little girl. What happened your lips ? Well of all the nerve ! I've a jolly good mind to go back and give her the thrashing of her life.

She laughed delightedly, and leant again on the low mossy wall. Divine, Olympian river. Of an entirely other character than the sweet English streams, or the winding waters of France. And how familiar it was to her, from Father's memory of it. If it *was* your river you would know it always, across years of absence. You would be unable to confuse its great

5

character. Father hadn't much of a brain, but his feelings were often accurate ; he was impressionable.

What happened your lips ? Well. what *did* happen them ? She took out her mirror again. Funny how they dropped that preposition. Perhaps the child was right. Perhaps for " Mrs. Kernahan's place "—no, it's no good. I'll feel twice as frightened if my make-up isn't what I'm used to. Anyway, why *should* they like me ? Here to-day and gone to-morrow. A duty call by Tom Kernahan's daughter. I suppose I should introduce myself as Angèle Kernahan. But surely they'll understand that that's an impossible name for the stage ? Angèle Maury. That's my name—oh, they can take it or leave it. Damn the whole lot of the Kernahans ! Why am I getting so worked up ? But did you ever face anyone yet without getting worked up ? Mother, Mother, where is all your calm, your modesty ? Have I got none of it ? None of your philosophy, none of your sense of proportion ? And yet none of the ease of Father ? *Athènes me montra mon superbe ennemi.* It must be ages since she heard Mother studying that speech—a long time now since Jeanne Maury had any practical hope of playing *Phèdre. Athènes me montra* . . . Drumaninch. Not Athens, thanks be to God. I feel quite natural leaning on this wall. Perhaps Father often leant here. That's a neat little bird, drinking on the stone. Nice little fat white chest. Bad figure really —too dapper. Oh, he's gone. You could get to know about birds here—if you wanted to. I wonder if I really ought to barge in on these cousins ? After all, they've never written— never even wrote to Mother when Father died. They *should* have answered her letter then. It's cooler. Perhaps I'd better go on and get this thing over. What possessed me to start it anyway ? I expect the others are still drinking in Ennis. They'll hardly get to Galway to-night. I wish I had a drink. I don't drink enough to please Bob, I know, but I could do with a stiff drink now ! Mother would disapprove of that—she despised Dutch courage. Perhaps that's why she never played *Phèdre.* Oh, if she were alive I wouldn't be here, that's certain ! If she

6

were alive I'd never have gone on that silly motoring trip ! That's the fat little bird again. Come on, pull yourself together. Mrs. Kernahan's place. A big ivy wall and a gate in it. What happened your lips ?

The road curved away from the water ; below the mossy wall wooded land thrust out, hiding a great bend of the river. Rich trees towered up, and the wall beside her grew high— tufted and scrolled with ivy.

She came to the gate. It was set in a deep curve of approach. It was low and wide and of heavy iron. It needed paint and its pillars were mossy. It stood wide open to a neglected drive. The hexagonal lodge beside it had ogival windows and looked wild and poor, but as if fully inhabited. There was no-one in sight.

It looks very foreign, Angèle thought confusedly. This was a curious, childish reflection from her, who was at ease in many countries. Foreign to what, to whom ? Rich grassland swept away on either side, broken by trees and by neglected clumps of bamboo and rhododendron. There were soft crack-lings, as if birds or badgers moved—but she saw no creature save a small blue butterfly that went ahead of her.

The drive turned sharply and, before she was ready, before she had expected it, the house she sought laid its shadow over her. She started back almost as if struck, and her heart began to pound.

It's too big, she thought, excusing her sense of panic.

It was a plain, large house, washed with cream paint that was dilapidated. Its face was late Georgian " squireen," smooth and blank. Five big windows across the first floor ; four similar windows and a wide doorway below ; and further below, basement windows half-visible above a kind of moat which was spanned by a flight of stone steps to the doorway. Flat-roofed, with a narrow cornice, and solid flat chimney-stacks. Stone flower-pots, full of geraniums, at the foot of the flight of steps. Ilex trees close about. Silence, pride, and shabbiness.

The door was open. Angèle went up the steps. There was a wrought-iron shoe-scraper fixed in the stone. There was a

7

bell handle which suggested that if it was pulled it would reverberate loudly very far away. Angèle wondered what to do. The hall was large and square. There were fox-masks and a barometer on the walls and a fish in a glass case. There were dahlias in a bowl on a black oak table. A kind of hunting whip, she thought, lay on the floor. She wondered how it was used—it had a bone handle at one end and a small leather thong at the other.

"Well, glory be to God ! Didn't you ring the bell at all, Miss ? "

A big maidservant stood in front of her. She had come out of a room on the left and was carrying a loaded tray. Her smile was very pleasant.

"I—I was just going to. Is Mrs. Kernahan at home ? "

"To be sure. They're all at home, Miss. Wait awhile till I put down the tray and show you in." She edged her load on to the table with the dahlias. "'Twas a hot walk, faith, to come visiting ! Who'll I say is here, Miss ? "

"Well—they don't know me. I'm their cousin from France. My father was Mr. Tom Kernahan——"

"Their cousin from France, is it ? Well now, you'd be talking ! Divil a bit did I know they had a cousin from France, the creatures ! They'll be delighted with themselves to see you ! Come in at once, let you, to the mistress ! She's in the drawing-room, inside. Sure isn't it grand for them to have you coming visiting them all that way ? "

Angèle was calmed by the pleasant voice, and she entered the drawing-room without panic.

"The children's cousin, ma'am—all the way of the road from France, praise be ! "

The Second Chapter   AUNT HANNAH

THE drawing-room was two rooms, with folding doors open between them. There was nobody in the first of these—only white walls, a ringing chandelier, much furniture and many curious old objects. And a sharp blaze of daylight, flung in from the hot, wide sky reflected on a wide water. Angèle had almost to shade her eyes to see her way into the inner room.

This too was full of relentless light—and curious objects. But there were people, female shapes, in the semi-circular embrasure of an enormous, outflung window. The girl advanced towards two blurred heads, half-closing her eyes. The northerly aspect of the entrance façade, with its sober ilex trees, had seemed almost cold, had indeed suggested a somewhat menacing detachment from the bright day ; the hall and the maidservant's voice had been cool and almost friendly of shade —so this assault of light was unexpected, and unsteadied her.

" What's that you're raving about, Delia ? The children's cousin—from *France*, did I hear you say ? " The voice was chuckly and uneducated. A civilized and soft one answered it lightly.

" You did, Dotey. You heard her say it."

The latter speaker extended a pretty hand, with a silver thimble on the middle finger, towards Angèle.

" This is unexpected," she said amiably. " I would get up and welcome you properly were it not for these embroidery silks. Come nearer. You should have written, and been properly received."

" It was the merest chance—a sudden idea, as I was in Mellick——"

" How improbable, your being in Mellick ! Yes—I suppose you are a bit like him—fair-haired anyhow, even fairer than he was. Would you recognize her, Dotey ? "

" Now how would I, Hannah, and I not knowing who in this wide world the girleen is ? "

The pretty woman laughed.

" That's the point. Could you guess ? "

Angèle smiled cautiously from the pretty, ladylike woman to the fat woman called Dotey. Silence fell for a second or two.

" She is Tom's child, Dotey. Would you have known ? "

9

"Tom's child? You mean Ned's and Corney's brother—poor Tom that died in Paris?"

The pretty woman nodded. Her eyes were on Angèle and were reflective.

"Who else?" she said. "And I don't even know your name," she said to the girl.

"Angèle is my name. Angèle Maury."

"Surely—Angèle Kernahan?"

"Well yes, of course. But as I am on the stage, like Mother, I use her name. Angèle Maury seems a better name for the stage."

"Perhaps. Certainly *Kernahan* was never a stage name. Won't you sit down? You must be tired. How on earth did you get here?"

Angèle sat down on a small chintz-covered chair. "I took a train from Mellick to Drumaninch, and walked here from the station."

Dotey had an amiable, shining face and she beamed placidly at Angèle—but the latter half-perceived that under the placidity she was startled, was waiting for information, waiting for her cue. The girl wondered who she was. She wore no hat on her shining silver head, and looked like a fixture, in a basket chair with her feet on a footstool, and a thick man's sock, which she was darning, stretched on her left hand. She could hardly be a casual visitor—yet she did not seem to be a member of the family, or to know the family history.

"Well now, what next?" Dotey said, as if amazed at Angèle's plain statement. It occurred to Angèle that she had the mannerisms of someone accustomed to play for time and afraid of asking simple questions. Yet she did not look as if she was afraid of anything. She looked a comically comfortable woman. Her breath smelt strongly of peppermint. "And what's that foreign name you said you have, alannah?"

"Angèle," Angèle repeated.

"French for Angela," the pretty woman said. "It's easier to say in English."

" Ah, but I hate it in English ! Please call me Angèle."

" Of course—whatever you wish."

The girl was interested, neither attracted yet nor repelled, by the curiously exact yet unwarmed courtesy of this pretty woman who she knew must be her Aunt Hannah, Mrs. Ned Kernahan, the mistress of the house. This gracious, yielding reply, for instance, to her impetuous plea for her own name, fell at first very kindly on her nervous ears—but did it or not leave a cold echo ? Your name, what on earth is it going to matter to me, you silly stranger ?

" ' Angela ' means ' messenger,' " said Dotey. " Isn't that right, Hannah ? "

" It is. And what message does this messenger bring ? "

The pretty smile reassured Angèle.

" Why—none," she said. " Only Father always talked a great deal about Drumaninch and Waterpark House, and used to plan our coming here sometime, Mother and he and I——" she paused.

" Indeed ? " her aunt encouraged her, but more as if amused than simply interested.

" So, as I was motoring with some English friends, I couldn't resist calling here before I left Ireland. I—knew he would have expected me to do so. He—loved Drumaninch very much."

" Indeed and he did, the creature, and every stone and stick that's in it, to the last beat of his heart," said Dotey in rich tones, seemingly sure of her ground now. But Mrs. Kernahan looked at her oddly, without a smile.

" How do you know that, Dotey ? "

Dotey looked almost startled, Angèle thought.

" Divil a bit do I know it then, child—and how would I, and I seated here in ignorance ? Only wouldn't it be right for him now to love the place he was born in, and them that he left here in it and they fretting for him ? "

" Well, he does seem to have been more pious about us than we thought." The attractive smile returned as Mrs. Kernahan addressed herself again to Angèle. " In any case, it was very right and natural of you to come and visit your father's home. I suppose you can't know that your Uncle Ned, my husband, died—was killed riding—a year after your father died. But your Uncle Corney, who has never married, lives here with us—and there are my children, your cousins. You will meet us all. I am Aunt Hannah—you have heard of me ? "

" Indeed yes—Father spoke of you all often."

" But you were very young when he died ? "

" I was twelve. I remember him well."

" Then you are twenty-five ? "

" Yes."

" A nice fit-in between Tom and Martin, isn't she now, Hannah ? "

" Tom is my elder son," Mrs. Kernahan said explanatorily to Angèle, " he is twenty-seven and Martin is my second son ; he is close on twenty-five. There is also Jo, my daughter, who will be twenty-two this month. But—we're so simple here—I'm afraid you'll find us the very epitome of country cousins——"

The door of the outer drawing-room opened and shut while Mrs. Kernahan spoke, and Angèle thought a faint shade of perplexity passed over her aunt's pretty face, but she could not turn in her chair to see why this was so.

" Why, Mother, who has turned up that's going to despise us ? "

The male voice was musical, but the speech so rapid and careless that Angèle only just caught its meaning.

A heavy-shouldered young man in shabby clothes came and stood by Dotey's basket-chair. When his eyes fell on Angèle his expression of amusement changed to a mask of polite surprise. But the girl felt that she was being shrewdly examined and that the examiner had no idea at all of her identity.

Mrs. Kernahan spoke frivolously now, though Angèle found no frivolity in her eyes, and was in fact startled and hurt by what she said.

" It's a pity you're looking so disreputable, Martin, just

when you have to meet a cousin you didn't know you possessed."

Angèle started—then drew back defensively into her chair. Martin turned sharply from her to his mother.

" What cousin ? "

" Uncle Tom's daughter—Angèle Kernahan, from Paris. Shake hands, and be nice ! " Mrs. Kernahan laughed.

Martin, bending, took Angèle's hand in both of his.

" I'm delighted ! Delighted ! Oh, Mother, how has all this happened so suddenly ? All the time I've been in Paris—and me not knowing I had *relations* there ! " He laughed so kindly into Angèle's eyes that she laughed too, though offended and bewildered. " Are you sure you aren't some impostor or other ? " He went on : " How do you account for this girl, Mother——" he yielded up her hand and sat down near her on a stool. " Have you examined her papers, Dotey ? Sure wasn't Uncle Tom the bachelor of bachelors, the wanderer with the broken heart ? "

Dotey went on with her darning.

" God's ways are wonderful, child," she said.

Martin returned to his assault on Angèle. He did not seem to see her discomfort.

" But how did you prove to Mother that you are this cousin she didn't know we had ? "

" She knew," Angèle said coldly. " I didn't have to prove anything."

Martin's expression of interest and goodwill did not change even to increase. Angèle, raging in her heart that she had come to this house in friendliness, suspected gratification in him as she spoke, and that he had even so calculated the dialogue as to make her say what she had said.

" H'm," he said, softly and coolly. " It seems we children are still in the nursery. Even so, we could play with our cousins. What was the big mystery, Mother ? "

Mrs. Kernahan picked up a skein of yellow silk, and eyed it critically.

"No need to be impertinent, Martin," she said with great good humour. "These old stories seem very funny, no doubt, to clever young men—but there it is—your father didn't wish you children to know of—your French relations, and I did not feel any right to go against his wishes. Perhaps when you were older he would have told you, had he lived. I really have no idea whether he would or not. And for my own part —well honestly, Angèle must pardon a busy, preoccupied person if I say that the important matter of her existence had long ago escaped my memory."

"To be sure, Hannah dear," said Dotey. "Sure anyone could understand that."

"I see, Mother," said Martin, and his eyes rested on her reflectively as she threaded a length of embroidery silk. She seemed peaceful, interested in what she was doing. She did not look towards him or towards Angèle.

"And as things are—look what a nice surprise it has made for you on this hot, boring evening," said Mrs. Kernahan, and suddenly smiled with great sweetness at Angèle. "A very lovely, rare surprise."

"No ; it's unfortunate that I came," Angèle said without smiling. "I can only beg your pardon, all of you—and go."

"What nonsense, child !" said Mrs. Kernahan. "In any case, where would you go to ? Where are you staying ? At the Royal Anglers' ? " She laughed and Dotey chuckled richly in echo.

"You're staying here, I'd have you know," said Martin. "You're staying for the rest of the summer, if I have any say with you ! You've no idea of how all this mystery of you interests me ! "

But Angèle was stubborn, and unused to slights.

"Why did my uncle not want it known about Mother and me, Aunt Hannah ? "

Dotey creaked in her basket-chair and beamed at Martin.

"You're a terror entirely on your socks, Mr. Clever," she

14

said. " Wouldn't you have any mercy at all on a blind old woman ? "

" My husband was surprisingly strict about some things—— "
Martin looked half-surprised, half-amused.

" Uncle Ned strict ? " Angèle said. " Father seemed to think—— "

" Oh yes—I know. Your Uncle Ned had his faults like everyone else. But about some things he was strict—perhaps excessively strict."

" Even so—what had that to do with Mother and me ? "

Mrs. Kernahan laid her little circular embroidery frame on her knees, and looked very kindly at Angèle.

" I wish you wouldn't force this unpleasantness, child. After all, it is all in the past, the prejudice of the dead—and you are our cousin and our guest—— "

" Oh rubbish, Mother—cough it up ! "

" Tch, tch," said Dotey. " Mr. Highbrow with his continental manners ! "

Mrs. Kernahan smiled.

" True enough, Dotey—we must often wonder about the benefits of Martin's extended education." She chose another silk. Angèle noted the design of her embroidery—it seemed to be a cross for a maniple or a stole.

" What was the matter with Mother and me ? "

" Why, nothing at all, if you ask me, child. But your uncle had had years of annoyance from your father and had never heard anything good of his lazy life abroad. So when he married—an actress, a penniless actress—— "

" As long as I can remember Mother earned every penny we ever had in our family—and often we were quite rich—— "

" I'm glad to know that. Don't be impatient with me, Angèle. It's you who are forcing the distasteful topic, after all."

" I don't see anything at all distasteful in it," said Martin. " It's lively—and full of surprises. That about Father being so prim, for instance ! And about there never being anything

15

good heard of Uncle Tom ! The idols are falling all right this evening ! "

" If I brought you children up to some illusions which I once had myself, Martin—perhaps when you are my age you will see why. Anyway, I am not giving Angèle my *own* opinion on this old story which is naturally hurtful to her. Take it or leave it, Angèle, but your Uncle Ned had obstinate views about stage people and about Frenchwomen—and your father's marriage was the last straw. His patience was exhausted——"

" Like Hitler's," said Martin.

" ——He washed his hands of the whole business, forbade me to mention it again, and forbade me to let the children know they had connections he wished them never to meet."

" I see. And when Father died, and Mother wrote to tell Uncle Ned——"

" Well, perhaps my husband was sorry—but what was the good of trying to make friends then, with strangers ? In any case, he was to follow his brother very soon, you see."

Mrs. Kernahan resumed her embroidery. She looked very pretty, very vulnerable. Her silvered brown hair was soft and untidily curly ; her crumpling, fair skin looked as if it would still be delicious and cool to touch ; her eyebrows and lashes were brown and delicate still. She wore a dress of grey and white foulard ; an old-fashioned hoop of diamonds swung loosely with her wedding ring on the third finger of her left hand. She was left a widow not long after Mother, Angèle reflected. Say thirteen years ago, in 1926. She must have been in the flower of her best attractiveness then. If Mother was alive now she'd be fifty-one—I suppose she's a bit younger than that. She looks younger—forty-eightish. I suppose ordinary people would say that she's much more attractive than Mother. Angèle smiled.

" What are you smiling at ? " said Martin.

She was embarrassed by the insistent tone of his question and the impossibility of answering it truly. She could hardly say : at how much more attractive my mother was than yours.

"Nothing," she said. "Well, I just thought of Mother for a minute."

"Where is your mother, Angèle ? " Mrs. Kernahan asked kindly.

"She is dead, Aunt Hannah. She died in Paris two years ago—after an operation."

"Tch, tch," said Dotey. "Tch, tch—may the Lord have mercy on her soul ! "

"That is very sad for you, Angèle," said Mrs. Kernahan. "You are alone in the world now ? "

"Yes. Of course I have relatives in Paris—Mother's people. They are very kind—very dear to me."

"Ah, that is a good thing. You—you——" Mrs. Kernahan paused delicately. "You earn your living ? "

"Yes. Mother left a little money ; but I've been fairly lucky about work, and so I still have most of her savings. I'm an actress too. But I told you that."

Her aunt nodded.

"What mystifies me still is how an actress from Paris comes strolling in here, of all things, this quiet evening ? "

Angèle was relaxing unconsciously. Her aunt's smile was quite ravishing sometimes, and she felt real friendliness in Martin. She laughed now, softly, half-absent-mindedly— thinking of Bob and Rhoda and the rest getting drunk in Ennis.

"Yes—it's funny right enough ! You see, I was in two films that Jean Rouart made in France last year—and in January this year they decided to make English versions, so he brought me along. It's useful being bi-lingual sometimes."

"So you're on the movies, childeen ? " said Dotey. "Well now, what'll we be hearing next ? "

"Only that you're on them yourself, Dotey," said Martin. "Did they make the English versions ? And what were the films called ? Did you have good parts ? Did I ever see you on the screen in Paris ? "

17

"I had a small part in a ghastly film called *Flamme d'Amour*, and a better one in *L'Eté s'en va*. We've just finished the English version of that."

"I didn't see either. I believe Rouart is a good director?"

"Very good, I think. But he gets mixed up with bad scenarios, He wants to film *War and Peace*, if he can ever get the money!"

"Lord—he'd need money—and nerve."

"He has the nerve. He once said—but he was drinking champagne at the time—that if he gets the money before I'm too old, he'll cast me for Natasha."

Martin looked at her gravely, as if in conference with Jean Rouart.

"He must think you have talents," he said.

"Ah, but I'm twenty-five already!"

"All very interesting, children," said Mrs. Kernahan, "but it doesn't explain why you're sitting in my drawing-room, Angèle."

"Oh, I forgot, Aunt Hannah. We've been hanging around in London waiting to start the second film—and it was very hot, and some friends I've met in England asked me to come driving round Ireland with them."

"I see. And where are your friends now?"

"On the way to Galway, I think. We came to Mellick last night from Kerry—and this morning—oh, I don't know—being in Mellick made me think a lot about Father, and the stories he used to tell me of Waterpark House and everyone here——"

"What did he tell you, Angèle?" Mrs. Kernahan's voice was very gentle.

"Heaps of things. The river, and this house, and fishing—he loved talking about Drumaninch."

"H'm—I see. Well?"

"Well, suddenly I got tired of the others——"

"What are they like?" Martin asked.

"Oh an actress and her very new husband, and another girl, a painter, and a cameraman from the studios——"

"They don't sound a very steady sort of party for you, Angèle, if I may say so," said Mrs. Kernahan.

Angèle laughed.

"No, they're not a bit steady," she said. "But they're nice."

"Why did you abandon them then?" said Martin.

"Well, I've told you. I was thinking of Father, and Drumaninch—and I grew tired of them."

"Good girl," said Martin. "But you mustn't get tired of us all of a jump like that!"

"She's not very likely to give herself time to, Martin dear," said Mrs. Kernahan. "You see, she belongs to the world—not to our old backwater."

Angèle felt chilled again. This woman's tranquil dissociation of her and hers from everything else on earth was curious, and unattractive. So she rose against it once more, feeling suddenly with passion that she was Tom Kernahan's daughter and a grandchild of this unwelcoming house.

"I came here because Father always insisted so much that I belonged to Drumaninch," she said.

"His way of proving it was odd, however," said Aunt Hannah. "Have you any luggage, child?"

"I left my suitcase at the station."

Martin took her by the wrist and made her rise with him.

"Come on and we'll see if Jo is back with the car yet. If she is we'll go for the bag, you and I."

"That's a good idea. Angèle's room will be ready by the time you get back." Mrs. Kernahan's voice was soft and hospitable again.

Angèle, unnerved by so many currents of mood, had nothing left to say, and allowed herself to be drawn across the inner drawing-room by Martin. She was still, absurdly, feeling something of the shock which the rude, cruel child by the river had inflicted. What happened your lips? Was this Aunt Hannah cruel too, in the same cold, casual way? In the arch of the folding doors she turned, smiled reluctantly back at the two women, who smiled with what seemed again to be kindness at her. Her cousin led her through a long open window of the other room, and down some wrought-iron steps into the garden.

Mrs. Kernahan did not resume her embroidery. She gazed out towards the brilliant river, and Dotey peered at her, did a stitch of darning, and peered again.

"You'd better go and see about her room, Dotey." The voice was gentle, faraway—but Dotey bounced under its immensely veiled command. She rolled up her darning with frenzy and creaked herself out of her basket-chair.

"To be sure I'd better, child! Glory be, what's on me at all to be dreaming this way, will you tell me? "

Mrs. Kernahan did not tell her, but continued to look outward to the river ; the fat old woman trotted nimbly from the room.

The Third Chapter   THE COUSINS

"THE river is very loud," said Angèle.

"Yes ; there was a lot of rain—until to-day," said Martin. "I like it loud like that, over the rocks."

"It throws up a terrific light. I can hardly look at it."

Terrific light, the terrific light of day, suits you, Martin thought. It suits your white face and gold hair.

"There's almost no fishing now—no real fishing, like the old days, at all," he said.

"I saw the Royal Anglers' as I passed. Father used to talk a lot about the goings-on there—and Mrs. Cusack."

"Well, she's still there."

"The hotel looked absolutely dead."

"There's a way round by the ivy wall to Mrs. Cusack's snug. I'll take you there one evening—she'll want to see Uncle Tom's fair daughter," he said with a sudden nervous flourish. "Hi! Hi there, Jo! "

At a plank bridge they had crossed a haha which divided

the garden from the sloping river field, and now Angèle saw a girl some distance off and a little below them on the river path. She was coming in their direction, and now at Martin's shout looked up, paused a second and then waved and came diagonally over the grass, between wild shrubs. She was a heavy-shouldered, large-headed girl of medium height; she moved like an athlete, and seemed ill-suited by the sprigged cotton dress she wore. Her dark wavy hair was bobbed and fell thickly against her neck. As she drew near Angèle saw that she was like her brother Martin in being pale of skin, dark-eyed, and attractive-looking with the attractiveness of intelligence rather than of beauty.

" Jo ! I give you two guesses who she is ! "

Jo smiled with disarming shyness at Angèle from under her shadowing brows. She pushed back her hair from her forehead.

Angèle stretched out her hand.

" I'm your cousin," she said. " A cousin you didn't know you had, I believe."

" That's it," said Martin, laughing at Jo's doubtful eyes. " This girl," he took Angèle's left hand, " is half a French-woman, and she is Uncle Tom's legitimate daughter, no less! You know, Jo—Uncle Tom, who never looked at a woman again ! "

Angèle saw Jo frown at him very slightly. Evidently his joke was in bad taste. But she smiled at Angèle.

" Good Lord, I am glad you came ! A French cousin—marvellous ! "

The last word was said softly and slowly, and as if its full meaning was intended. Then silence fell, somewhat awk-wardly. The three went on over the grass, without apparent intention. It seemed that no more could well be said at present about this surprising cousinship—but Jo, more shy than her brother but like him in disposition, like him had easily made Angèle understand that the surprise was welcome, and seductive to the imagination.

Jo had a béret and some rosary beads in her left hand.

" Were you at the chapel, Jo ? " Martin asked her.

" Yes. For Benediction."

" Benediction on a Tuesday ? What's coming over that famous lotus-eater, Father Dooley ? "

" It's the Octave of the Assumption."

" Ah, of course ! How careless I'm getting ! " said Martin. " Do you know, Jo—this girl's an actress ! "

" No ? " Jo turned the words over. " I—wouldn't have thought of that," she said.

" Why ? Don't you think she looks like one ? "

" Oh, maybe ! I don't know. If you mean exotic, painted and that—perhaps yes. I've never seen an actress off stage, so far as I know. But——"

" But what ? " Angèle pressed her.

" Well—I'd have thought you were something brainier. You don't look at all stupid ! "

They laughed.

" I wish Mother heard you ! " said Angèle.

The light from the river still hurt her eyes ; the air was full of small sounds and smells which were strange to her ; she felt and indeed perceived great beauty all about her, but beauty made up of so many new subtleties and controlled by such arrogance of character that she could come to no simple decision of pleasure about it. It must wait. She felt tired, and wished she could look at the river without having to screw up her face.

" Is this a way to the station ? " she asked.

" Lord, no. I forgot. Jo, is the Ford in the yard ? "

" Yes. But you aren't going the minute you've come, are you ? "

" No. My bag is at the station."

" She's come on a visit, Joey ! Dotey is this minute wheezing about the Round Room making her bed, I hope ! "

" Oh—I ought to go back to the house then, and help old Dotey ? "

" Nonsense. What's Delia doing ? Come on to the station for her bag."

"All right."

They turned back, crossed the haha again and went along the grassy drive ; beyond a thicket of ilexes and rhododendrons they passed through an arched gateway into an enormous stableyard, surrounded by a high stone wall. Everything in this vast space seemed very neat and in its right place. White-washed stables with red doors and with skirtings of shiny black tar ran around two sides ; there was a whitewashed coachman's house in one corner and near it the white wall broke into a great archway which led, Angèle saw, to another large stableyard ; a long row of open coach-houses held an orderly array of farm-carts and pony-traps, and a battered-looking Ford saloon ; an iron pump and a water-trough stood in the middle of the immense cobbled space. Two children in pinafores played with a collie dog under the trickling pump, and on a mounting block near the coach-house a youngish-looking priest sat reading a newspaper. A groom came out of a stable, carrying a saddle.

"No sign of Mr. Tom yet, John-Jo ? "

"Ne'er a sign, Miss Josie. But 'tis early yet, and he coming from Clonmore."

The children by the pump stared at Angèle, and John-Jo eyed her cautiously as he crossed the yard.

"Here's the old bus. Want to drive, Martin ? "

"No. You do. I'll talk. I want to, for once."

Jo laughed at him, and opened a door for Angèle to get in, then went round and got in beside her at the driver's seat. Martin got into the back of the car. As they backed out of the coach-house they passed very near the mounting block, and the priest raised his eyes and met Angèle's. She was startled. They were insane. They were wide, blue, desperate, and the mirrors of complete confusion. The face was un-shaven ; the mouth hung open and saliva trailed from it, a lock of mouse-coloured hair hung loose across a great, white forehead ; but in contrast to the dereliction, physical and mental, of his head, the priest's worn black clothes were neat,

23

Angèle observed. He spoke aloud as they passed him, and Jo and Martin each waved a hand in a gesture of friendly reassurance which seemed second nature to them. The car went through the archway and reached the drive before anyone spoke.

Martin laid his hand for a second on Angèle's shoulder.

" You were frightened that time," he said kindly. " I am sorry."

" Ah yes," said Jo. " We're so used to poor old Bernard that we're always forgetting to explain him to people."

" Who is he ? " Angèle asked uneasily.

" John-Jo's brother. He lives here in the yard with him. He's stark mad, poor chap, and as good and kind as your guardian angel. How many years is it now that he's here, Jo ? "

" Oh, Lord knows ! About twelve, I'd say. It seems he was a genius at school, and at Maynooth. And then, in his first curacy I think it was—but of course we never mention it to John-Jo, so I'm not sure of the details—there was some kind of trouble. And the poor fellow went mad. So John-Jo was sent for, and he brought him back here. And then he seemed to calm down. He likes being with John-Jo—and the kids."

" Will he ever get better ? "

" I don't think so. He never says anything that a normal person could call lucid. But he reads the papers, and seems to have a pretty good visionary's conception of what the world is in for soon."

The world. Angèle looked with interest at the empty road ahead, along which she had walked alone not more than an hour earlier. In that little time her attention had been curiously deflected from " the world."

" I wonder what's really being settled in Moscow ? " she said.

" Well, they've made a trade agreement," said Martin. " But Ribbentrop is staying on—he's very keen on old Molotov, all of a sudden."

"What Russia decides just now doesn't matter at all, I think," said Jo. "She's playing for time, like all the others."

"Uncle Emile wouldn't agree with you about Russia," said Angèle.

"Who's he?"

"Mother's eldest brother. He lives in Paris."

"Whereabouts, Angèle?"

"You know Paris?"

"I've lived there, more or less, for the last two years."

"When you weren't just anywhere south-east of the Alps," said Jo.

But Angèle had turned in the car and was smiling back at Martin.

"Then do you know Rue d'Estrées?"

"Somewhere across the Boulevard des Invalides? Yes—I believe I used to get robbed by a *blanchisseuse* in that very street, when I lived in Cherche-Midi."

"You lived in Cherche-Midi? Ah!"

"Is that your part of Paris?"

"I think we always lived in the *6me*. Rue des Saints-Pères is the first address I remember, and then Notre Dame des Champs, and for three years before Mother died, Rue Madame. And I went to school to the Lycée Fénélon—Mother was nothing if not a traditionalist—so you see I got to know my own *arrondissement*. Indeed, all through childhood, I hardly remember leaving it except to see a performance at ' *la Maison* '——"

"What's that?" asked Jo.

"The *Comédie Française*. Worshippers and pensionnaires like Mother never call it anything but ' *la Maison.*' *Maison de Moliere*, you know."

"I know," said Martin, watching her. "But why did you ask me about Rue d'Estrées?" His attention was on her, and he wanted her facts. Angèle noted this with warming heart.

"Because that is where Uncle Emile lives, and *Grand' mère* and my cousins. And it's almost the only other place I knew outside my *arrondissement* when I was little. Uncle Emile has a clock-making shop and *orfèvrerie* in Rue d'Estrées. Did you ever take your watch to be mended at Auguste Maury et Fils ? "

" I wish I had. Would you have been around ? "

" Not living there. But until a few months ago we might have met any day at Uncle Emile's door. I'm awfully attached to all that family—especially since Mother's death."

The car pulled up in the sweet-smelling lane by the little station-house, and Martin got out.

" I'll find the bag all right. Don't you stir, Angèle," he said.

Silence fell a moment between the girls. Jo switched off her engine, and Angèle marvelled, as she had done before, at the profound quiet of this countryside.

" What's that lovely smell ? I noticed it when I arrived."

" Myrtle, mostly. But probably a mixture. Drumaninch is very spicy in summer." Jo paused. " It was a pity we were never told about you, Angèle. Have you brothers and sisters ? "

" No."

" It must have hurt you, your reception. Did Mother seem —unkind ? "

" Well—well, no. Indeed, in a way she was very kind."

" She *isn't* unkind, you know." Angèle noted the anxious stress. " But she lives entirely in Waterpark. I mean, whatever concerns Waterpark constitutes her life."

" I can see that that would be enough for a very full life, really."

" In a way, yes. And devotion can make people seem cold-hearted, perhaps. Mother has always been very devoted to us. Well, mostly to Tom, I suppose. But she's just."

This might have seemed a queer speech to Angèle was she not still sore from her first conversation with Aunt Hannah. But there was a gentle quality in Jo's face which made her seem not at all her mother's daughter, and which made all the more touching this anxiety to keep the screens in position, and to dismiss an offensiveness which must not be admitted to exist.

" Is Tom your mother's pet ? "

26

" Well, he's the eldest—and he's always been at home—not like Martin and me, who went away to school and to the university and so on. The two of them live for Waterpark, and they are tremendous pals—because of that mostly, I suppose. Tom is awfully good to Mother, I must say."

Martin came out of the station with Angèle's suitcase. The old porter was with him and came to the door of the car to speak to the girls.

" Good-evenin' to you, Miss Josie. I was on the watch for you for the bag. So you got there safe, Miss ? To be sure you did. I was just after hearing it from Miss Toomey anyway, and she waiting for her sister off the Dublin train. It seems she was below at the house, seeing Mrs. O'Flynn about one matter or another . . ."

They all laughed and waved to the old man as the car moved on.

" To be sure she was ! " said Martin. " Trust Miss Toomey. And now, Jo—I know it's against your principles, but this whole situation calls for a drink—and Angèle and I are having one. So pull up at the right place, like a good girl, and make no fuss whatever ! "

" Much good it would do me to fuss ! " said Jo. " All this drinking ! No wonder Europe is the way it is ! "

" Hitler and Mussolini are teetotallers," said Angèle.

" Good girl ! " said Martin. " Ah, too clearly do I see that you're after my own heart."

Jo pulled up at the end of the street just beyond the Royal Anglers'.

" While we're about it we might as well give Miss Toomey *plenty* of news," she said, indicating the little grey house beside which she had parked.

The three crossed the road.

" And no doubt her sister, hot off the Dublin train, will be able to explain to Miss Toomey what a real exotic, from the real world, we've landed ! "

He pushed open a gate in a great wall hung with ivy, and

27

they passed through a tangle of kitchen garden to a back door of the dead hotel.

"The snug," said Martin. "Mrs. Cusack is an entertaining relic."

They went through two doors, the second heavy and covered in green baize, into a large and lofty room, furnished in Victorian mahogany and leather. Daylight was obscured at the windows by flower-pot stands crammed with geraniums and maidenhair; there was a cage of canaries; the walls were covered with glass-cases containing stuffed fishes; there was a gilt-framed mirror over the mantelpiece and there were some large, signed photographs which seemed to be of personages. At a table near the fireplace an old woman sat, drinking tea and eating a mutton chop. A book was propped against the teapot, and she read as she drank and chewed.

The air of the room was astonishingly stale. Angèle noticed that a fire burnt in the grate.

"'Snug' is the word," she said softly.

There was a semi-circular mahogany bar in one corner. The three went towards it.

"Maggie May is at hand," the old woman said, without lifting her eyes from her book. Instantly Maggie May appeared from behind a looped-up red curtain and stood within the mahogany semi-circle. She was thin and middle-aged, with a narrow face of masculine and distinguished cut. She nodded pleasantly to Martin, but spoke in tones of surprise to Jo.

"Good-evening, Miss Kernahan. This is an unusual sight, you in the snug—but I'm hoping it's only the way your hand was forced."

"That's right, Miss Ryan—my hand was forced."

"'Tis no harm for the once, I suppose," said Maggie May, but she seemed uncertain, and looked at Jo with concern.

"What do you like to drink, Angèle?" Martin asked her.

In spite or perhaps because of the enervating heat of the room, Angèle felt a longing for a drink that would be sharp and potent.

" Could I have gin and French vermouth ? "

" I hope we both can. And you, Jo ? But it's far too hot for sticky brown sherry, I warn you."

" May I have cider ? "

" Lord, the stuff people drink ! "

" A nice glass of lemonade would be better for you," said Maggie May.

" I expect so, Miss Ryan, but I think I want cider, somehow."

Maggie May inclined her head, and prepared the drinks. Angèle admired her cocktail. It was a large one, served in a very fine old glass, and with ice and lemon peel.

" Lovely," she said. As she lifted her glass she smiled a little, first at Jo, and then at Martin. " I am drinking this to my two new cousins," she said.

Martin put his fingers on her wrist to stay the glass.

" There are three," he said. " You can't leave Tom out of your first toast to us."

" But I haven't seen him."

" That's neither here nor there—he's your cousin too. And the pick of the bunch."

" Then he must be nice indeed ! "

Martin bowed his head mockingly.

" He's a nice chap all right. Isn't he, Jo ? "

Jo nodded over the top of her cider-glass.

" Very well, I include Tom. I drink to you all," said Angèle, and sipped her cocktail.

" That's very forgiving of you," said Martin, " considering everything——"

" It's a pity you didn't know about me when you were in Paris, all the same. Why were you living there ? "

" Travelling studentship from the University. And they'll let me have another year or so of the idle life, they say, Hitler permitting. And now they're equally willing to oblige Jo, it seems—if there's any Europe to study in this winter."

" Brainy pair. Oh, I hope it'll be all right ! "

" You don't sound very certain—and who could be ? "

Jo looked grave.

" What is it ? " Angèle asked her.

" Nothing much. Only—I'm not sure that I'll take my studentship, even if there isn't a war."

Martin frowned.

" Please, Jo—take it. Please ! You've no idea the benefit it'll be ! "

" I'm not sure. It's such a delay. After all, I've been four years now marking time at University College, and I have a perfectly good M.A. degree. That ought to make me useful enough."

Martin looked unhappy.

" I want another drink," he said.

" Let me buy you one," said Angèle.

" By no means ! Maggie May ! The same again, please."

" I don't want any more cider," said Jo. " I'll never get through this."

" Why don't you want the studentship, Jo ? What would it delay ? "

Jo smiled at Angèle suddenly, brilliantly.

" Oh, let's leave it," she said. " I don't know what I'm talking about."

" Fine," said Martin. " Let's leave it indeed ! And here are our drinks, Angèle."

" You know very well what you were talking about, Miss Kernahan," said Maggie May, " and it surprises me very much to hear you. Take care for fear the cock will crow this minute ! "

" Attend to what concerns you, Maggie May," said the old woman in the corner, without lifting her eyes from her book.

Martin looked across the room to her and smiled.

" What page are you at, ma'am ? "

" Page five hundred and fifty-one."

" And as many to go ? Has the young lady lost her virtue yet ? "

Mrs. Cusack lifted the large book into both hands, smiling broadly.

" . . . ' he had never known such gallantry as the gallantry of Scarlett O'Hara going forth to conquer the world in her mother's velvet curtains and the tail feathers of a rooster.' "

She took a hairpin from her poll and, placing it between the pages, closed the volume slowly, lovingly.

" Isn't that a caution ? " she said aloud, but addressing no-one. " Her mother's velvet curtains and the tail feathers of a rooster."

" She'll come to no good," said Martin.

" That's as may be," said Mrs. Cusack severely and poured herself another cup of tea. " Maggie May, you'll oblige me by informing Annie that this chop she's after placing before me is no less than a disgrace to her. And pour me out a glass of rum this instant to counteract the injurious consequences."

Martin took the glass of rum to her. She poured it into her tea.

" Mrs. Cusack, do you remember our Uncle Tom ? "

She dismissed him pityingly with a wave of her hand.

" I don't forget gentlemen. There aren't so many, by the standards of Helena Cusack. And I've had occasion to tell you, Martin—to your shame—that, as it happens, your Uncle Tom was a gentleman."

" I know. That's why I thought you'd be interested——"

" That you've brought his daughter in to see me, is it, as was fitting ? "

Angèle and Jo laughed, and the former rose and crossed to where Mrs. Cusack sat.

" Who told you ? " Martin teased her.

" No-one has any occasion to tell Helena Cusack what it is her blood privilege to know. I saw your father in you when you lifted your glass," she said to Angèle, " and you have a French name. What telling would I need ? "

" And Miss Toomey wasn't in at all, for her drop of gin ? " said Martin.

"What Miss Toomey was or wasn't is equal—I pay no heed. I have my intuition to suffice me." She shook hands slowly with Angèle. "Your father had a ' cachet,' " she said, " or as Lady Octavia might have said, God rest her soul, he had a kind of a ' panache.' "

"That's one thing about the snug," said Jo, "you can always brush up your French here."

"There was them that said he had no call to his fine goings-on."

"Nor had he either, in terms of honesty—if Angèle will excuse me," Martin said. "How long did it take you to get his drink account settled by Father, Mrs. C. ? "

"There's a coarseness about you, Martin, and about this whole generation, that wasn't in your uncle. The Kernahans are respectable people, and well respected in Drumaninch, I'm not denying—but your Uncle Tom would have been incapable of saying the like of what you've said."

Angèle laughed uneasily.

"Poor Father ! I'm afraid that's true."

"He was a gentleman, explain it as you may. And Helena Cusack grants the title to few—knowing full well ! "

"Knowing full well," Martin murmured with pleasure.

"The old Colonel now, above at The House, was another, God rest him, Lady Octavia's husband. And then there was His Majesty Edward VII, the Prince of Wales as he was, of course, in my knowledge of him." She waved towards a very large photograph near her on the wall. "The prototype he was—a kind of Galahad, as you might put it."

"Might you ? " Angèle ventured in amusement.

"I hope you like the gentlemanly company your father keeps, Angèle," said Jo.

Martin came from the counter bearing more drinks.

"Here's another drop of rum for your tea, ma'am," he said to Mrs. Cusack, who almost gave him a smile for it.

"I'll take it without the tea," she said. "The squeeze of a lemon, Maggie May."

32

Angèle eyed her third gin and French uncertainly. She had been hungry and nervous before she reached Waterpark House, and although the friendliness of Jo and Martin had somewhat relaxed the latter condition, she did not yet feel the ground easy under her feet—and she was still very hungry.

" You know, I'm not really as good at this sort of thing as you'd like me to be."

" Go on. You've often before had three drinks—and I want you to slacken, to get happier."

His eyes were very questing and kind.

" Don't get her upset, Martin," said Jo.

" Of course I won't. But you've a long, sober evening ahead of you, Angèle—I warn you ! "

She thought of Aunt Hannah and the vast echoing drawing-room, and she accepted her drink.

" But it was more than my turn to pay," she said.

" No ; not to-day."

Mrs. Cusack smacked her lips on a mouthful of rum.

" The upper ten can carry its drink, be it lady or gentle-man," she said. The tone of her pompous old voice never varied. " This young lady will be no exception. I understood your father. I knew—though there was many that didn't, and some of them having the education, you'd say, *to* know—but I knew he'd never settle down with some craw-thumper's daughter of the shop-keeping class. It was the *beau monde* for him, if you get my meaning."

A girl in jodhpurs and short-sleeved yellow shirt came into the snug. Jo and Martin smiled at her and she at them. She had an open, friendly face and she was pretty in the rustic Irish style, with high cheekbones and wide-set eyes. Her body was too solid to appear to advantage in the clothes she wore, but she looked active and muscular. Her curly, short brown hair fell loosely across her brow.

" Hello, Norrie ! "

" Well, Jo Kernahan—what next ? In the snug ? "

" And what about your virtuous self, Miss O'Byrne ? "

33

Martin asked, standing up. " And now we've caught you at it, what do you usually have ? "

" Whatever Jo is risking will be about my strength, Martin. Thank you very much. But really I shouldn't. I'm in a hurry, and I don't know if that kid of Flaherty's is to be trusted outside, holding Rapparee."

" Rapparee is safe enough, if the kid isn't," said Jo. " We're celebrating the arrival of this cousin we didn't know we had. Let me introduce you. Miss Norrie O'Byrne, Miss Angèle Kernahan."

The two shook hands and murmured graciously.

" What a nice surprise for you all," Norrie said, and was too polite to ask any of the questions that rose in her quick eyes. After a pause she turned away, as if shy and in some relief, to Mrs. Cusack.

" Father wants to know are you ever sending up his barrel of porter, and to collect the empties, Mrs. Cusack. And he says to tell you that if war breaks out in Europe and he's left without a decent quota of sherry, he'll have your head on a pike on the chapel gate, so he will ! "

" The doctor was ever a man with a taste for violence," said Mrs. Cusack. " There'll be *no* war in Europe, tell him, and Helena Cusack will attend to his needs at her convenience."

" It'd be better if you could make it *his* convenience," the girl said good-humouredly. " Anyway, don't say I didn't give you his message. Good Lord, Martin, I can't drink all that ! " She pulled a face at the glass of cider he gave her.

" It'll cool you down, chaste huntress. So we're having no war, ma'am ? "

" No war, Martin."

Angèle was feeling lucid and happy with her third drink.

" I almost believe that," she said and smiled at Jo.

" I knew he'd get you drunk ; he's very silly," Jo said gently.

" No war for *us* anyway, thank God," said Norrie.

" Who are ' us ' ? " Martin half-asked of no-one in particular.

His eyes were on Angèle and he was thinking of France. " Someone said some time that war is indivisible."

" Not Dev, I imagine," said Jo.

" Whoever said it isn't getting my vote," said Norrie. " Thanks for the lovely drink, Martin. I must be off now."

" So must we," said Jo. " You two have had all that's good for you. Come on."

They stood up and saluted Mrs. Cusack, who received their courtesies absent-mindedly as she searched for her place in *Gone With the Wind*. As they passed out through the baize door, they encountered a tall, thin man in worn flannels and an old tweed hat stuck with trout-flies.

" Good-evening, Major Vandeleur."

"Ah, good-evening, Miss Kernahan, Miss O'Byrne. Good-evening, Kernahan." He had a husky, nervous voice and unhappy eyes. As he entered the snug Mrs. Cusack's voice sounded, lower and less authoritative than it had been.

" The Major's usual, Maggie May. Come over to the arm-chair, let you, Major——"

The young people went through the sunlit kitchen garden, which seemed amazingly sweet and airy now.

" She's a revolting old creature," said Martin.

" She's very unreal," said Angèle. " Will she never have anything *real* to tell me about Father ? "

" No. She lives in fantasy."

" Except about money," said Norrie.

" Yes—she's a terror on money. But everything else is a dream she dreamt when she was a stillroom maid at Druman-inch House. The Vandeleurs' place. When Edward VII was Prince of Wales he stayed there—and she made cakes for him. The seed cake she still makes when the dream drives her."

" And who is the Major ? "

" He is the last and only Vandeleur—and the only man in Ireland who gets credit from Helena Cusack now. Indeed, I don't think he ever pays her for anything."

" Sure, how could he, the poor wretch," said Jo. " God

knows how he lives at all—in a little tin shack on the side of the river."

" Why, what's happened to Drumaninch House ? "

" The Holy Trinity Fathers have it for a seminary."

Norrie O'Byrne glanced sideways more than once at Angèle.

" Do you think she's a bit like Tom, Jo ? "

" Well, now you say it—I suppose she is."

" She's Uncle Tom's daughter anyway," said Martin, " and as our Tom is supposed to be very like him, I suppose the two should resemble each other."

" They haven't met yet ? " said Norrie.

" No."

" I thought not, as he said nothing about her."

" Is Tom home then ?   Did you see him ? "

" Yes, I was a bit of the road with him.   I left him at your gate.   Gráinne threw a shoe.   These new roads are hopeless for hacking."

She took her bridle from Flaherty's kid, and swung into the saddle.   " Lucky I can mount even with all this drinking," she said.   They all smiled at her, and got into the car as she rode away.

" Well, you keep on meeting us," said Martin to Angèle.

" Why—is Miss O'Byrne a relative ? "

" Not yet.   Not till she marries Tom."

" Oh !   She's engaged to him ? "

" Not within miles of it," said Jo.   " Poor Norrie ! "

Angèle felt amused.

" What *is* the position, then ? "

" The position is that she intends to marry Tom," said Martin.

" She's been intending that since she left school seven years ago," said Jo.

" Give her a chance, Jo," said Martin.   " Norrie is used to her own way.   Time is on *her* side, and against her opponents."

Angèle risked another idle question.   She might as well get the hang of this family.

" Is she—unsuitable in any way ? "

"On the contrary. Dr. O'Byrne is most respected round here, and an old friend of the family. And Norrie's as good as gold, and knows almost as much as Tom himself about horses and cattle and land. She isn't penniless either, and there's no match the Doctor would prefer for her——"

"Well then?"

"Exactly," said Martin with a laugh. "Tom will be weaned some day—and then he'll want a wife."

A frown passed over Jo's face.

"Damn those kids," she said ; and a few of them scattered before the car as it swung in at the entrance to Waterpark House.

"Did you think Norrie good-looking, Angèle?" Martin asked her.

She glanced back to him in doubt.

"Well—yes," she said politely. He laughed.

"She's all right," said Jo. "She's very nice." And then, with a gentle, laughing look towards Angèle, "We can't *all* be water nymphs."

"That's so," said Martin. "The standard's been shot up a bit on poor old Drumaninch to-day !"

Angèle smiled at her two cousins.

"You are very nice to me !" she said.

"' *Oisive jeunesse, A tout asservie,*' " Martin was murmuring as they got out of the car.

"Go on," said Angèle.

"' *Par délicatesse J'ai perdu ma vie* '—I don't exactly know what it means," he said.

"No," said Jo, "but this girl suggests it, I agree."

The yard was emptied of children as they walked across it from the coach-house, but Bernard, the priest, came to them. He searched Martin's face ; he did not see the girls.

"There must be a way," he said in a clear steady voice. "I think of it without resting—there must be a way to save the sons of man. Christ died for the redemption of sinners, Martin ! Couldn't we try that, in the name of eternal pity? Look at here—what's coming !" He waved the newspaper in his hand. " Can't we die again, some of us, some of us—for the sins of the world ? "

Martin answered him in a gentle, conversational manner.

" We can, Bernard. You're right, I think ; it seems to be the only way. It's going to be tried anyway, Bernard. I promise you that."

The wild eyes shone, almost smiled.

" Praise God ! " he cried. " Praise God for the noble hour and His Merciful Redemption ! "

He went on his way.

" What you said comforted him ? " said Angèle.

" For a minute, poor chap."

" The thing is to answer what he says as literally and *reasonably* as you can," said Jo.

Angèle gave a little shiver in spite of the warmth of the evening. She felt hungry and very tired.

" You look dead all of a sudden," said Jo.

" I am tired, I think. I had too many drinks."

" What did I tell you, Martin ? "

Martin looked somewhat anxious.

" Oh, but I'm perfectly all right, Jo," said Angèle. " Only—it seems to have been a very long day."

She let her mind look back along it, and was shocked at how far away and vague its morning seemed. She was used to movement, to change of scenes or of companions, but she had neither a forgetful nor an easily adapted temperament ; she kept her thoughts a step or two behind immediate events, as a rule—a form of absent-mindedness which made her sometimes seem to miss her cue of casual reaction. But now it struck her that it was not the day which had been long, but only these last two evening hours of it—and, retentive of herself and of her background, she tried to shake off a foolish sense of having been, against her nature, most rapidly engulfed —when she had only desired to be accepted.

I'm tired. I'm being silly. Mother would tell me to forget myself.

" Is that bag very heavy ? " she said to Martin.

" Not at all," he said.

" I hope there's something decent for supper," said Jo.

Angèle felt cheered by this first reference to food.

The sky seemed as full of light as if there was never again to be a nightfall ; yet the evening star was up and the exaggerated quiet around made the voice of the river seem almost as if heard at midnight.

As the three turned by a great yew tree and came to the front of the house they saw a man and woman pacing away from them across a shaggy lawn.

" Hi there, Mother ! Here we are ! " Martin called out, and the two figures turned and came back.

Aunt Hannah looked graceful, Angèle thought ; her open parasol, lined with dark green silk, made a good frame for her head against the brilliant light. The fair young man beside her stooped and she spoke to him ; he wore riding clothes and looked slim and strong. He tapped on his gaiter with a leather-thonged whip such as Angèle had noticed on the floor of the hall two hours before.

Aunt Hannah smiled prettily as she came forward.

" What on earth have you been up to, children ? We began to think you were lost ! Angèle, you look tired. Oh, this is your cousin Tom."

Tom stretched his hand and pressed Angèle's cordially.

" I'm delighted at this," he said. " We all are. It was a fine idea to come and see us."

As Angèle returned his friendly smile she observed that the details of his face were a match in simple beauty for his beautiful outline. No wonder they " plug " him, she thought, with a faint twinge of mockery that half-surprised her. He has just the innocent, " dumb " beauty for which Hollywood pays thousands a week.

" Thank you," she said. " You're all being awfully nice, considering the surprise I am to you."

" Oh that ! You'll have to forgive poor Father, Lord have

39

mercy on him! Mother's just been explaining that old foolishness to me. It must seem silly to you, I know——" Tom's
voice and face were very kind; he clearly wished to set this
new relation at her ease.

"It hurt her, naturally," his mother interposed. "I could
see that." Her tone was very gentle, and with what she said
she seemed to wish to dismiss, for everyone's sake, an unfortunate but finished topic. She put her hand on Tom's arm
and moved on towards the house.

"Where's Angèle's bag to go, Mother?"

"In the Round Room, Martin. And, Jo, will you take
Angèle upstairs, child? Supper will be in about ten minutes.
The poor traveller must be starving!"

"I am hungry," Angèle said, and smiled at her aunt's kind
smile.

"Come on," said Martin, and took her arm as they ascended
the steps to the house. At the threshold she looked back.
Aunt Hannah was pulling dead leaves from a geranium in a
stone pot; Tom's head was bent and he was smiling as if in
assent to something his mother had said.

The Fourth Chapter   UNCLE CORNEY

WELL now, who'd have thought it, if it wasn't myself, reflected
Uncle Corney.

He had not thought it; he had learnt it all from Delia
and Mrs. O'Flynn in the kitchen. The arrival of a French
cousin; the unrevealed marriage of his dead brother Tom.
A Parisienne, he mused. Poor Tom, poor old son. I'm glad
to hear it, late and all in the day. Two bottles. I'll take up
two bottles, faith, by way of no harm. He chose a Moselle
of 1933.

He came out of the cellar, locked it and went along the
wide stone passage, carrying the wine carefully. He sniffed

with disgust as he went and, passing the open kitchen door, called out :

" Smell of hens, Mrs. O'Flynn, smell of hens ! Enough to make a man vomit ! "

" Divil a hin, Mr. Corney ! Don't be annoying me now and I whipping the mayonnaise ! "

He went up the basement stairs and crossed the hall of the house to the dining-room.

He was a man without a mind, but he had many inchoate tastes and fads and an amiable, affectionate disposition. He smiled as he heard the stir of voices, and then entered the dining-room wearing an innocent, blank expression.

The family was seated at the long mahogany table ; Hannah at the head, Tom at the foot ; the new-comer at Hannah's right hand instead of at Tom's, Corney noticed fussily. He was fussed by such niceties.

He went towards the sideboard with his bottles.

" Ah, Corney ! " said Aunt Hannah lightly, " we'd almost forgotten you. We've had a great surprise—and now you're going to have one."

" What's that you say, Hannah ? A surprise ? "

It would please his sister-in-law to tell him what he already knew, so he let her do that, and blinked in astonishment. Angèle stood up as he came towards her and what he saw when he looked at her openly touched him at once. For he was erratically responsive to what he called beauty, and he had loved his brother Tom, the father—as indeed memory could see now when she smiled—of this grace and fairness.

Hannah told the little introductory story nimbly, without waste of words. Corney nodded to express complete astonishment—he got a pleasure of his own always out of such harmless cheating—and kept his eyes in wondering appraisal on Angèle. Tears came into them—easy, but real—as he took her hand.

" It's a delight to see you and welcome you," he said. " You're lovely, God bless you ! You do him and your mother great credit, so you do."

41

He won Angèle by his graceful acceptance of her mother.

"Oh thank you," she said. "I'm very glad to meet you. Father used to talk a lot about you, Uncle Corney."

"Uncle Corney!" he repeated in pleasure. "Then you knew about me, when you were a baby?"

"Oh yes—of course!"

"She's starving, Corney. For Heaven's sake let her have some supper. Do sit down again, Angèle."

"Indeed sit down, child; and you and I are going to drink a glass of wine to this happy day."

He pushed her chair in, smiled at her and returned to his bottles. Angèle reflected that if her father had lived he might well have grown to look like this foolish elderly man. She did not yet see the resemblance everyone claimed between her cousin Tom and her father. The former seemed to her too young and scatheless, perhaps even too uninteresting, to resemble anyone so complicated to imagination as a father. But Uncle Corney, though silly, looked as though life had played on him and mattered to him, and before he got bald he must have been handsome in the fair, Kernahan way of her father and this new Tom. Certainly she felt related to him at once, and saw a sad hint of her father.

She could hardly keep from wolfing the cold chicken and salad and the superb home-made bread and butter.

"But, Uncle Corney, I've begun drinking tea," she said regretfully.

"So have I," said Martin. "But I don't let that bother me when Uncle Corney brings up a bottle."

Dotey had wheezed from her place and was setting out tall green hock glasses.

"Why *two* bottles to-night, Corney?" Hannah asked him.

"Faith, you'd think I was inspired," said Corney. "But when I was below I thought I might spare myself another journey to-morrow through the smell of hens."

"May the Lord forgive you, Corney Kernahan," said Dotey. "Don't you know well there's no hen sets a foot below there?"

42

" I didn't speak of hens, Dotey, but the smell of hens."

Corney drew a cork, tipped a little wine into his own glass and then came and filled Angèle's.

Dotey passed behind Tom's chair to place a glass where Martin sat.

" You can give me one too, Dotey."

" But, Tom, hock gives you a headache," said his mother.

" This is Moselle—a green bottle," said Tom. " Much better. Anyhow, we must drink a toast—you and Dotey and everyone, Mother."

Mrs. Kernahan smiled at him.

" I'll drink any toast you propose, son—but out of this teacup, if you don't mind ? "

" And it's no use wasting the poison on me, Tom, for well you know I wouldn't raise it to my lips," said Dotey, who adored a glass of wine.

" Well we know," said Martin, who had once found Dotey gulping down port behind the pantry door.

Uncle Corney went from glass to glass contentedly, with his long green bottle.

This room was on the north side of the house, away from the river, and its windows were shadowed by ilex branches. Angèle felt herself relaxing in it, and looked about her with interest. She had never seen an interior like this. Her knowledge of English life was only of recent months, and limited to flats, hotels, and the week-end cottages of film people. Her mother had brought her up with a most loving and civilized care, and holding as closely as was possible to the fixed traditions of French bourgeois and family life, but Jeanne Maury's profession had necessarily created much changefulness of place and conditions, and indeed a fundamental sense of insecurity, which was always gallantly fought indeed, and never openly acknowledged. But with a father who had neither the temperament nor an occupation which imposes form on life, with no brothers or sisters, and with a mother whose breadwinning took her away from home almost every evening and for a great part of many days also, Angèle had grown up in a design of urban adjustments, made secure always because of her mother's trustworthiness, but retaining inescapably a character of *faute de mieux*. She relied more than most children on school life and on the plans and co-operation of school friends. Also she had her cousins in Rue d'Estrées ; she had the books and personal treasures of home, and a succession of dearly loved cats ; and there was always Séraphine, her mother's faithful, hard-faced *femme de ménage*.

The life had advantages. Uncle Emile said that it fitted one for life. Angèle was uncertain about that. But it was unusually educative, for often the *Comédie Française* sent a company for a season abroad, to Germany or Holland or Italy or Spain, and this meant that, however far afield her mother was, Angèle joined her for the school vacations. She was accompanied on the journeys by the indignant, disgusted Séraphine ; they travelled second class very respectably, and with a neatly packed basket of excellent food. These recurrent long holidays in foreign countries had always seemed happy and memorable to Angèle ; particularly in her father's lifetime, for always in new places he became very gay, and devoted himself to his little daughter's pleasure more than he troubled to in Paris. Looking back on her mother's professional tours, it amused the grown-up Angèle to recall that her father apparently never thought of staying in Paris during them. Where Jeanne went he went without debate. Certainly her parents were much in love, and her father, quite rightly, preferred his wife to his little daughter. But a parent might, perhaps, in the exacting circumstances have considered the occasional sacrifice of his own preference—for his child's sake. However, Angèle knew well that had she, when old enough to reflect on these things, made such an observation to her mother, Jeanne would simply have pretended not to see her point. Herself she constantly made sacrifices of her own time, pleasure or comfort, without a second's thought, could they by an iota increase her little daughter's happiness or sense of security, and to that end she made free use of the kindness and goodwill of others. All except " Tom," or " *Ton* " as she pronounced him. He was untrammelled ; and his pleasure, Angèle reflected now, must always have been her mother's most passionate preoccupation—perhaps often in those hard-worked days challenging and even defeating her scrupulous devotion to her daughter. But this was only to guess at secrets laid away for ever now with Jeanne Maury, who, having three passions—for " *la Maison*," for her husband, and for her child —served them and gave them union and form, in French fashion, and against difficulties about which no-one, so far as Angèle knew, had ever heard discussion or surmise. Family life, in fact, her family life which she had so much loved and which had had the charm of being unusual without ever becoming in any sense casual, crude or embarrassing to her, had been nevertheless, Angèle came to see, a long battle against expediency and its attendant degeneracies of bohemianism and *laisser aller*. Jeanne Maury obeyed, as she could and as she understood them, two traditions—of art and of domestic life. But she did so in small apartments in the sixth *arrondissement*, and in modest provincial and foreign hotels ; she did so whilst earning the whole livelihood of three people, and whilst deeply in love with and so very much at the mercy of an entirely irresponsible man whose whole nature was bohemian, and who probably cared no more for her integrity than that its un-waveringness made it possible for him to live at ease.

Nothing then of all the memories, habits, and precepts of Angèle's childhood was truly of natural or accidental growth, springing from spirit of place, or from long roots or the certain hope of perpetuity. Nothing of all that had seemed so sweet and right could ever have been taken for granted ; all depended on an idea, a personality, and a struggle ; all could at any moment have ceased entirely to be.

When after Jeanne's death Angèle had pondered all this, surveying what was over, the perspective added much gravity and tenderness to her love for her mother ; but also appre-hending now the necessary loneliness and strain underlying what had seemed merely natural to her young heedlessness, it made her afraid—afraid of fixity of idea, of the isolations of self-reliance, and the awful menaces of faithful, narrow-tracked love. Her mother's life alarmed her often to consider ; for it had been excellent, ordered, and happy, and yet, examined in detachment, it was only a desperate balancing act from beginning to end—and she had never played *Phèdre*. It was a frightening thing to be her daughter, to feel so much of her in oneself, and to have been brought up to live as she lived, by her high standards, in her crude and hard profession.

Here in the house of her father's childhood she came on something very different. She had only the most generalized clues to it, and was prepared, indeed even determined, to go slowly in nearer approach, but at least she sensed around her an assurance which possessed this family without its volition, and depended on no living will but only on a sense of place and on the sunken years.

It was a relaxing idea, a relaxing air. The room was shabby, dark, and cool, and completely unidentified with fashion. A great row of vast silver chalices—trophies of some kind—stood along the sideboard. There were steel engravings in fine frames, and little bright hunting pictures worked in silk. Over the mantelpiece there was a painting in oils—a romantic, suggestive picture, to which Angèle's eyes returned in wonder —of a wild grey horse, bare-backed and prancing, against a stormy landscape. There were roses on the table and much good food and old-fashioned silver and china, not all of a piece. Delia came into the room sometimes with a teapot or a dish of scones, but Jo and Dotey changed the plates and saw to things. The walls had a dim gold sheen, for they had been papered—it must have been a long time ago—as if in Spanish leather, embossed and gilded. The heavy curtains at the windows had been frayed and faded at their edges by the sun and hands of many years. Outside there was an incessant noise of crows, but from here hardly a hint of the roaring river.

" Angèle ! "

46

She turned her eyes again from the picture of the beautiful horse over the mantelpiece. It was her cousin Tom who had spoken her name. He was standing now in his place at the end of the table. The greenish, darkened light filtering in behind him dimmed his beauty by a shade, made him even seem a little sad, although he was smiling.

He lifted his glass.

"A toast," he said. "Our dear cousin, Angèle."

They all rose about her, laughing and repeating "Angèle."

"Coupled with the name of her father, God rest him!" said Corney.

They drank to her and sat down and she smiled at them gratefully. Her smile rested on Tom, who was looking at her.

"Thank you all very much," she said. And then, to Martin: "May I drink now?"

"Certainly you may. It's a lovely wine, what's more."

"All this picturesqueness, but you're getting no chance to eat, Angèle," said Aunt Hannah kindly. "Get on with your supper now, please, everybody!"

"You'll be staying some time, won't you, Angèle?" Tom asked her.

"Well, I'd like to stay a few days, if I may, Aunt Hannah?"

"'Few days'!" said Corney. "You'll do better than that by us, child! Anyway, this is no time at all for beautiful young women to be running loose in England and France—with the Germans up to no good again, as usual!"

Hannah laughed.

"Really, Corney, what do *you* know about the Germans?"

"Only what I've seen in my time, Hannah, and read in the papers."

"Ah well, you always *were* credulous."

"And praise be to God," said Dotey, "but who's to know truth from false in those wicked, lying, immoral rags?"

"You know perfectly well, Dotey," said Martin, "that your solicitous Dev. doesn't let an immoral rag within three hundred

47

miles of you. This country is Heaven's ante-room," he said to
Angèle, " whether we like the idea or not."

" It's a good idea," said his mother firmly.

" Anyone hear the six o'clock news ? " asked Tom.

No-one had.

" You don't have to just now," said Martin. " He'll take
Danzig and Poland any day now. When he does there'll be
some news."

" For those who're interested," said Hannah.

" Yes, Mother," said Martin, very quietly, too quietly.

Angèle felt a pang of sympathy with her aunt. For this was
how Frenchwomen had been talking of late. Mothers of
sons. Before Munich. And in March, when Czechoslovakia
was taken. Not in phrases of such total detachment—how
could they ?—but with a similar passion to put this threat out
of reach, out of reckoning. Tante Julie, Madame Barbou,
Madame de Guy, Séraphine. All mothers of sons. All, like
General Gamelin, " *avare du sang français.*" Oh, rightly, rightly.
There had always been too much generosity of blood and life.
Aunt Hannah was very safe indeed compared with the women
of France, and she was perhaps a bit smug and brutal about
that, a shade too uncontrolledly set on preserving her own
safety, *sauve qui peut.* But she was no fool. She saw ahead,
and no doubt understood many things she affected to dismiss
unexamined. No doubt she was extremely glad she lived in
Eire ; extremely devoted to Dev. Angèle understood all that,
and half-guessed her aunt's thoughts as she watched her serene
blue eyes turn tolerantly from the impertinent Martin to rest on
Tom, who was eating apple pie and cream in great contentment.

And then the blue eyes moved back to Angèle.

" Forgive me, child," said Aunt Hannah. " Your Uncle
Corney's war-mongering deflected me—but of course you
must stay with us just as long as you like, and I think it is clear
that we all hope it will be more than a few days."

" Thank you, Aunt Hannah."

How polite she is, Angèle thought—and then, with some

48

uneasiness, how impeccable, when she gives herself time to think things out.

"We must show you round," said Tom. "This is your native heath, after all, Paris or no Paris!"

"Do you swim?" asked Jo. "We'll take her over into West Clare, Martin, and show her the Cliffs of Moher."

"You're for it, my poor girl," said Martin to Angèle over his wineglass. "We'll rubberneck you all right."

"Norrie says she and the Doctor are going to Carahone on Sunday," said Tom.

"Oh of course—Garland Sunday," said Jo.

"What's Garland Sunday?"

"Well—they celebrate some local saint," Jo told her, "and there's a lot of praying and dancing, and a fair——"

"Ah, like in Brittany?"

"Yes, or like the village *romerías* in Spain," said Martin. "Have you been in Spain?"

"Yes. One summer, when the *Comédie* toured the chief towns of the north——"

"*When* did Norrie tell you of the Doctor's plan, Tom?" Hannah asked him.

"Just now. I met her at Duggan's Cross, and she rode with me as far as the gate on her way home."

"Rather a roundabout way home for her, surely?"

"She was taking a message to Mrs. Cusack for her father, she said."

"Yes. We met her in the snug," said Martin, and Angèle noticed that Jo raised her brows at his observation.

"Tch, tch, Martin, 'tis you have the bad ways," said Dotey. "The *snug*, God help us!"

Hannah was looking severe, and she spoke to Angèle apologetically.

"I don't really know what 'the snug' is, Angèle—but I do know that it was *not* a place to take *you* to, and I can only apologize for Martin—*and* indeed for Jo, of whom it astonishes me to hear that she has set foot in the place."

49

Jo flushed.

"Oh, I've been there before, Mother," she said, with the effort of a schoolboy who has *got* to sail under true colours.

Angèle plunged into the affair dutifully.

"As for me, Aunt Hannah, I'm afraid I'm perfectly used to cafés and—bars and things, everywhere. You have to be, in my work, anyway. And the snug was awfully nice and quiet —really!"

Hannah's eyes remained severe.

"You poor child!" she said to Angèle, coldly and reflectively. "But Jo, you see, is rather differently placed—and here in Drumaninch, you understand——"

Corney muttered softly:

"Oh what harm? What harm? Sure, they're only young!"

"Oh God, Mother—it's 1939, even in Drumaninch!" Martin's voice was husky with exasperation, and everyone, except his mother, glanced at him nervously.

"I know that, Martin," the latter said, and then smiled her peculiarly gracious smile, first at him and then all round the table. Angèle marvelled to see Martin smile back at her and look happy. There seemed no principle in such government, but only a trick which eluded definition. "More apple pie, Angèle? Or some fruit salad? Sure? You, Tom? Had enough, son?"

"Yes, thank you, Mother."

"Then, if you're all ready——" Hannah stood up, bent her head and said grace inaudibly with a quick, small sign of the Cross. Everyone else did likewise. Angèle's eyes fell again on the painting of the grey horse. Corney watched her with pleasure.

"You keep on looking at that picture, I notice," he said to her.

"Yes. It seems lovely. Is it very good, Uncle Corney?"

Hannah laughed as she passed under it on her way to the door.

"'The White Elephant' I christened it long ago—very wittily," she said.

"Come here till you study it," Corney said to Angèle, and she went round the table to the mantelpiece. Martin stood and watched her, and sipped more wine. Jo and Dotey began to clear away. Tom held the door open for his mother.

"Come on, son," she said and took his arm. They left the room together.

"It isn't by Géricault," said Martin.

"I wouldn't know anyhow," said Angèle, "but I think it's lovely. Is it yours, Uncle Corney? Did you buy it?"

"I bought it. Ah, you have an eye for things, like myself!" He took hold of her by the elbow and discoursed about his picture—how he had bought it for a song, well, for twenty-five guineas, at an auction in Dublin ten years ago; how Hannah thought it trash, if you please; "but your Aunt Hannah, although she is the best and cleverest of women, has her blind spots, I suppose—anyway, she doesn't care for things like this, does she, Martin?"

He raised his thin, freckled hands as if to stroke the picture through its glass; he ran his fingers slowly along the ornate frame. "I never learnt about these things when I was young," he said. "I wish to God I had!"

"Corney's a connoisseur *manqué*," said Martin to Angèle. "You may have noticed that this house is rather fully furnished? Corney's doing. Auctions are his vice. It's a pity he *isn't* a connoisseur, I think."

Angèle half-agreed, but thought he looked very happy at this moment with his picture, connoisseur or not.

"Faith, I think I *am* a connoisseur," he was saying contentedly under his breath.

Jo came and sat on the edge of the cleared table.

"*Why* do you like the picture of the horse, Angèle?"

"Oh, I suppose because the colour is lovely, and it's so freely painted, and it has a romantic quality—don't you think?"

"Romantic—yes!" said Martin. "It's a French canvas, and

51

curiously enough there are indications that it was painted in Géricault's lifetime—or anyway some time during the period of Ingres and Delacroix. It's imaginative and free, as you said, Angèle. I sometimes wonder what it is doing here ! "

" Some day I might *prove* it to be a Géricault," said Corney.

" You won't, Corney. It's student work. Some young hopeful painted it by chance, on his one good day."

" Poor chap ! " said Jo.

" Anyway, if you could prove it a Géricault, how long do you think ' The White Elephant ' would be allowed to stay with us ? "

Jo frowned, but Corney, who had drunk much wine, chuckled in acceptance of the query. Angèle, turning away from the picture, leant an elbow on the mantelpiece and looked attentively about her.

" I like this room," she said.

Martin looked about it and then smiled at her.

" That can only be a way of saying that you like family life," he said.

" Well—I do."

" I expect you like a lot of things, Angèle," said Jo. " I mean, see their point, and can be moved by them, as they come. But I doubt if you would be absorbed by any one thing—you see, I think you've—well, imagination."

The girls' eyes met reflectively, but Angèle said nothing.

" Imaginative—and free, like the picture," said Martin. " Is there any more Moselle, Corney ? "

" To be sure there is," said Corney, and happily uncorked the second bottle. " I must keep a drop of this for Bernard, though."

Angèle and Jo would have no more wine, but he filled his own and Martin's glasses.

" I'll take you round the place to-morrow," he said to Angèle, " and I'll show you things your father liked, and places we used to play in when we were kids. Tom, poor old son, he never came back after all, though he swore he would.

Well, sure he had a better life than some of us—and sign's on ! " He lifted his glass again to Angèle. " We should have known your mother, child. He should have brought her here. Your Uncle Ned would have been as glad to see the three of you as I am to see you, and——"

" But, Uncle Ned——"

" Never mind all that old muddle," said Jo. " What did your mother look like, Angèle ? "

" Have you a picture or a photograph of her ? " asked Corney.

" Yes. I have some snapshots with me. I'll show them to you to-morrow," Angèle said gratefully. " Shall we go to the drawing-room now ? " she suggested, because she felt it was rude of her so much to prefer the absence of her aunt and the peaceful talk of these three friendly ones in this shadowy room.

" Yes, come on," said Jo. " Mother was upset about the snug, I'm afraid——" she added in a worried voice.

" Yes, I'm sorry about that, Jo," said Angèle. " I'd no idea——"

Martin laughed.

" Ah, these things crop up ! Family life, that you're so fond of, Angèle ! "

Angèle smiled and did not say that what he dismissed so airily now had seemed to unnerve him during supper.

Corney replaced the cork in his bottle of Moselle and tucked it under his arm.

" I must go across and have a word with Bernard," he said.

They all moved towards the hall.

Corney spent many evenings " having a word " with Bernard, whom he held, with heat, to be quite sane. A bit sad in himself, the poor fellow, that's all. And why wouldn't he be, if that's the way he feels ?

" Don't let him have too much wine, Uncle," said Jo. " Really, you know, it *can't* be good for him."

" Jo child, you have some curious female notions," Corney answered.

Tom met them on the dining-room threshold.

"We're wondering what's delayed you all," he said. "Father Gregory is here, and Mother wants to introduce Angèle."

, Corney sloped off quickly towards the open hall door.

"Tell your mother I won't be long," he said, and the three young Kernahans smiled inattentively at the formula.

"I'm not in vein for the Prior of the Holy Trinity," said Martin, and strolled after Corney to the hall door. But he paused there, leant against the lintel and lighted a cigarette. He smiled back at Angèle. "I hope I'll see you again before they pack you off to bed," he said, as Tom opened the drawing-room door and the two girls vanished ahead of him.

Martin drew strongly on his cigarette and watched Corney trotting past the ilexes and round the great yew trees towards the yard. Bad action, he mused. The fellow's old for his age; can't be much more than fifty-five. He was the youngest of the three. I wonder what he has to say to Bernard to-night?

Corney trotted on, already launched on his "few words." He talked to himself habitually. But this evening he was unusually moved, and images and memories jostled thickly in him, in confusion.

You'd think she'd be livelier, more of a playboy, Tom's child. But she's nervous—anyone could tell that. And why not—none of us knowing of her or the sky over her. Shame for him to put that on her, and on the whole of us. Would he never learn sense, that fellow? Ah! I missed him. I'd have been glad to know he was happy and settled. I could have gone over to Paris to him maybe—and stayed there a bit. There's no knowing what would have come of it, if I knew where he was, the scoundrel——

He went into John-Jo's house, where he found Bernard finishing off the night-time hair-plaiting of John-Jo's two little daughters. They were in long calico nightgowns. Bernard had just brushed and plaited their hair. John-Jo's wife was washing her son Barney in the scullery.

"Aren't the lot of you in bed yet?" said Corney. He was fond of these children and they smiled at him friendlily now. "I'm afraid I've no sweets to-night, Pegeen, but would sixpence be any use to ye instead?"

He put down sixpence on the table.

"Thank you, Mr. Corney."

"Is Barney ready for night prayers, Nelly?" Bernard called out.

"Here he is, the ruffian, and I don't know will he ever wash clean for me," said Nelly, coming into the room, pushing before her a little freckled boy in shirt and pants. "Ah, Mr. Corney, good-evening." Then, seeing the sixpence. "Now you shouldn't do that, sir. You have them destroyed. It's rolling in money they are, them three. But sure I might as well be talking to the wall."

The three children dropped on their knees by Bernard's chair and the mad priest said their night prayers with them. His voice was grave, and led them gently, waiting for them, helping them. His eyes were very sad, but quiet. The prayers were long. Corney often heard them, but the mingling of the little voices with the deep one always gave him fresh pleasure. Mad indeed, he thought. If Bernard's mad, so am I. So are plenty of us.

". . . Jesus, Mary, and Joseph, let me breathe forth my soul in peace to you. Amen. In the name of the Father and of the Son and of the Holy Ghost. Amen."

The children said good-night, and Nelly shooed them up the stairs in front of her. Bernard picked up a prayer book from the windowsill and put it in his pocket. Corney took two tumblers from the dresser, and they walked out into the yard. They seated themselves on an old mounting-block pushed up against the wall of the house. Corney poured out wine for them. He raised his glass to let the light pour through it. The last of the warm day was streaming into the wide, clean yard and fell on them blindingly where they sat.

Bernard sipped some wine. Evening and the talk of the

55

children at tea, and the little domestic jobs he did with skill and care for Nelly, usually quieted him and brought him to lucidity, which again, by making him unhappy after an hour or two, drove him back into confusion and anguish. Wine was not good for him, but it pleased him that Corney liked to sit and drink with him.

"A beautiful evening," he said gently. "It's escaped my mind all day, the Octave of the glorious Assumption. I wonder did I even advert to it at Mass this morning? *Assumpta est Maria in cœlum.* It's easy to believe it, Corney, when you look at that sky. It isn't an article of faith, though." He turned and smiled very politely at his companion. "This is a very fine wine. Have you any news this evening, Corney?"

"Plenty of news," said Corney. "Plenty to think about. You never knew my brother Tom, Bernard—of course not. The last time he cleared off from here was in 1909. Thirty years ago, God save us! Who'd have thought things would stay so clear in the head after thirty and forty years? I remember sitting on this very block with Tom, when we came in from school one day, and we tried to splinter the paw of a fox-terrier pup we had. I can't remember now what happened to the poor little puppy after, but I remember him screeching, and Tom telling me to stop shaking and give him a hand. We can't have been more than kids, because it was before we went to Clongowes. Well, anyway, Bernard, to cut a long story short—here have some more in your glass—Tom's daughter has turned up to-day——" Corney paused and stared in front of him. "It was a pleasant surprise. That's why I'm thinking about him, Bernard. He's very much in my mind to-night, you'll understand——"

Soft whinnies of brood mares came from the upper yard behind them. The Kernahans, fighting a slow vanguard action against the government of Eire, still owned two hundred of their original four hundred and thirty acres on which Tom raised dairy and stock cattle, and experimented with grain cropping. But the family's original fortunes—founded by

56

Tom's grandfather who had bought Waterpark from the Vandeleur of his time—was based on fine horse-flesh, for which the Kernahans were said to have a particular flair and gift; and Tom's heart was in this tradition, so against the run of the times he still bred bloodstock, and would not foresee a day when there would be no thoroughbred horses in Waterpark stables. The stud farm, about a mile away across the land, housed two very expensive stallions. Altogether he had a heavy and dangerous burden on his shoulders, but it was traditional, his father had carried it, and he loved it.

Corney sighed a little at the whinnies from the upper yard. Often he was unconscious of them, but to-night his nerves were somewhat exposed. He thought vaguely, unwillingly, of the anxiety such thoroughbreds had always been. He was afraid of horses, though he had fits of pretending to be Kernahan of the Kernahans about them. Indeed, when he still had some money he had gone the length of posing as a judge of a horse, and had bought and sold a few. But the money had not lasted long. Ned had taken most of it, at some bad period or other— and in return for two thousand pounds, handed over when he was thirty and in love with Ned's wife, Corney was given the right to live free of all charge in Waterpark House for the rest of his days. It was all he had wanted then, and since then he had come to want very little.

The pottering, dependent life suited him. The small income he still retained was derived from house property in Mellick, and fluctuated somewhere just over one hundred pounds a year. He manœuvred fussily with the source of this income, borrowing and mortgaging, but somehow it continued to exist, enabling him to buy wine and to bid for junk at local auctions. He had a vague idea too that sometimes he ran up bills he couldn't quite settle. This was easy to do, for the Kernahan name was good for credit in Mellick, and Waterpark House was a safe address to give in shops. It was probable that Tom settled some of these accounts, without bothering Corney. He was a good boy. Corney sighed again when the mares whinnied.

There was no place like Waterpark, nowhere else for a Kernahan to live and die, but it was a load to carry ; a heavy load on a young fellow.

Hannah was a great support to Tom, of course. Everyone said he couldn't run the place at all without Hannah. Father Gregory, who seemed unable to keep away from the house, Corney thought irritably, Father Gregory thought Hannah a saint. " A walking saint, Tom," Corney had heard him say, " that's what your mother is. And no man could have a greater blessing than that at his side." Corney wasn't a judge of saints, but anyone could tell Hannah had her wits about her, and knew her own mind. There was no doubt she was a great help to Tom. Corney had entirely forgotten what it was like to be sick with hopeless love for Hannah, as he had been from first sight of her until—until when ? How does hopeless love die ? When is it gone ? Corney remembered nothing of the love itself, but very occasionally the cold remote fact— that he had been in love with Hannah. He chuckled cunningly nowadays when this occurred to him, jolted out of dead impressions now and then by some quicker flip than usual of Hannah's authority, which suggested that she still believed him her slave. The idea tickled Corney, who knew his own peaceful forgetfulness. He supposed it must be that women don't understand that such things pass. But how had she ever known it, to presume on it in the many years when it was ashes ? There was never a word of it spoken to her or anyone. The battle for Hannah had lain clear between Ned and Tom.

" I saw her, Corney—a fair young girl. She stood here with Martin some time to-day. I can't remember. She looked innocent, Corney. Like her cousins. All the young look innocent now, in the light of what is coming ! Oh Lamb of God, that takest away the sins of the world, oh precious Blood of Christ—these innocent flowers of the old tree of evil, Corney——"

Corney took Bernard's hand and pressed it kindly.

" There, there, old son—maybe it won't come at all. God

is good, they say. And sure anyway didn't we get through it somehow, the last time?"

"Were you in that other war, Corney?"

"No. I volunteered for the South Irish Horse, but they rejected me. Said I was C3, if you'll believe me! And Ned didn't go either—he had a wife and two children already, and the whole of this place depending on him. He made a good deal of money out of it, I can't deny. But Hannah was anti-British even then, and wouldn't have let him join up, if he'd wanted."

"Ah! Then it's easy to talk! For us that didn't see it then with our eyes of flesh, talk of it comes easy! Or else we're madmen, it may be, or devils, devils!"

"Tom was in it though—this girl's father, Bernard. I remember Ned hearing some way that he was attached to a French regiment, and doing liaison work with the British. I remember we were delighted it was for the French he was fighting. And then in 1917 Ned had a postcard from him to say he was invalided out. That was the last news I ever had of him until nine years later, when Ned told me he was dead. The letter they had about that came from Paris, and it was in French and Hannah had to translate it to Ned. I never saw it—I can't read a letter in French any more than Ned could. *Mon père, ma mère* is all I remember of my Clongowes education."

"The sun is gone," said Bernard. "It'll be night soon, Corney." He shivered. "I hate the night. Mother of God, I hate the darkness!"

"Have some more wine, old son. Your memory has left you, Bernard, but mine is lively enough for the two of us to-night. I loved him very much, Bernard. When we were kids I don't think I minded who was alive or dead so long as I had Tom. And I never saw him again after that day Ned struck him above in the house, and he left for Dublin on the four o'clock train."

Tears were on Corney's face now; he stared about him as if

finding strangeness in familiar objects. He was disconcerted by this vivid renewal in him of a bad day in his life—but it had all come back with this girl, Angèle.

"You see, Bernard, the two of them wanted Hannah O'Reilly, and Tom got her. You'd wonder in a way why he did, because Hannah had her head screwed on, and Ned had Waterpark and whatever Tom had was nearly all gone, faith, by the time he was twenty-five. But Ned was good to him, and before they met Hannah they ran this place and the stud farm as a partnership, and they were getting on well—in spite of both of them being a bit wild. Ah, but then they met Hannah O'Reilly!"

Bernard was turning the page of his prayer book.

"I can't see to read the Breviary," he said. "It's time I read Compline, Corney, and I can't see. I'm going in to the light. We must pray. There's no time for all this talking and idling —there's no time left to save the world! Do you hear me?" He raised his voice. "Are you inside, Nelly? Have you a light? All this talk, and the night around us! Light me a candle, Nelly!"

He rose and strode into the little house, anguish restored to its command of him. Corney looked after him in kindness.

Poor son. Poor Bernard. He noticed the half-empty wineglass left forgotten beside him on the block. He emptied it, and poured the last of the bottle into his own glass. He's spared a lot, all the same. Corney was drunk now, and his glass swayed in his hand. He smiled with cunning towards the bright evening star above the house. Hannah O'Reilly. There she sits inside, talking to a priest that says she's a saint. Well, I know nothing against her, and that's a fact. She's a good mother, and she's had her share of trials. Tom, you villain, you set yourself out to get her, and you got her—and I was glad, faith! I was fond of poor Ned, but I always liked you to have your wish, boy. You were good to me, Tom. I'd never have lived through Clongowes without you—I know that, old son. Ah well—Corney burst into a laugh—

that was a day all right when you told myself and Ned that you had asked Hannah to release you from the engagement ! What's this you said ? " You wanted her, Ned," sez you. " But take my advice and get over that. She's lovely," sez you, " and so is steel. Ned. Hollow-ground steel." And then Ned hit you so that I thought he'd break your jaw, and the two of you fought and shouted all day, by God !

Corney finished his wine, leaning against John-Jo's white-washed house. He would like to know what really came between Tom and Hannah. Hollow-ground steel. There was something in what Tom said—God's truth there was a gleam in it, poor son. But you were a hard one for her to school anyway, and I'll never know now. It was the devil of a jilt all right, and the O'Reillys in their draper's shop so proud of their beautiful daughter landing a Kernahan. It was hell and all—straight into her teeth. No wonder they pitched the story the other way—could you blame them ? Ah Tom, there's been occasion to smile here sometimes, over the tale of your broken heart. God help us, women are simple.

Corney rose, leaving the glasses and the bottle on the block, and shuffled lazily back towards the house. He wiped his eyes as he went. He said to himself that Angèle was a quiet sort of girl, for a Frenchwoman. But beautiful, in a queer sort of way. She looked as lovely as a flower when she stood before the picture of the horse and smiled at it.

He dried his eyes again and put his handkerchief away. He sniffed the sweet night and thought of his dead brothers and of the past.

The Fifth Chapter   ON THE CLIFFS

" I'M playing thirty-six holes at Carahone to-day," said Dr. O'Byrne, " if I have to sabre a path through the sporting clergy ! "

" A Tommy gun would be better," said Martin.

61

"Some more, Angèle? Look, here's a claw!" Tom leant over the grass with a piece of bright lobster in his hand.

"Lovely," said Angèle. "I'm ravenous."

"I'd better break it up for you."

Tom pulled himself nearer along the turf, laid the claw in a napkin and rapped it with the handle of a knife.

"There you are! Where's the salt?"

The picnic was well set—in a stretch of brilliant turf, about fifty feet inland and downward from the very lip of the highest Cliff of Moher. It was a hot, clear day with even here only a gentle breeze. Westward, left and right of where the picnickers sat, the cliffs, declining, exposed an open sea, quiet and luminous, yet hardly bluer than the blue sky. The land shelved downward to the east in a composed, stripped pattern of green turf, grey walls, and little houses painted white or pink or blue. There were no trees in sight. A few sheep grazed, and gulls and curlews cried; an empty road twisted between the fields like a slack white ribbon.

Angèle considered all of this with wondering pleasure. Sharply outlined, clear, immaculate, and seeming on this day to overflow with light, the scene, dramatically balancing austerity with passion, surprised her very much and made her unwilling to cry out in hasty praise. Yet though so individual, so unlike other recollected scenes of beauty, it struck at her heart nostalgically, she felt; something it upheld of innocence, of positive goodness, familiarized it at this first encounter to emotional memory. It was austere and proud, and extremely regional—yet it assaulted, even teased, imagination. Perhaps its beauty was in essence tragical; but it made Angèle feel very happy as she drank it in—made her laugh indeed.

But everyone seemed inclined to laugh easily to-day. The expedition was going very well. Two cars had set out from Waterpark House after breakfast, and ten o'clock Mass. Tom had driven Dr. O'Byrne's car, with Norrie at his side, and the Doctor and Jo at the back. There had been some protests about this. Martin had wanted Jo to drive the Ford and to sit at ease in the back of it himself and show the scenery to Angèle ; and Hugh Delaney, " Red Hugh," Jo's faithful hanger-on, had hoped to sit wherever she sat. But the Doctor liked Jo's company, and was a man to have what he liked ; and Jo said she'd prefer to drive home rather than out, as by the time they left Carahone that night, she wouldn't, with all respect, have much confidence in Martin's driving. So the Ford, following the fine, shiny Buick, carried Martin and Angèle in front, with " Red Hugh " making what he could of Corney's company at the back.

" My usual luck," he said truly enough. And sang " I Ain't Nobody's Darlin' " for a while.

" Poor old ' Twenty-Two Misfortunes,' " said Martin.

" Yes—but why always twenty-two ? " Hugh asked, as he had asked before.

But he was no wet blanket. He sat on his heels near Jo at lunch, and plied her, and himself, with plenty of food. Dr. O'Byrne had brought a very large cocktail shaker, well filled with dry Martini, and Corney had devoted the evening before to making hock cup and pouring it carefully into cider flagons —so everyone had plenty to say.

It amused Angèle to watch Jo keeping her suitor at bay. Angèle had met him before. He had come to Waterpark to play tennis on Friday, and also to ask Jo to sail on Lough Derg with him to-day. Instead he had been invited to join this party. His way of courtship was complete subservience, a flow of silly jokes and silly songs, and regular presentations of fine boxes of chocolates. Angèle felt that if any method was to succeed with Jo this was not the one. She had teased her cousin about Red Hugh on Friday night.

" He's silly," Jo said with impatience. " He's been going on like this almost as long as I can remember. And believe it or not, he's been *eight* years in University College, and only just scraped through his *third* medical last June ! " Jo was honestly incapable of understanding people who failed in ordinary university examinations.

" Oh, I expect he does his best ! "

" But why go in for exams. if you can't pass them ? "

" Aunt Hannah seems to like him ? "

" Yes. He's nice and polite. She'd probably like me to marry him. He's an only child, and his mother's rich and absolutely spoils him. They've got a pretty house on Lough Derg, and I don't think it really matters whether Hugh ever gets through Finals or not."

" *Could* you marry him ? "

Jo looked at her wonderingly.

" But, Angèle, I told you. I'm going to be a nun."

Angèle had no answer. In a few days she had grown very fond of Jo, and she hated this idea of her religious vocation, hated it as she noticed both Tom and Martin did. She was sorry that Red Hugh was not a more formidable suitor. However, he fitted into a summer picnic—slim and coppery-haired and very tuneful with his foolish songs.

" The distinguished foreigner is laughing at this noble panorama," said Dr. O'Byrne.

" Yes. It's exhilarating," said Angèle.

" Good girl," said the Doctor. " I'm glad you don't play tragedy in the wrong place. 'Exhilarating' is the word for County Clare. I've driven foreign ladies to view our beauty spots in my time—I bet you have too, Corney !—and I've been disconcerted sometimes by the—well, the melancholy thus engendered."

" I'd like to see you disconcerted, Father," said Norrie.

" I'd like to see the lady—foreign or native—that could disconcert him," said Martin.

" But the ladies—God bless them ! " Dr. O'Byrne raised his Panama hat and his glass to the girls. " The ladies *are* disconcerting. That's their function, Martin. Woe to her who can't unnerve us ! "

" Then perhaps I should have wept at this ? "

Angèle waved her hand towards the shining, wide-flung country.

" But no means ! A laugh is a terrible weapon, Mademoiselle

64

Angèle ! And I'll engage you can weep too, when that suits your book. You're an actress, after all ! You can time things ! "

The big, Roman-nosed, burly man delivered this piece of chaff without conscious malice. He liked Angèle and he thought her attractive. Not straightforwardly pretty, which was what he thought best on the whole for a woman, for her own and her husband's sake ; but the French girl's curious distinction and sensitiveness,· her fairness, her narrow bones, her air of race and of originality he accepted as both beautiful and novel ; and he was a lively man, with a taste for novelties. Also her story interested him, as he had liked her father and often wondered what became of him in the world beyond Drumaninch. So it pleased him to watch her, talk to her, and observe her in contact with her new relations. But—he had one great devotion—to his eldest child, Norrie. His wife was a poor thing, having long ago become devitalized by child-bearing and perhaps by the too-muchness of his personality ; she had taken refuge in religiosity and excess of domestic fussing ; she never went out except to the church, and had long been regarded as not quite " all there " by Drumaninch. The Doctor never mentioned her, to praise or blame. He loved his work, his children, and the sound of his own voice ; but most of all he loved Norrie, and he knew where she had set her heart : he intended her to have what she desired. There was no particular hurry, he had always thought ; there was no threat from elsewhere, and so long as that was so, Dr. O'Byrne, genially selfish, was glad not to lose his daughter yet awhile. But he was realistic and knew that now she was twenty-five her happiness should not be left many more years unformulated. Any time from now on, he had been thinking lately, that the young man could be brought to the point, would be a good time. And though he still shrank from his own loss, he was lately considering the wisdom of a talk with Hannah Kernahan about her elder son. So now, intuitive and much more observant than his rotundity of speech suggested, he liked better to see this exotic French girl smile on Martin than, as a moment ago, on Tom. And altogether, in amusing himself with the novelty of her, he tended, only half-consciously, to *stress* her exoticism, and to hold her off at some length from Drumaninch habits and tastes.

" Yes, I'm an actress." Angèle's smile flicked him back the equivalent of his own light challenge. " It's useful training, for some things."

" *We* haven't seen much of the actress in you, Angèle," said Martin gently.

" You need no training for living with us," said Tom. " Have some more mayonnaise. You, Norrie ? "

" After you with the mayonnaise, Norrie," said Corney, who was seated on a little rock with his plate on his knees, a straw boater tilted over an eye and a hatguard floating from it to his lapel. He looked like a figure from a faded Edwardian snapshot.

" You're a brave man for your age, Corney," said the Doctor. " Lobster mayonnaise, and potato salad, and far too much of this very fresh bread ! And as for your hock cup— you ought to be shot, man ! It's a terror ! "

Corney chuckled.

" I'm a very good hand at an old-fashioned cup," he said.

" I'll say you are," said Red Hugh. " Come on, Jo—try a little more of it ? "

" No, thank you, Hugh."

He leant across the tablecloth filling other glasses, and singing softly about " my echo, my shadow, and me."

" Ah ! A triple personality," said Norrie. " That explains a lot."

" But hardly his fidelity," said the Doctor. " Eh, Jo ? "

The latter, producing more food from a luncheon basket, half-frowned over her shoulder.

" There are some jam-puffs here," she said, changing the subject, " and really they look as if Mrs. O'Flynn has surpassed herself."

People who had begun to eat apples and bananas gladly accepted some jam-puffs as well.

" Great God ! " said Dr. O'Byrne.   " *Si jeunesse savait !* "

" *Si vieillesse pouvait*, Father," said Norrie.

" *Touché*," he admitted.   " But not you, Corney ! "

Corney bit into a puff and jam ran down his chin.   He dived with a napkin to save his fine silk waistcoat.

" I'm a younger man than you, O'Byrne," he chuckled.

" Well, you won't be much longer, let me tell you ! "

When lunch was being packed away Martin refused to let Angèle assist.

" I want you to look over the cliff," he said, taking her hand and pulling her up off the grass.

" But I'm not sure that I dare, Martin !   Nine hundred feet, did you say ? "

" Every one of them.   Come on."

" Be careful," said Norrie.

" I *hate* these cliffs in a way," said Jo.   " They're too much of a good thing really."

Martin kept hold of Angèle's hand and they mounted towards the edge of the terrible headland.   The crisp turf seemed to vibrate under their feet, and it was bright with many little flowers—windflowers, wild pansies, orchids.

" How surprising and lovely all these delicate things are up here," Angèle said, bending down to touch a windflower.

" That one's rather like *you*, as it happens," said Martin.

" Oh, I'm tough."

" So is a windflower.   That's a principal part of the comparison."

" Must I really walk to the very edge ? "

" I've got your hand.   Look, I can hold it very tight ! "

She winced and laughed.   They were near the edge now and the wind was stronger.   It blew Angèle's hair across her eyes.

" I'd much rather kneel down for looking over," she said.

" All right, coward.   We'll kneel down."

So they crept to the edge and lay flat, looking over.

The water lay cold and still, very far below, profoundly shadowed by the great uneven wall of rock which stretched to left and right. There was no sound, either of bird or wave ; little frills of foam came and went on the quiet side ; a lonely black canoe, seeming absurdly small and with three tiny shapes of men in it, moved outward, escaping from the shadow of the cliffs into blue water.

Martin worked a fair-sized piece of stone out of the turf, balanced it in his hand a second, and then dropped it. There was no sound, no splash.

" It's like dropping something over the edge of the earth," said Angèle.

" Yes. Are you impressed ? "

" I—I suppose so. But one can't estimate these gigantic things. Three hundred feet would be just as much a drain on my self-confidence ! "

" Then it depresses you ? "

" Well, if I lay here too long it might. But not really—not to-day." She looked away from the cliffs, up to the sky, as she spoke.

" You're enjoying to-day, Angèle ? "

" Oh, yes ! Aren't you ? "

He turned on his elbow and looked at her. She saw many answers to her question race across his eyes ; then with one of his odd switches to gentle simplicity, he smiled and said :

" I am. Immensely. It's a marvellous day." He took a packet of Player's from his pocket and, sheltering the flame of his lighter inside his coat, they both lighted cigarettes. " When I was a very raw new student in U.C.D.," he said, " only a day or two up, I think, I strolled into the Abbey Theatre one night by myself, and *Man and Superman* was on. I'd never before seen a play by a living playwright, and I'd never seen naturalistic acting. It just knocked me sideways. It was, I suppose, an absurd experience, excessive and out of proportion every way—but I wasn't eighteen yet, and I was a country lout."

" What made you think of it now ? "

" Well, somewhere at the end, when he's caught and all the talk's no good, he says to her, ' If we two stood on the edge of a precipice now I'd hold you tight and jump.' Words to that effect. Of course the preceding fireworks support the case—but the panic is on general principles—intellectual—and most men could claim a share in it sometime."

" Only I suppose they can't get the women to jump ? "

" Well yes—that's the argument in a nutshell. Angèle, are you going to play old hell with me ? "

" Oh, no. I like you terribly, Martin. There's no ' old hell ' —we're relations, after all. First cousins."

" I don't think we need pay much attention to that. If they wanted the forbidden degrees observed they should have announced them in time ! Not that this is a proposal of marriage, by God ! "

" I don't want a proposal of marriage. I'd loathe to be married."

" But you like family life."

" Yes. I think it's a perfect thing. But it's not for me. I'm quite unsuitable. I'm fond of too many other things. I'm far too selfish."

" Ah, you're a pet ! No, let it blow into your eyes—you're looking heavenly."

He twisted a strand of her dishevelled hair about his finger, then let it slip away. They smiled at each other uncertainly.

" I think you're a bit of a pet," Angèle said gently. " But——"

" But what ? "

" I don't know. You're *all* pets, the three of you. You're a bewildering discovery."

" Ah, no ! The shoe is on the other foot. No need for *you* to be bewildered. Are you—are you in love with anyone ? "

" No."

" Have you ever been ? "

" From what I read about it—no, I haven't."

They both laughed.

" Well, you'll have to make a start, you know. You're getting on ! "

69

" I've nothing against it."

The others were shouting for them. They shouted back and scrambled to their feet.

" Jo's right," said Angèle. " I think these cliffs are too much of a good thing."

The Buick was already moving down the mountain road. Tom waved to them from the wheel. Jo and Red Hugh were waiting in the Ford.

Driving down to Carahone the three supported Hugh in his singing. They sang " South of the Border " and they ate chocolates from his huge presentation box.

" Where *is* Carahone ? " Angèle asked.

" Straight ahead. Down there against the very edge of the sea," Martin pointed. " The sun is so strong on it it's almost invisible."

The little group of white and pale washed houses was indeed only barely discernible against an arc of yellow sand and through a kind of nimbus of light. It looked like a very delicate sketch of some imaginary seashore town.

" Oh, it's lovely ! " Angèle cried. " It doesn't look the least bit real ! "

" You wait ! " said Jo.

" Here's a truffle, Jo," said Hugh. " Shall I put it in your mouth for you ? "

Jo took it in her hand.

" I can manage, thank you," she said. " This isn't the Brooklands track."

" ' When you whispered *Mañana* I wished I could stay ' . . ." Martin sang, very loudly and delightedly, and they all joined in.

The Sixth Chapter   CARAHONE

CARAHONE, close up, was not at all like a very delicate sketch of itself. It was packed with people, cars, merry-go-rounds, aunt sallies, and brass bands.

70

The Ford squeezed itself into the Golf Club car-park, not far from the Buick.

Dr. O'Byrne was busy already round the crowded club-house, hiring caddies and arranging a foursome—Norrie and he against two brothers called Hogan whom he liked to play with. The others were going to try the fun of the fair.

" Sure you'd rather play golf, Norrie ? " Jo asked her.

" To be sure she would," said her father, who liked her game. " She's got some sense in her head."

" I'm dying for a round," said Norrie. From her voice and face it was impossible to suspect her of any other inclination.

" We'll probably bathe later on," said Martin. " What time do you get to the tenth ? "

The tenth hole of the golf course lay very near a good bathing stretch of Carahone strand.

Norrie looked at her watch.

" Round about four, with luck."

" We'll look out for you then," said Tom.

" Oh, we'll see how the game is," said the Doctor. " There mayn't be time to knock off for her swim."

" Yes, there will, Father."

" We'll bring your things anyway," said Jo. " They're in the car—aren't they ? "

The party divided then.

" Poor Norrie ! " said Hugh. " Rotten business, golf."

" She plays a great game, I believe," said Tom.

" Where's Uncle Corney ? " said Angèle. " Is he coming with us ? "

But Uncle Corney had had a great deal of hock cup, and now he found a deck-chair and a mad old antiquarian parson whom he liked. So they left him in peace.

" I'll see you later, the lot of you. I'm looking forward to a waltz with you to-night, Angèle, in the Town Hall."

The three Kernahans, Angèle and Hugh set off over the grass towards the town.

71

There was distraction at every step. Tumblers performing on little mats ; a gipsy family with cards to tell and toasting forks for sale ; an old man singing a wild weird thread of traditional song ; a woman selling rosary beads and some purplish-brown seaweed.

" Ah, dillisk ! " cried Hugh.

" It doesn't look very fresh, ma'am, your dillisk," said Martin.

" I think it looks grand," said Tom.

To Angèle's amazement the three boys filled their pockets with the crackling purple stuff, and each gave the woman sixpence.

" What on earth ? "

" Try it."

They each held her out a handful. They were already chewing some themselves. She laughed as she bit into a piece.

" What'll it do to me, Jo ? "

" Make you very thirsty. I think it's awful stuff. I'd rather chew a shoe-lace."

" Frightfully good for you," said Martin. " All the vitamins —including E."

" What's so special about E ? "

" Don't you know about vitamins ? "

" Well, not one from the other. This is awful stuff—what do you call it ? "

" Dillisk. No, you must have some more," said Tom. " It's an acquired taste—like olives."

" That's what I call a sea," said Hugh. " Have you seas like that in France, Mademoiselle Angèle ? "

During the dillisk talk they had seated themselves on a little flat wall at the edge of the village and just above the wide, flat beach. Families were bathing, undressing, paddling, eating, shouting ; old country people sat about and dozed ; vendors and entertainers were everywhere ; but the uproar was simple and *extempore*, clearly not the habit of the little

72

place, and just beyond it the immaculate ocean swung full in ; glittering, gentle waves that broke with hardly a sigh on the pale sand, at the end of their long journey.

Angèle smiled admiringly. She found the whole scene enchanting.

" There are good seas in France," she said. " But nothing better than this anywhere."

" What'll we do first ? " asked Jo. " The merry-go-rounds, or the *café chantant* ? "

" That'll be much better to-night," said Hugh.

" There are sports in the Convent field," said Martin.

" Gárda Ryan of Carahone is the Munster high-jump champion. Would you like to see him do his jump, Angèle ? " Tom asked her.

" Not as much as I like sitting here," she said. " Fancy there being a *café chantant* ! "

They all laughed at her serious wonder.

" We think of everything," said Martin. " We ought to look at all the stalls, don't you think, Jo ? Up one side of the street and down the other ? "

" Yes, let's do that."

They moved into the village, getting wedged at once in a thick crowd. The main street was wide and hot, and filled with crazy, battered old booths and lively people. They moved along, pausing to admire or buy or argue, or have a bet on the three-card trick. Tunes from radios, accordions, and bagpipes made a crazy fugue, delighting Hugh. Far off in the Convent field the Carahone Brass and Reed Band was playing " Roll out the barrel."

" Find the Lady. Try your luck, Miss. Five to one against. Find the Lady."

Jo became engrossed in the three-card trick.

In a sweet shop someone had put on a gramophone record of " Madame La Marquise." The shrill French singing startled Angèle. Martin took her arm.

" Makes you homesick ? "

73

" Well, it reminds me of how far away I am."

" Do you mind ? "

" I would if it were to be for long."

" I can identify ten different tunes this minute," said Hugh.
" You're on the wrong card again, Jo ! Here, let me bet for
you ! "

" What on earth fun would that be ? " said Jo.

Tom wondered idly how the golf foursome was going. He
had never tried his hand at golf. His life was made up of hard
physical exercise, so he had no need of the conventional week-
end discipline. And he was by habit non-gregarious, pre-
ferring those pursuits which could be enjoyed at home, or
alone. The O'Byrnes liked golf—and bridge and things.
Well, they were very good at them. Mother really wouldn't
have enjoyed a day like this. He was glad he hadn't succeeded
in making her join them—it would only have tired her. He
knew she had really hoped he would stay at home with her,
and as usual was too unselfish to say so. Perhaps he should
have stayed. God knows there was plenty for him to do and
Sunday was always his best chance with accounts—but it was
a long time since he had had a sight of West Clare, and he loved
it. Doon Point, of course, a bit farther on, was a better place
than Carahone—it was where the summers of childhood had
been spent. But all this coast was lovely and familiar.

Tom stood tall above the crowd ; he took a long breath of
salt air over his neighbours' heads, and looked back along the
street to the strand and the breaking waves. Grand day for a
swim.

Angèle and Martin were fooling at a booth, choosing
picture postcards and haggling with the woman over objects
made of bog oak or Connemara marble. Jo still strove to
" find the Lady," counselled and worried by Hugh. Tom
thought the latter rather a fool, but—anything seemed better
than that Jo, their one dear sister, should be a nun. Affection
between the Kernahans was an active, constant force, a rhythmic
anxiety which they concealed fairly well, but which held

74

placidity off from them, and made them all a shade neurotic. And Tom had yielded more to it, had built more on it, than his brother and sister. He was acutely sensitive to its assaults. He remembered childhood with devotion, and was constantly hurt and made anxious by the breaches which the grown-up years made and made again in a unit which once had been impregnable.

He was fifteen when his father was killed in the hunting field, and after the Christmas holidays of 1927-28 he had not returned to Clongowes. Everyone said that his place was with his mother, and that he must be a man now. He adored her, and was very glad to be a man for her sake. But he missed Martin and Jo when term began and they went back to their normal life. And afterwards when the University took each in turn, and sometimes vacations were spent abroad, and there were Martin's travelling studentships—Tom went on being lonely for the vanished life of his first fifteen years, for the companionship of those two beloved equals, for irresponsibility and freedom and shared secrets and private jokes—all vanished overnight when he became, too soon, a man for his mother's sake. With nothing of boyhood left save its sentimental memories, and a deep, interdependent family love—its persistent and often troublesome witness.

To forgo adolescence is a pity. Tom was more introspective than he knew or than was perceptible, but he was not self-conscious, and he did not think of himself as having forgone anything. The most he would ever have allowed himself to think, but *not* to say, was that in the twelve years in which he had been his mother's support and companion he had sometimes missed his brother and sister very much indeed, and more vaguely, the habitual intercourse with contemporaries which they enjoyed ; and he had felt inadequate and dull sometimes as he tried to compensate an adult for griefs and losses which he knew himself too young and raw to measure. This inadequacy made him sad—for he worshipped his mother, and he knew, from the very earliest echoes of childhood, that she was wonderful, especial, like no-one else, and quite undeserving of the trials she had undergone, and carried with such dignity.

She had always been a legend, and her children did not discuss her. Nor did Tom think it right to ponder too much the details of her life, about which she herself was reserved. But he knew that, against her will, in marrying one man she had broken the hearts of his two brothers, created an unmended family quarrel, and in her innocence done much harm to the weak, wild characters of the three Kernahans. He knew that married life had not been agreeable to her, and that his father had been wild and violent sometimes; he remembered his sudden oaths and shouts. She had lost children, one in childbirth, and one, a little pretty daughter, at eighteen months old. There was always financial anxiety—sometimes very grave—and there was his father's secretive and careless way with money, from which Waterpark House was only now and very cautiously recovering. But Mother had loved him; and had to see him carried into the house in time to die; had to go on without him, struggling against the vast confusion he left, keeping things afloat somehow while Tom, very hurriedly, very nervously, learnt to wear the shoes of a much older man. In the early days of his mother's widowhood when he sat, all goodwill and attention, in conclave with lawyers and bankers, with relatives and with creditors—he gathered up these fragmentary proofs of the perfection he had long ago accepted and delighted in; he heard from advising priests and admiring nuns and tearful family friends that his mother was wonderful, a saint, a credit to her sex, that she had suffered as few are called upon to suffer, and that he must never forget, and must always bear in mind and——

He never forgot; he had never needed telling. From his first years she had been beauty, grace, and goodness personified—and he took his place in charge of her with an immense and proud delight.

He had worked very hard and had learnt how to carry large anxieties; but in return he lived in the place he loved best on earth, and he had not only his mother's love but also her counsels and good sense perpetually at his disposal—with her smile and prettiness thrown in as added bounty of which he never tired. Always she pleased his eyes as no other woman did ; always, if she wished to, she could make him laugh. It seemed a good life to him—worthwhile and lucky and founded on traditions and duties that he understood.

It had its darker side, known only to himself, and to his confessor. There were shames and needs which a mother could not possibly be expected to imagine ; there were loneli-nesses which her understanding would, thank Heaven, never compass, and sins of which she would never hear hint or rumour. But the worst phase of these things had come and gone before he was twenty ; and they were the private problem of any man, and the Church was there, after all, to help him solve it. It might sometimes seem as if early manhood was easier, more naturally controlled, in those who were more free than he, who were not so tenderly loved by so sensitive and devoted a parent, But were things, Tom wondered, so fine and simple for Martin, say, whose private life was his own, and who presumably did as he pleased in foreign parts ? Tom did not know. He imagined Martin might be no wiser than himself. But a man had to manage his own temptations by the light of his own soul, wherever he lived. And perhaps it was no bad thing to be spared the more obvious occasions of sin. Anyway, one learnt a kind of self-discipline, as pre-sumably others had to learn it. And living with goodness made a man value it ; made him contemptuous of his own inclination to evil.

But these were occasional reflections, for solitude, and in mo-ments of self-questionings ; they were not bothering him to-day.

" Can you shoot, Angèle ? "

" Ah ! He wants to show off now," said Martin. " We must let him do his stuff, I suppose—but it's embarrassing, I warn you, Angèle. Always raises a crowd, and infuriates the gallery-owner."

Tom picked up one of the loaded revolvers lying on the booth table, and began to shoot while Martin was still talking. He stood a long way back from the booth, and seemed as if aiming wildly through the lookers-on and other shots. The clay pipes and clay birds moving past the screen at the back of the gallery went down in pieces, as steadily as if by automatic device. Children shouted with pleasure. Tom picked up another revolver and repeated his exhibition of marksmanship. The crowd cheered. "Ah sure, it's Mr. Tom Kernahan—I wouldn't doubt him," said a delighted voice. "Grand, sir ; grand entirely," said the booth man wearily. Tom smiled at Angèle suddenly, picked up a third revolver, and once again hit six targets in six shots. The children shrieked and danced.

"That'll do," said Martin. "Leave the poor man a few clay pipes to get on with, for God's sake."

Tom smiled at the man, and paid what he owed him.

"But take your prizes," said Jo.

"If you take more than one there'll be a row," said Martin.

"Have the fish slice ; you deserve it," said Hugh.

Tom's eyes wandered dreamily, Angèle thought, over the display of dolls and salad bowls and photograph frames. She wondered which of the horrors he would choose. All the admiring children were eager to see him have a splendid prize.

He picked up a small conch shell ; it was pink-lipped and creamy and deeply curled. It had " A Present from Carahone " written on it in gold. He held it to his ear and nodded.

" May I have this ? " he asked the booth man, who assented with evident relief.

The children were disgusted.

" An auld bit of a shell ! " they said.

Tom moved on up the street beside Angèle.

" Would you like the shell ? " he asked her.

She was surprised.

" Are you—giving it to me ? "

" Yes. Listen—you can hear the sea in it fine."

Moving her gold hair aside, he held it to her ear. While she listened their eyes met, and paused in reflection.

"It's very loud," Angèle said, and moved away gently from the shell and his hand. But he took her hand and placed the pink conch in it, looking down at it with pleasure.

"It's a good shell," he said. "Please take it, Angèle."

"I'd love to," she said. "Thank you very much."

"If we're to be at the tenth by four we ought to go and get our bathing things from the car now," Jo called to them through the crowd.

"O.K.," said Tom. They turned to make their way back.

Martin, who had dropped behind to finish an argument at the souvenir and postcard stall, joined them. As he met them his eyes fell instantly on the shell in Angèle's hand, but he said nothing. He thrust his own hands deep into his coat pockets.

When they got out of the main street and on to the grass track that led to the Clubhouse, Angèle caught up with Jo and took her by the arm. I expect she's had enough of Hugh for the moment, she said to herself. She did not examine further into her momentary need of the sane, dear company of Jo.

"Did you win anything, Jo?"

"No, I'm down seven shillings. But I love betting. A race meeting's my idea of Heaven."

Angèle smiled at the future nun, but found herself unable to make even jocose reference to Jo's vocation.

"Is it far to where we bathe?"

"No. Just a bit along the strand. But it's away from all these mobs, I'm glad to say."

"I'm not much of a swimmer, you know."

"Oh, no-one can really swim here. The waves simply bang you about. They're much stronger than they look—even on a day like this. You see, there's no breakwater. They come straight in from the open Atlantic."

"Fine for me!" said Angèle.

79

"Oh, we won't let you drown, I promise." They were diving round inside the Ford now, finding their bathing things. Angèle placed the shell in the little shelf of the dashboard.

"It'll be safe there," said Jo. The two smiled at each other.

"It was nice of Tom to give it to me," Angèle said.

"Oh, a natural impulse," said Jo, on a dryly humorous tone she sometimes used, which made her seem older than she was.

They shut the doors of the car. Hugh was hovering about. He wanted to carry everything.

"All right." Jo gave him some towels. "But go on ahead, will you? Angèle and I won't be long."

He went off obediently, singing to himself.

"Poor chap!" said Angèle.

"Oh, he doesn't mind. Anyway he's very polite, and he thinks that means that you and I are going to the 'ladies' in the Clubhouse. Which in fact we might as well do."

After they had done so they collected Norrie's bathing things from the Buick, and set off by the edge of the golf links, just above the strand. They could see the three boys ahead of them.

Jo looked about her, at the sky and the sea and at all the simple, rollicking people below her on the sand, with eyes which were full of searching, keen affection.

"Are you very fond of this place, Jo?"

"Not as much as I am of Doon Point. That's a bit far for one day's driving, and anyway the O'Byrnes hate it, because the golf is rotten there. But Carahone was always our first sight of the sea, on the way to Doon, when we were kids. And anyway, it *is* marvellous, don't you think?"

"Yes." Angèle thought sharply of the summer holidays of France, the villages and *plages* of Normandy and Brittany all given over now, like this little place, to innocent summer delights, to family life. Tante Julie was probably fast asleep this minute under a striped umbrella on the beach at Sainte-

Madeleine-sur-Mer, with Uncle Emile at her side, asleep also, very much unbuttoned, and with a handkerchief over his face. And Fernand and Bette and Joséphe were bathing, or pillion-riding or eating ices or making calf-love, they and their simple, shopkeeping friends—all set on the full bourgeois delight of the annual holiday.

" There will be a war, I suppose, Jo ? "

Jo looked at her quickly.

" Funny you said that. I was just thinking that certainly there will be. The worst ever."

" It seems absurd."

" Yes. But I think it is inevitable now—don't you ? "

" H'm. Munich was awful. I was in Paris then, and in spite of the relief—and God knows it *was* a relief !—somehow the feeling everywhere was awful. I've never seen anything like the way people cried in Paris during those days. Nobody said very much—there didn't seem a thing to say—but all the women, shopping and sewing and in the trams and everywhere, just had tears in their eyes or on their faces all the time. I was glad Mother wasn't alive."

" Why ? She had no sons ? "

" No—but she was so noble, so terribly French. She couldn't have borne all the tears, and the unexpressed sense of tears and humiliation. It was terrible, to feel so relieved and so ashamed. But we all did."

" Well, that's over now, I'd say. There'll be no more relief to be ashamed of soon."

" You'll be all right here ? "

" Oh yes, Eire will be neutral, which is only the clearest common sense, politically. But that's beside the point. Little patches of immunity like ours are going to be small consolation for what's coming. Being neutral will be precious little help to the imagination, I should think."

Angèle's eyes were on the three young men ahead.

" Still—it *will* keep your brothers safe," she said.

" Yes, I suppose so." Jo's eyes rested on them too and

were gentle and reflective. Then a curious half-smile crossed her face. " But it's queer you should have turned up, *now* of all times, you Frenchwoman ! "

" That's an odd thing to say ! "

" Is it ? For two pins I could make an analogy between Eire and Europe and the boys and you."

" Ah ! "

The two girls glanced at each other quickly, cautiously. Then Angèle shook Jo's arm with affectionate impatience.

" It would be a lot of nonsense, Jo—not a bit like you."

" That's all you know. But anyhow I know there's no sense at all in being protective."

" Are you protective ? "

" I think protectively. That's as far as I have the nerve to go—and it's too far. But I don't want dullness for either of them, and yet Heaven knows I don't want trouble ! "

" You'll have no say in what they get."

" True for you. And I can always pray for them."

Angèle's heart vibrated anxiously to the simple love in Jo's voice. She looked out over the sea and tried to distract her uneasiness by admiration of the radiant day and the immense, noble scene. She had observed the lives of others sufficiently to believe that there could be dullness in what Jo meant as " trouble," and that trouble often lived with dullness. But she said nothing of this. She was conscious of the dreamy innocence which underlay Jo's firm intelligence, and which probably made the latter think that because she, Angèle, was a foreign actress and made up her face shamelessly, she was experienced and formidable. Jo might not ponder on whether or not this new cousin was still a virgin ; she would shrink from that crude curiosity and hope for what she held to be the best. Martin, on the other hand, probably hoped for the worst, Angèle thought with a smile. He was used to unconventional love, and afraid of the upheld traditions of his respectable class. Afraid also of vows and of attaching too much weight to personal feeling. And Tom ? Well, at a guess she'd say that Tom's sensibilities ran exactly counter to his brother's, though perhaps arising from an exactly similar kind of fear. But Tom had given no sign towards her of anything more than brotherly goodwill. Until to-day. But when he gave her the shell and held it to her ear she had seen his blue eyes cloud suddenly and then as it were recede from her into a very deep blue darkness. And she had felt her own heart sink unaccountably.

I wish I *were* experienced and formidable, she thought now, and, falling into the idiom of her cousins, I wish to God I were !

Dr. O'Byrne was seated, with the two Hogan men, on a little hillock beside the tenth green and overlooking the strand. He was in high good humour with his foursome, and was allowing Norrie thirty minutes, carefully timed, for a swim. She was sitting on the beach with the boys, and waved a welcome to Jo and Angèle.

The three young men withdrew to undress behind a sand-hill. The girls found a sheltered place between two large rocks. When they were ready and walking down over the sand in rubber helmets and dark *maillots*, Norrie eyed Angèle and said with good-natured grudging :

" Lord, you *are* slim ! It's inhuman ! "

" That's what I think," said Jo.

" All the same, I'd give my soul for such a figure," Norrie admitted.

" Oh, don't be silly. You both have pets of figures," Angèle said nervously. She felt acutely aware and shy of her exotic whiteness and lightness against the brown muscularity of the other two. Also, she was afraid of this wavy, glittering sea that already lapped her feet and was very cold.

The boys came whooping towards them.

" In with you, you cowards ! What's all this dallying ? Come on ! "

" Now, Hugh, splashing is barred, do you hear ? "

" Do you hear, Hugh, you cad ? "

They all advanced hand in hand against the breakers.

Martin was at the end of the row and he had Angèle's hand in his. His eyes ran over her, and they blazed with a sudden excited tenderness.

"It's absurd," he said. "You'll break in pieces! And you say you're tough!"

"Well, I am, in a way!"

"But this is the Atlantic Ocean!"

"Yes. And to tell you the truth, it frightens me a bit!"

"That's as it should be. I'll take care of you, Angèle. Come on, get wet or you'll freeze. Dive under this next one with me, and then swim."

She did as he commanded, holding his hand for the dive. They came through together breathless and laughing. "Swim for the next one before it breaks," Martin said.

They swam in and out of the troughs of the waves, on the incomparable, exhilarating tide. Martin stayed with Angèle, reaching his hand to her whenever an advancing wave looked like breaking too soon over her unready head. She heard the shouts and laughter of the others, and heard Hugh singing contentedly "When you whispered *mañana* . . ." Martin took it up and yelled it. His dark hair streamed across his forehead; he looked very happy.

Angèle felt happy too, buoyed up and strong in the strong water. She looked inland at the lovely summer peace and the holiday people; she looked up to the immaculate sky; she smiled at Jo's brown, wet face emerging from a wave nearby, and at Tom, streaking about racer-fashion, his profile buried in the sea.

She turned and swam on her back, half-shutting her eyes to make the sky seem bluer. I'm glad I'm here, she said, and a shiver of pleasure went through her. They're pets and I love them all. There's nothing to worry about in that, surely? And to-day is heavenly. Fifty wars can't alter that. When you whispered *mañana* . . . she swam along, still on her back, content with her modest prowess against the Atlantic.

"You're doing fine," said Martin. "Steer inland now.

You're out of your depth, and that might scare you if you
got tired."

"It would indeed."

They swam side by side towards the beach.

"I miss your hair dreadfully," Martin said. "I would have
liked to see it floating about you like some marvellous, strange
sea-weed."

"That's all very fine, but would you have liked sea-weed
hanging stickily around me for the rest of the evening ? "

"I suppose not. Still, that helmet thing is too contemporary, too brisk, for your Gothic face."

"It suits Jo. Makes her look marvellous—like a head on a
coin."

"Yes. She's a bit Roman-looking, I always think. But
you—do you know what you're like, Angèle ? I got it
suddenly last night. You're like something on the walls of
Chartres. One of those great angels, or perhaps it's Saint John
the Beloved——"

She laughed, well pleased with him.

"Oh Martin," she said, "you do know how to please."

They were in shallow water now, and halted and stood up.
The others were on their way in too, Norrie and Hugh racing
each other, with Tom ahead to umpire. He came and stood
with Angèle and Martin.

"Good for you, Norrie ! Keep it up ! "

"Come on, Hugh ! You can't be beaten by a girl, man ! "

"There's a horrible wave coming ; look out, Norrie ! "
Angèle cried.

But the breaker was fast and strong and crashed over racers
and lookers-on almost as Angèle cried out. They all went
down together with childish shouts. Angèle emerged from
the tumble, propelled to her feet by Martin, who was gripping
her right arm, and by Tom, who had firm hold of her left. She
was out of breath, and gulping with salt water and delight.

"You're too thin for this tough business," Tom said,
smiling at her. "It takes a bit of weight to bathe at Carahone."

"Oh no, it doesn't—I've done fine. Haven't I, Martin? Are you all right, Norrie?"

"You won, Norrie," said Tom.

"Naturally," said Norrie.

"Liars all," said Hugh.

Jo swam in sedately.

"I'm sorry I missed that wave," she said. "It was the biggest to-day. Did it wind you, Angèle?"

"Ugh, I'm cold now," said Hugh.

They all ran over the sands to where their clothes were.

"Marvellous swim," said Jo.

"Oh, marvellous," said Norrie. "Tom says my trudgeon is greatly improved, Jo, but that he'd like to give me a real coaching at Doon Point."

"You can't do it in this sort of water," said Jo.

Angèle pulled off her rubber helmet and shook her hair into its usual freedom. How well she will suit him, she found herself reflecting, half sadly and half irritably, of Norrie and of Tom.

When the bathers were dressed and eating bars of chocolate produced from Hugh's surprising pockets—"though tea is what we really want," said Jo—Dr. O'Byrne addressed them humorously from his hillock. In good fettle to resume his game he mocked their vain sport against the breakers, and quoted Greek at them. ("He has about six lines of Homer, and he uses them like a genius," Martin said to Angèle.) The Doctor went on to be witty about a caddy whom he had dismissed with emphasis and heat at the ninth green—"One of your saintly knock-kneed fellows, with the holy eye of a weasel. A fine example of indifference to material ends, as I told him——" in short, the Doctor required Tom to be so good as to caddy for him and for Norrie, for the eight holes to be played back to the Clubhouse. "The leisurely exercise will be good for you after all that spectacular work out there——" The Doctor waved a contemptuous hand against the sea.

Tom agreed and said he'd love to caddy.

"You'll die of hunger," said Jo.

"You'll be bored to death," said Norrie.

"I'll be neither," said Tom. "Have you any more chocolate to spare, Hugh ?"

So the party divided again. Angèle watched Tom sling two heavy golf bags over his shoulder and stride away over the hill, his head a little bent to hear what Norrie was saying to him. Somewhat to her surprise he did not look back at all before he and his party disappeared. She recalled that it was thus that she had first seen him five days ago, with his back turned and his head bent to listen to his mother's voice. She turned away and went towards the town with Martin, Jo, and Hugh, in search of tea.

Hugh, politely carrying almost all the bathing gear, trotted ahead with Jo. Martin walked with Angèle ; it was very hot now, and he refused to hurry ; he carried his tweed jacket slung across his shoulder.

"Tea will be hell at the Clubhouse," Jo called back. "We'll try to squeeze into the Dudley Arms."

"O.K.," said Martin.

He eyed Angèle reflectively a minute or so. Then, offering her a cigarette, he said :

"I don't even ask you what you're thinking about."

She raised her brows.

"Because you're thinking about Tom."

She was surprised, but smiled as innocently as she could.

"Well, I *was* at that minute, funnily enough."

"It's a fool's game," he said. "Don't do it—I beg you. I'm not speaking entirely from selfishness. At least I think not."

"You're terribly imaginative. But say I *were* ' thinking of Tom ' as you mean it—what harm could it do me ?"

"It could upset you very much. And there'd be the devil to pay—to *no* purpose, I tell you ! "

"But what do you mean ? Are you Tom's keeper, or the family chucker-out, or what ? "

87

" Oh, no. *I'm* not Tom's keeper. I just happen to be on your side."

He hitched his jacket farther across his shoulder, and the contents of its side pockets fell out and scattered round them on the grass. Angèle, kneeling with him, helped to pick them up. Some keys, a pencil, two or three letters, a notebook—and a little box, made of mirror and cockleshells, " A Present From Carahone," which she had been fingering and admiring on the souvenir stall when Tom began his spectacular shooting at the next booth. The eyes of both rested on this ; neither moved to pick it up. Martin looked from it to her and smiled.

" After the hero's presentation of the shell," he said, " I couldn't very well offer it."

" Oh, Martin—why ? "

" Would you take it now—to save me looking foolish ? "

She was touched, as she had been before, by the sensitiveness that lay under his volubility and attack.

" Give it to me for a better reason. You *never* look foolish, I promise you."

He paused ; then he picked up the little box, made a grimace at it, and handed it to her, smiling.

" All right. I'll give it to you, as I'd give you anything —except perhaps the awful vow at the altar—because I've fallen for you like hell, and don't know what in God's name to do."

" No-one half as nice as you has ever done that," Angèle said slowly. " I—I can't help feeling delighted."

" That's a nice answer. Come on, get up now or the natives'll think we're doing penance for something." They stood up. " Here's your box, so. I'll keep it for you till we get home, to save embarrassment." He put it back in his pocket, and they walked on.

" Don't let it fall out again, please."

" I won't. I was deflected—perhaps opportunely—from what I was saying about Tom. But anyway I could never

88

prove my disinterestedness, I suppose. So I'll let it be. Only remember—it's every man for himself now, and God for us all ! "

" I have been warned."

For the rest of the amusing day Angèle gave herself up to pleasing Martin and being pleased by him. They were most of the time in crowds and with other members of their party, so intimate talk of themselves was barred, but she liked the subtle tenacity with which he conveyed his feeling to her without embarrassing her ; she liked the adroitness whereby he induced her nerves to acknowledge his inner excitement. She told herself not to worry—for once to let events get ahead of her direction, and to find out from undergoing rather than from evading them what was in fact happening to her emotionally in the house of her cousins.

She was still a virgin, which, at twenty-five, was considered amusing by theatrical friends in England and in France. When they laughed at her she found herself unable to explain to them that whereas they had apparently spent their youth in exuberant or miserable quarrel with their parents, she had been so lucky as to love and rejoice in her mother, and find herself at home in the standards fixed by that love. To such a plea they would have countered, no doubt, their Freudian rules-of-thumb, and been more amused at her than ever, to her further confusion.

She had never really fallen in love, she supposed, after she had outgrown her privately worked-out passions of school-days—for famous actors, for school friends, and once, a very painful mania for an elderly, handsome playwright, a friend of her mother's, who had surreptitiously petted and flattered her and then suddenly disappeared from the list of their intimates. Angèle suspected that her mother had discovered his liking to stroke and kiss a fifteen-year-old girl, and had dealt with him according to her principles—but nothing was said that hinted at this discovery. When she left school and began her studies for the stage, admirers appeared sometimes ; but she lived at home, was more chaperoned than her contemporaries, and her young men had to conform to the rules of respectable society. And it happened that none of these young men did more than amuse or reassure her. It was a comfort to be able to attract the male—but that was all. She had two formal proposals of marriage before she was twenty-two, and one of these her mother favoured—perhaps because she was already ill then and feeling anxious about her child's security—but Angèle was allowed to take her own decision.

It was very shortly after her mother's death that she got work in Jean Rouart's film studios. She fell half in love, as she soon discovered most young women did, with the great director ; and when he singled her out for a second lead and for " star " development, she adored him for a time, not unnaturally. He admired her professionally, and was generous and earnest in encouragement of her, found her " *extrêmement photogénique*," and made it clear that he thought she had both the kind of beauty and the kind of talent he was in search of. But he neither fell in love with her nor pretended to. He had mistresses, but those who knew him best in the studios said that he never fell in love. The studio all day ; champagne and talk of the studio half the night ; then sleep until it was time to return to the studio. That was his life. Angèle recovered from being in love with him and worked hard under his encouraging difficultness. There were other men who wanted her, in Paris, and afterwards in England. And love, sex, what-you-will, was a constant topic in the circle of her profession ; so it was thrust upon her, and, because she was observant and reflective, she had at least a vicarious knowledge of it, and a normal desire to test its value. She was willing to fall in love, and if not on the very highest, most exacting terms, at least in some measure which her private, half-ashamed inhibitions would accept as worth the racket. But save for her brief, foolish mania for Jean Rouart she did not do so. Two years of grown-up, freelance life lay between her mother's death and her arrival at her cousins' house. For her work they had been exciting, and had fed her very strong ambition more than she permitted anyone to know ; she was secretive about the things that mattered to her, partly because she had been trained against exhibitionism but also out of a need to protect what she held very passionately to be her own. She intended to be what she had watched her mother fail to be—a great actress. But she was in no hurry ; she wanted no cheers yet, nor any of the head-wagging despondency of the know-alls ; she had been bred in the ups-and-downs of the theatre ; she knew its life and its literature, and she saw her way through. But she knew that what she wanted to accomplish could not arise from a cold centre, from loneliness and emotional uncertainty. Still, even over that, she preferred to believe there was no hurry. But she did experience panic sometimes, in spite of her almost-mania for inner patience. She was twenty-five already ; war might swamp all personal hopes at any minute ; Mother was gone, and she had no counsellor, no background ; and the love she knew she needed, for growth, for comfort, for en-lightenment, for authority, still, in the disguises it wore when thrust close home to her, seemed, for all her attempts at reason-ableness, an ugly or rather silly adventure, inacceptable. She was frequently haunted, in her personal fears, by her mother's lovely voice rehearsing a line she was never to speak. *Athènes me montra mon superbe ennemi.* Yet her mother had known and lived with love. Angèle wondered if, wherever she was now, she ever saw or smiled at her daughter's egotistical panics. She wondered if her mother knew that the reasonable success and promises of two years were not enough ; that the vivid sense of loss death had imposed, being unsubstituted as yet by any positive feeling that could match it, was turning bleak and difficult now in a heart that had perhaps been only too well taught by example not to forget, not to be cheap.

Tea at the Dudley Arms was not "hell" perhaps, but it was a warm, slow business, and punctuated by lively social encounters. Many acquaintances greeted the Kernahans and were presented to Angèle ; it was clear that news of her unforeseen arrival had spread through Mellick and surrounding society, and that there was a certain amused curiosity abroad about her.

Martin was uncompromisingly short with any males who wanted to be civil to his actress cousin.

"Frightful place, this hotel," he said. "Let's clear out of it. All these Dublin jackeens and Mellick vamps—trying to turn poor old Carahone into Le Touquet!"

"God help us!" said Jo.

They pushed their way out into the street again at last.

"I wish it was Le Touquet," said Hugh. "And I bet you do too, don't you, Mademoiselle Angèle?"

There was a tug-of-war in the Convent field, between a team of fishermen from Doon Point and a Carahone team. It was a tremendous display of muscle and heart, and Angèle and the Kernahans won a great deal of money when at last Carahone went over the line, defeated. They celebrated their relief with a ride on the flying chairs in the next field. With Martin riding beside her and holding the back of her chair, Angèle flew round and round above the people, above the little town, sometimes it seemed to her above the sea. To the music of *The Merry Widow*. She felt afraid at first, and then very gay and exhilarated. From her strange, whirring perch she looked out over the shining, open scene; she looked at Jo, riding recklessly and excitedly just ahead of her; she looked at Martin, singing and smiling at her.

"How do we stop?" she yelled to him.

"We don't!" he yelled back. "Didn't you know you have to jump for it?"

When they landed at last, she looked with dizzy pleasure at the fair green and the crowding people. She was out of breath, and everything seemed unnaturally brilliant for a moment. Martin had his arm round her.

"Good girl! You aren't sick?"

"Anything but! Oh, it was marvellous! What a day we're having!"

"Dear kid!" He stroked her hair back from her face. "Yes, it's all over the place. Where's your comb?"

"Come on for another go!" said Jo, who was enchanted with the chairs.

"No, no—drinks now," said Hugh, and Martin supported him.

On their way back to the Clubhouse they met Uncle Corney, his straw boater tilted wildly and his eyes very bright with contented cunning. He was chewing dillisk, and his pockets bulged with souvenirs and sweets he had been buying—for John-Jo's children, for Delia and Dotey, and for his enemy, Mrs. O'Flynn. But the cunning on his face was for "a dirty little old bit of a dish I'm after picking up, Angèle child, in a tinker's stall above there——" he patted his coat to indicate treasure in his inside pocket. "Sixpence she said she must have for it—but faith, for the fun of the thing, I beat her down to fourpence halfpenny! And if ever I saw a genuine bit of early Sèvres——"

So everyone seemed happy, and the cocktails they all drank at the Clubhouse seemed an unnecessary grace. The golfers were tired and exultant; Dr. O'Byrne and Norrie had lost the first round, and had taken a very fine revenge and were satisfied. The Hogan brothers were gallant with the girls, and the younger of them, attaching himself ruthlessly to Angèle, no matter how Martin beat him off, told her that "the stage was a madness with him—literally a madness."

Everyone grew lazy on the Clubhouse veranda; the day was cooling and a fresh breeze blew up from the wide bay; fun and music, though unabated in the town, sounded gentle and even a little sad from here; tired golfers passed in and out of the Club, sometimes pausing to greet the Kernahans or joke with Dr. O'Byrne; car engines roared and cars departed one by one; the smell of the sea was pungent.

"There's going to be one of those intolerably fine sunsets," said Jo.

"Royal Academy 1880," said Martin.

"Just my cup of tea," said Tom.

He was seated on the veranda steps, some distance from Angèle, but he looked at her as he spoke, as if he sought her smile. She smiled, wondering what exactly they meant to him, these rare and hardly perceptible attempts he made to reach her ; more ruefully she wondered why she always felt these attempts, and seemed at hand each time to salvage them. The personality of this eldest cousin was simple almost to absurdity ; even his physical beauty was too right and natural, too modestly carried to seem influential ; and he sat even now at the feet of a pretty Irish girl who was said to love him, and with whom he seemed gently, almost oafishly, content. What then were these rare, light flutters—which might by the unkind be called girlish for their delicacy—towards her smile, in search of her eyes ? And why did she catch them up, across much stronger things, and welcome them ?

"What an intellectual treat it would be for us poor yokels, Mademoiselle," said the younger Mr. Hogan, "if we could only have an opportunity to hear you exercise your glorious art ! Lady Macbeth now, say ! I'll engage you'd rouse us up in Lady Macbeth, Mademoiselle ! "

"Lady Macbeth was a diseased elderly woman in bad physical shape," said Dr. O'Byrne. "I could diagnose her for you, Hogan—and you wouldn't like it. Give our beautiful young artist a chance, man ! "

"But art knows no age, now does it, Mademoiselle ? "

Jo and Hugh brought sandwiches from the Clubhouse.

"No use trying to get anything else to eat in Carahone to-night," said Jo. "We'll give you something better when we get home, Angèle."

As they ate their sandwiches, the party discussed its next moves. They thought they'd like to try a *café chantant*, one of the short half-hour concerts of local amateur talent, receipts for which went to the poor of the parish. Then they might dance awhile in the Town Hall.

"I'm in great form for a dance," said Corney. "I'll

show you the old-fashioned waltz, Angèle. I'll teach you to reverse."

"I used to waltz with Father when I was little, Uncle Corney. I could reverse then, but I've forgotten it now."

"Well, you're mapping out a fine programme. You're a lively lot, I will say," said Dr. O'Byrne.

"Do you mind, Father ? " Norrie asked him. "If you like, I could drive you home now."

The others murmured in protest.

"No, I don't mind, my girl. I'll smoke a cigar here with Canon O'Flynn, and you too, James, if you feel that way," he said to the elder Hogan. "I'll expect the lot of you back here when I see you. And you needn't trouble me before the nine o'clock news, if you please ! "

Angèle had forgotten for hours that now seemed countless that there was such a thing as the nine o'clock news, with a whole world waiting on it in fear. She wondered if the others had forgotten. She looked about with sudden general love, as if she were a sister to these cousins, had sat here with them often before, and shared all their summers, all their childhood. She felt the peace of the moment as sharply as if she knew an alarm bell was about to clang against it instantly.

"There'll be no news to-night," said Hugh, with that sensitiveness he had, as of a kind, silly dog, who must take away from things a threat he does not see.

"We might get Nevile Henderson's reply to Hitler," said Martin.

"Aye ; and much good that'll do," said the elder Hogan.

"True for you," said Dr. O'Byrne. "Ah, now he's muzzled Moscow, I should think he'll chance his arm any day," said Dr. O'Byrne.

There was silence. Angèle thought of France, and of her cousins larking about at Sainte Madeleine-sur-Mer. She found Tom's eyes on her again.

"It won't happen," he said, looking at her. "It simply *can't*."

95

Dr. O'Byrne took out his cigar case, and smiled at the young people.

"Whether it can or can't is mercifully going to be none of your affair this trip," he said. "Be off with you now to your *café chantant* !"

A bell was being rung outside the tent. "Walk up, walk up ! To the *café chantant* !"

There proved to be no *café*, but quite a lot of *chantant*. The tent was very hot and packed with people. Two men danced a very complicated jig. They were champions, and wore medals which danced with them. The old fiddler who sat on a stool to accompany them wore medals too. The dancers were rigid, serious, and skilful. Angèle wondered how the rickety little platform bore their force, but they were very agile. She had never seen dancing like this ; it had a cold, fanatical character all its own. She could not say she liked it ; in any case it was too entirely novel for hasty acceptance, but it was extremely severe ; formal and beyond compromise. It had none of the sentimentality or sensuousness of other folk dancing ; it was simply a very difficult exercise, skilfully executed. When it was ended, she looked at Martin for interpretation.

"It's amazing," she said to him. "It's so austere that it's almost shocking."

He laughed.

"That's well observed," he said. "This national dancing blows the gaff on us, I always think. If you like it proves why Dev. is making a success of us. We're a prim, stiff-backed lot !"

"You like to stress that idea, I notice," she said amusedly. "Oh, listen ! "

A little chubby innocent priest had launched into a rendering of " Pale Hands I Loved." He was singing it almost falsetto, and with the greatest possible *verve*. It was impossible not to smile at him. The younger Mr. Hogan fidgeted nervously at Angèle's left side.

"A trifle unsuitable, I fear, Mademoiselle? A very fine song, of course—but hardly the thing, perhaps? And yet Father Kelly is actually a saint of a man, would you believe it, Mademoiselle? A veritable little saint, they tell me."

The little saint was cheered to the echo, and for *encore* obliged with "Love Thee, Dearest, Love Thee," very lovingly sung.

Gárda Ryan, the long-jump champion, received an ovation when he stepped on to the platform, which visibly shook under his tread. He sang "The Minstrel Boy" as if he intended his voice to assault his country's traditional enemy across the sea; the audience sang the last verse with him. His *encore* was "The West's Awake," sung even more defiantly, and with still more co-operation from the front of the house. Recalled for a third time, he mopped his scarlet face, beamed delightedly, and sang "The Low-Backed Car" with friendly, effective humour.

"Father used to sing this," Angèle whispered to Martin.

She had adored the song in babyhood, and the witty, graceful lines came back now ingrained with dear associations. Her mother, smiling but a little impatient—perhaps in a hurry to the theatre—trying to make her eat her supper; her lazy blue-eyed father taking her whole attention with his curious song, the words of which had always been so puzzling:

> ". . . But Peggy, peaceful goddess,
> Has darts in her bright eye
> That knock men down in the market-town,
> At right and left they fly . . ."

Mais je t'en prie, Tom—assez de cette affreuse chanson. Nous n'en finirons jamais . . .

Angèle encored the Gárda passionately, but she really only wanted to hear "The Low-Backed Car" again, and she knew there was no hope of that.

"Rough, very rough," said Mr. Hogan sadly. "It's very kind of you to applaud such a crude effort, Mademoiselle!

But now here's Mrs. Cudahy appearing, and I can promise
you a real treat—a beautifully cultivated voice—*bel canto*,
don't you know?" The accompaniment began. "Ah,
Gounod's delightful ' *Bursooze*,' is it not? Yes, yes, I thought
so . . ."

The concert dragged a little after the "*Bursooze*," but it
ended very merrily indeed, when the Convent schoolchildren
performed an action song in Irish. The song was about the
delights of see-sawing, and the children see-sawed bravely,
as they sang, on a long plank balanced across a barrel. The
performance was much admired, and wits and relatives in the
audience shouted advice or encouragement to Sean and May
and Josie, who shyly signalled sometimes in response. And
almost at the last bar of the song the barrel started to roll
impromptu, the plank lost its poise, and the solemn children
were hurled and scattered all over the platform and upside
down into the laps of the front stalls. The nun who was
accompanying the song sprang from the piano in wrath and
dismay, but no-one was hurt, the applause was earsplitting,
and that round of the *café chantant* was held by all to have been
a riotous success.

"Great value!" said Hugh, drying his eyes from a good
laugh as they came out of the tent. "Great value entirely!"

"Ah, I'm afraid *Mademoiselle* must find us sadly primitive,"
said Mr. Hogan.

"For God's sake stop *Mademoiselle*-ing her!" said Martin
rudely. "She isn't your governess, Hogan!"

Mr. Hogan was hurt.

"I beg your pardon, Martin; but I still believe in a little
formality, you see. I hope I don't annoy you, *Mademoiselle*?"

"But of course not, Mr. Hogan. You're very kind indeed,
I think."

"That's very nicely spoken of you, Mademoiselle. And
may I perhaps have the honour of a dance with you now—
this one?"

They were inside the tin-roofed Town Hall, and Tom was

buying tickets for the free-for-all dance which was going forward.

" Thank you very much."

" Oh, the honour is mine, I assure you."

Martin was in a sulk now.

" I thought you said you were dancing with me ? "

" Oh but I am, Martin ! " She smiled at him, amused at his scowling over all this nothing. " But you didn't say this particular first dance, did you ? "

" I don't know what I said."

" No-one can doubt, Mademoiselle, that you are the soul of correctitude in all your undertakings," said Mr. Hogan. " That goes without saying. Allow me ! "

He held his arm to her, and they moved into the dance. Angèle waved and laughed back to Martin, who suddenly laughed too, and blew her a kiss. As he did so, out of the corner of his eye he saw Tom looking at her as she was swung off from them in Mr. Hogan's arms. So he in turn looked at Tom and tried to assess the value of the shadow he perceived on his brother's face.

The Kernahan party danced with each other with enjoyment. Tom danced with Norrie, with Jo, and Angèle being engaged, with Norrie again. One of the " Dublin jackeens " who had been presented to Angèle at the Dudley Arms cut in and asked her to waltz, but against the defence of Martin, Corney, and Mr. Hogan he got away with nothing.

Angèle had a terrific waltz with Corney. He got the band— a quartette hired from Ennis—to play " Nights of Gladness " for it.

" I wanted the ' Blue Danube,' " he told her, " but the old codger at the 'cello said he couldn't risk it, God help him ! "

Corney was astonishingly skilful on the dancing floor, and he needed to be, for, though the crowd was thick, he took the waltz uncompromisingly at Edwardian pace. Alone among the 1939 shufflers and hesitators, he and Angèle whirled round the outer circle of the floor, everyone smiling and letting them pass. They took the corners like a couple of Derby triers, and every now and then arabesqued in reverse to the centre of the room, and back again to the outer edge.

"You're a marvel," said Corney. "You're Tom's own daughter every step of the way!"

Angèle's gold hair flew about her.

"Oh, you're a wonderful dancer, Uncle Corney!"

They whizzed, without seeing them, past Tom and Norrie.

"Corney's putting Angèle over the sticks all right," said the latter.

"Isn't he, though? She's very nice to him."

"Oh, it's a bit of fun!" Norrie looked up, smiling, at her partner. He was looking over her head in the direction towards which Corney had steered. She had thought that he would be smiling too, but he was not. He looked grave; he had apparently forgotten the two flying waltzers.

"You're not worrying about anything, are you, Tom?" She knew a good deal about his business worries. "Anything special, I mean?"

He looked down at her and shook his head. He smiled a little then, but not wholeheartedly.

"No—I'm not worrying."

She patted his arm very lightly.

"I'm glad. It's been a good day, hasn't it?"

"Very good."

But Norrie made a mental note that he was tired. He was never a very good stayer at mere racketing, she had noticed before. He seemed to need his own place and his own occupations more than most men. She was beginning to worry about her father too. It was getting on for half-past nine, and they really ought to be home before midnight. Tom and her father had hard days to get through to-morrow.

"Well done!" said Jo to Angèle, when "Nights of Gladness" was over.

"You're in good training, I will say," said Hugh. "Hardly out of breath at all."

" Oh it was lovely ! Thank you a thousand times, Uncle Corney ! "

Her cheeks were almost pink now, Martin noticed, and her eyes shone very darkly, almost as if they were navy-blue. He felt a little mad with sheer, edge-fine appreciation of her. I almost believe you could enjoy her for ever, he thought uneasily.

" Yes, you're probably right, Norrie," Jo was saying. And then to the others : " We're thinking it's time to go home, boys. It's a two-hours' drive, you know, and it'll be ten before we're started."

Nobody raised any real objection. Martin thought contentedly that his home was Angèle's also to-night, and that he would be with her for the long, cool drive. They began to edge their way towards the door of the dance-hall. They said good-night to Mr. Hogan as they went. He was sad.

" The night is only beginning, Mademoiselle," he protested. " And I have never before had the privilege of social acquaintance with an exponent of your great art."

Angèle murmured suitably, and Mr. Hogan begged and prayed so fervently for the pleasure of another meeting that Jo, half in mischief and half kindly, suggested that he come to supper at Waterpark one evening during the week. He gasped with delight in acceptance, as Martin almost punched him back into the press of dancers. " The poor ape ! " he said good-naturedly to Jo.

" I didn't get a dance with you, Angèle," said Tom. " I was hoping for the next."

" Ah, you're not in her class, old son," said Corney. " It takes myself to dance with you, Angèle—an exponent, as our friend Hogan would say. An *exponent.*" He chuckled contentedly.

They made their way back to the Clubhouse through crowds still pleasure-seeking. All the houses were open, and light and voices and radio music streamed from them. The street stalls were lit by naphtha flares ; the three-card trick man still desired all-comers to " find the lady." There was a smell of strong liquor; there were many smells, but that of seaweed and the sea overrode them all. The flying chairs still flew above the Convent field. Over to the left the sea gleamed and shivered, but the strand was empty now. Far away up the hill the brass band played " Let Erin Remember." Pairs of lovers lurked in doorways and odd corners.

" They're taking an almighty chance with Father Donovan's blackthorn stick," said Martin.

Dr. O'Byrne was pleased to see them and ready to go home.

" Who'll have a drink for the road ? " asked Martin.

Corney said they all should, but nobody else agreed, and a movement was made towards the cars.

" Any news ? " Martin asked Dr. O'Byrne.

" Something about incidents on the Polish frontier, I think," the latter replied, " but to tell you the truth I dozed a bit while they were crooning it out at me."

They all paused by the cars and looked about them. A great white star was climbing up the eastern sky.

" Is that Jupiter ? " Angèle asked.

" No other," said Dr. O'Byrne. " And Mars shouldn't be long behind him now."

" ' Oh my prophetic soul ! ' " said Martin.

" No need for that, Martin," said Norrie. " It won't be *your* war, I tell you."

Dr. O'Byrne laughed at her.

" That seems to settle it," he said. " In with you now, my girl, and good-bye to St. Fachnan and his garland ! "

" St. Felim, isn't it ? " said Jo.

" St. Fachnan," said the Doctor.

Hugh had started the engine of the Ford.

" I'll drive home for you, Jo," he said. " Come on, get in here and have a chocolate."

" The same goes for you," said Martin to Angèle, opening the back door of the Ford for her.

So Corney travelled home with Dr. O'Byrne in the back of the Buick, and Tom sat in front and drove for Norrie.

THE party broke up at the gate of Waterpark, where good-nights were said to the O'Byrnes ; Corney got into the back of the Ford with Martin and Angèle, and Tom stood on the footboard as far as the stableyard. Then Hugh said good-night and departed in his own long-nosed Fraser-Nash, the roar of his engine killing his last repetition for that day of " South of the Border."

The Kernahans and Angèle walked back to the house under the ilex trees. As Hugh's racing engine ceased to resound, the peace of the night struck almost painfully on the senses, and no-one spoke.

A bell began to toll midnight eastward through the trees. Angèle knew it was the stable bell at Drumaninch House.

" Poor Vandeleur, in his old tin shack ! " said Corney suddenly.

" I often wonder how he bears to live near that bell, poor devil ! " said Tom.

" But he couldn't bear to live away from it either," said Jo. " He can't bear life at all, I think."

" Except in the snug," said Martin.

Delia had left tea-things and food set ready on trays in the upstairs pantry. Jo put a kettle on the gas-ring there, and the others helped her to carry the food into the drawing-room. They set a table near the semi-circular window of the inner room. They moved and spoke very quietly in the quiet house. They lighted one lamp, but the night outside was brilliant and half-lighted the room. Tom flung up a sash and stood a minute looking out at the river. Its voice filled the room, but Angèle, having grown used to it, was aware of it now only as an increase, a stress, in an immense tranquillity.

" Do you hear that owl ? " whispered Uncle Corney.

Tom nodded.

They ate and drank lazily, making lazy comments on the day. Jo yawned once or twice, and Corney held his dirty little Sèvres dish under the lamp and purred over his own cleverness. Martin watched Angèle, and wondered what lay ahead, and whether war was really coming now.

Tom sat very still, near the open window.

" You're eating nothing," Jo said to him.

" I don't feel hungry, thank you, Jo."

" Why are you so mad on ' The Low-Backed Car ' ? " Martin asked Angèle.

On the drive home she had made him sing it through three times. Hugh had joined in to help him, but they had made a muddle of the words.

" Because Father used to sing it, when I was little. I wish you knew it properly."

" I know it," Tom said.

" It wasn't such a bad old *café chantant*, was it ? " said Jo.

" It was fine," said Angèle.

" Not nearly ' classy ' enough for Mr. Jamesy Hogan, though," said Martin. " My God, the way that idiot fell for you, Angèle ! "

" Ah, the poor creature ! " said Jo.

" He's no good on the dancing floor," said Corney judicially. " He waltzes like a Protestant curate." He swallowed a yawn, and got up from his chair wearily. " Good-night to you all. Good-night, Angèle, and thank you for that fine dance we had."

" Good-night, Uncle Corney."

He went off with his little dish, which he was going to wash at the pantry sink before he went to bed.

The others stood up and began to help Jo gather the plates and cups on to trays.

" Don't you bother, Angèle, you're tired. Could you carry *that* tray, Martin ? "

Jo set off towards the door with one load. Martin followed with his. From the outer drawing-room he looked back. Tom and Angèle were standing curiously still, he thought, by the cleared table. The midnight light from sky and river fell all round them.

Martin left the outer drawing-room and closed the door.

"I'm going to bed," he said dully to Jo, as he crossed the hall.

Tom turned from Angèle and looked out of the window.

"Do you like this ? " he asked her, indicating the wide view.

"Yes."

He took a step or two away from her, nearer to the window.

"Angèle . . ."

"Yes—say it ! Speak to me ! "

The long day of lightness and amusement had strained her nerves, but now in this exhausted, very still moment at the end of it she knew that she could stand no more of this boy's anxious tentatives towards her. There were pain and anxiety in her breast, but for once it seemed to her that she knew what she wanted. For how long, how cruelly, foolishly or rightly she had no way of guessing—her innocence denied her that, although her sense of orthodoxy would not spare her any of the outer barriers and dangers of what lay ahead. She saw them all as if in the unrelenting light that never seemed to leave this window, even at midnight ; yet they seemed, for this moment at least, secondary things, though grave, and this other, this knowledge, was pure certainty. For once she knew that a true feeling dominated her, and that she was neither afraid of it nor ashamed.

Tom turned from the window swiftly when he heard the tone of her voice.

"I've been asleep a long time, I think," he said, and he spoke fast now and his voice shook. "In a way, I've never been awake. But since you came, since I saw you—and all to-day—I see. I used to love all this "—he looked about him as if at things that were strange to him—" as if it were life, as if it were the whole of things. And now, if you weren't here, if you were to go, it would be meaningless. I see that you're the reason for it all—and that you are a part of it for me now, and that I must give it all to you—and keep you here."

He paused, and they stared at each other.

"Don't speak to me yet, Angèle. I think I'm mad. I know you belong to the world and the stage, and that you are foreign to all this, and couldn't bear it. And I know my own side of the story too. And we're cousins, and I'm not rich, and I have duties—but it *is* your home, in one way, and you have brought it to life, and it fits you. And if you go away—Angèle, I didn't know a thing like this could ever happen to *me*; will you tell me what I am to do?"

"I can't. I am in love with you. I don't know what to do myself."

Neither moved. The cold light from without fell between them. But Tom's face became irradiated, and his beauty so enhanced for a second that Angèle saw him almost as a stranger.

"You are in love with me, you said?"

"Yes. I don't know what to do. I love you."

"Then you won't ever go away?"

"I don't see how I could."

"My love!"

"Oh you! Oh Tom!"

His hands went out as if to touch her, but then fell back to him.

"There's plenty of time," he said, under his breath. "Oh, now there's plenty of time."

The door of the outer drawing-room opened and the full lights of the chandeliers blazed up. Hannah came towards them, looking very pretty in a faded *peignoir*.

"Still chattering?" she said. "And where are the others?"

"In the pantry, I think, Aunt Hannah."

"Well, it's time you were all in bed now, surely? Did you have a good day? How white you are looking, Angèle! I hope they took sufficient care of you?"

"Oh yes, thank you. It was a lovely day. I'm going to bed now."

"That's right, child. Good-night!"

"Good-night, Aunt Hannah."

She crossed the room, and looked back from the door to

Tom. He was closing the window, but he turned to see her go. The full lights showed her his face still shining with an extraordinary delight.

" Good-night, Angèle ! Sleep well."

" Good-night, Tom," she said, and smiled at him.

As she left the drawing-room she heard Aunt Hannah say :

" You're looking very lively, son. Come up to my room, and tell me the day's adventures."

She took her coat from the bench in the hall, and with it, folded in it, Tom's shell. A Present from Carahone. She unwrapped it from the coat as she walked upstairs, and stroked it closely with both hands. Dear love, dear love, her heart was saying. She could not think. She was brimful of joy, and fear.

In her room she found Martin's little box of mirror and shell laid carefully upon her pillow. She smiled at it absent-mindedly, and with Tom's shell still in her hands she went and stood at the window, which looked out over the river. She heard Tom and Aunt Hannah come upstairs, and as they entered the latter's room she heard his murmuring voice and her aunt's clear laugh of response.

The Eighth Chapter   DOTEY IS TROUBLED

MRS. KERNAHAN disliked going to Drumaninch village on foot, and indeed never did so. She said that the halting and chatting with this one and that which it necessitated was a bore. She disliked small talk, and declared, to her children's amusement, that most outsiders made her feel shy ; she said she preferred to gather up the humours of village life at second hand, seated in her own chair in the drawing-room window. She went to Mass at her parish church every Sunday, and scattered her charming smile on friends and neighbours at the chapel gate, before she got into the Ford again and was quickly driven home. And once a week or so, on her way back from Mellick whither she had gone to shop or to go to Confession, she might be seen leaning out of the car to have a passing word with Dr. O'Byrne, to ask old Sadie Ryan how she was, or to command Mrs. Geary to Waterpark for a day's scrubbing or carpet-beating. But she never walked about the village casually, as other people did.

Dotey ran her local errands for her. Very willingly— unless it was to the yard, to John-Jo's house, or to the kitchen garden. For in those regions she might meet Bernard, of whom she was afraid. " God help the poor creature, but he puts me in a holy fright, the very thought of him," Dotey said. " I've only to lay an eye on him to break out in a flood of perspiration, God forgive me ! " But a trot to the village, or to Drumaninch House with a note for Father Gregory— these were labours over which she never demurred, however inclement or hot the day.

" You're a sociable creature, Dotey," Hannah said to her amusedly sometimes. " You're wasted here, I fear."

Hannah was innocent in many ways. The high defences of her vanity had kept her innocent. Although she had Dotey helplessly and for ever in her power and knew this, she did not understand her at all, or think it necessary to do so.

On the morning after Garland Sunday the house was quiet. Tom had had early breakfast and gone off in the Ford to Mellick cattle fair ; Martin had not appeared at all so far, and was presumably still asleep, or lying in bed reading *Ulysses*, his mother surmised, or something equally disgusting—according to his undisciplined habit ; Jo was upstairs helping Delia with the bedrooms, and Angèle, very quiet and polite, had set off by herself for a walk along the river-bank. Hannah liked knowing where each person was and what he was doing.

The day was already so hot and bright that she apologized to Dotey for requiring messages done in Drumaninch. But the latter was as glad as usual to have this little outing. She was ready to go at half-past ten ; she wore a long black silk coat over her black flowered silk dress, and a black hat mounted high with purple and white flowers ; she wore black cotton gloves and carried her very shabby, fat black handbag in her shopping basket. Already as she stood on the doorstep she shone with sweat, but she set off with a smile.

The smile faded as she waddled down the drive, but her face was set in such an unalterable shape of placidity and good humour that even now, with her features relaxed and off guard, there was no sign in any of them of the perturbation she was undergoing.

I don't know ought I to say anything to Hannah, or would it be right for me to leave well alone, in God's name ? Sure, hasn't she enough on her mind—and she the best and most devoted of mothers !—without I bringing her this bit of trouble, the creature ? But sure, if I *don't*, if I hold my tongue, maybe 'tis ruined I'll see the boy, and his mother's heart broken before my very eyes ? And what'll I have to say for myself then, will you tell me ? I *owe* it to Hannah, that's what I do. I owe it to Hannah to protect her and her children, and to let her have the evidence of my own eyes, so I do. . . .

Dotey thought as she talked, in cushioned superficialities and pieties. She believed in whatever she found rambling round domestically on the surface of her consciousness, and used these familiars in all good faith for talking and for her ruminative processes. But underneath this soft layer which she took to be herself and which defined her as brainless and foolish, she had a couple of dominant instincts, which she knew nothing about, but which had in fact ruled her life from babyhood, making it exceptional within its circumstantial limits, and making an odd, original character of her—again within the very small range of her personality. Dotey was timid and greedy—and both excessively. She had all her life refused responsibility, loathed it and denied it ; with equal certainty she had insisted on material comfort. She wanted nothing of life save to be quit of its personal assaults, and to be well fed and well bedded. And without having to think at all, simply by following instincts of which she was unconscious, she had managed these two requirements uninterruptedly during her sixty-seven years. If the last twelve of these, spent in the house of her cousin, Hannah Kernahan, had exacted a little more of her than she had hitherto paid for her two desires, they had in recompense yielded a better measure of comforts than the earlier years. But Dotey, be it repeated, knew nothing of all this. All she knew was that when Mrs. O'Reilly died Hannah had offered a home to her mother's faithful old cousin and companion; and in return for that gesture of family feeling, she, Dotey, made herself as useful as possible to Hannah. In fact, she made herself very useful; she was often surprised at all she got through in a day; but the food and the comforts were certain, and she had free access to the pantry.

She did not want anything changed. She never had liked change, though when it forced itself upon her she usually adapted herself to it, for it was her natural, timid custom to be whole-heartedly on the side of the party in power. But now she wanted no change or disturbance at Waterpark House; she foresaw none that could better her own lot; and indeed the old woman knew, without ever facing it, that she was where she was—in what she would have called "clover"— only because her cousin Hannah liked to play the lady, liked to have leisure and to look pretty and at ease for her son, and for her priest-admirers, as cheaply as possible. What could be cheaper than Dotey, who did everything she was told to do and plenty besides, and to whom, as a blood relation, the awkward word "salary" had never once been mentioned in twelve years?

Dotey knew that when Hannah ceased to be full mistress of Waterpark, her own undefined position would either cease to be or would undergo much change; she knew also that Hannah dreaded the possible idea of a rival mistress in her house, a wife for Tom; and she knew, for she was all her earlier life an inmate of the O'Reilly household, the true, distressful story of Hannah's brief engagement to the first Tom

110

Kernahan. She knew that the blow that man had driven against a spoilt girl's pride had never been forgiven. She had seen the whole drama through from beginning to end in the O'Reillys' dining-room above the shop, and had marvelled silently at the rage and the commotion ! But there it was—and you might as well be idle as trying to make them go easy that can't. Hannah had ever the high opinion of herself, faith—and why wouldn't she ?—and the way she fell in love with that soft-spoken boyo was unnatural almost, to them that knew her. And then to be insulted the way she was, after making a show of herself with love, God help her ! Well, well—it's a miracle I didn't die on the spot, Dotey ruminated now, when that thin, quiet streak of a girl walked in last Tuesday and said she was Tom Kernahan's daughter, no less ! I declare to God if the fright of it didn't take the heart out of me. And wasn't Hannah the quiet one too, keeping the knowledge of his marriage and his child from the lot of us all these years, if you please ? But sure that was just like her—as proud as Lucifer always. Her own mother said it, time and time again. No-one will best Hannah, she'd say to me ; no-one will ever down that girl, Dotey, or go one better than her. I declare to God you could nearly be sorry for that poor young foreign child, with her smile and her story, and she expecting her Aunt Hannah to be delighted with her, God help us ! Ah well, I knew there was no good in it. I knew it that very evening, I felt it like a wave going over me. And sure wasn't I in the right, as I know to my sorrow this morning ?

Dotey was in the habit of eating a good supper—a second supper in the pantry by herself before she retired to bed. Some-times too she took a little plate of odds and ends to her room, to help her through the night. Last night, with Delia fussing round leaving trays for the picnickers, she had been unable to collect her plateful. But after everyone had gone to bed, about one o'clock, she thought she had better slip downstairs and find something—if she was to get any sleep at all that night. She had noticed a very nice cake with thick coffee icing that Delia left out for the picnickers' supper. Her mouth watered as she put on her slippers and dressing-gown.

She found the cake and some other eatables, and made a selection. She came upstairs again with her plateful, needing no light but that of the summer night pouring on to the staircase and landing. As she came to the top of the second flight she heard a bedroom door open. She stood very still ; from where she was she could see along the landing. She saw Tom come out of his room. He was still fully dressed and he had something white and flat, an envelope, a letter, in his hand. He went very quietly to the door of the Round Room, Angèle's room, bent down there, and slipped the letter under it. Then he went back to his own room.

Dotey, recalling this to herself, was of the opinion that she had all but fainted, that it put her heart across her, and that she would never be the better of it. Certainly it gave her a troubled night. It was a night to make her ruminate in fear, for her instincts deduced from it that already, without a word spoken or a suspicion raised, Hannah was no longer full mistress of Waterpark House.

Dotey didn't know what to do for the best. She was never one to disturb a hornets' nest or a sleeping dog. She believed in peace and quiet, in glossing things over, and in the bliss of ignorance. She knew nothing about love, or about the normal forces or activities of life. She was a great one for saying that God is good, and that He never forsakes the widow or the orphan ; she constantly murmured in piety of this one or that one that he had " his share of troubles," but she didn't think it did people any good to let themselves " get upset." She had never examined anxiety, or undergone a real pain, physical or spiritual ; she was a stranger to pride and violence and all extremes ; and of passion she knew nothing beyond her recurrent cunning need of, say, a piece of rich fruit cake or a glass of port.

But soft and unseeing, she knew Hannah. She had known her from birth. She knew her cousin's values, though she could not have defined them—and she knew them to be in-transigent. Whoever threatened them would get no easy passage ; Dotey quaked at the mere idea of such a battle, not only because she loathed all " upsets," but because in this one her own security would be at issue. She was Hannah's faithful man ; the one permanent nourisher of the now widely flourish-ing belief that Mrs. Kernahan was a wonder, a sainted widow and a martyr mother. A woman in a million. The greatest beauty of her day in Mellick, with the three Kernahan brothers —and not they alone !—at each other's throats about her. And now look at her—the best of Catholic mothers, unselfish and devoted, a most charitable and perfect lady, a widow who had suffered many's the dark trial all through her married life, and had had to keep her beautiful home together and bring up her children single-handed—an example to us all. Dotey was a perpetual spring of this talk. Priest-admirers came and went round Hannah as their careers dictated ; nuns grew senile and bank managers were moved on ; family lawyers died and were succeeded by their irreverent sons—and Dr. O'Byrne was ever a brusque, outspoken, and indelicate man. But Dotey stayed as she had been, and kept the platitudes in currency, believing every unexamined word of them. And somehow understanding that they were to the reserved and amusedly deprecatory Hannah what the pleasures of the pantry were to her.

She understood too, though by no means fully or deeply, but only with a confused, platitudinous acceptance, that Hannah worshipped her son Tom inordinately. " He's the pulse of her heart," Dotey said, " and sure, would you blame her ? Isn't it only natural—and a lovely thing to see, thank God—the saintly devotion of a mother and a son. Like Our Blessed Lady herself, at the foot of the Cross," said Dotey. She knew nothing of passion—of jealousy or possessiveness, or of being in love with the illusion of being exclusively loved, of coming first for ever in one fellow-creature's heart, of being irreplaceable and undefeatable once, just once. Yet for ordinary purposes she knew Hannah, and was loyal to her.

So she did not know what to make, save trouble, of Tom in the middle of the night putting a letter under the door of his French cousin's room.

She got to the village, shining with sweat, which increased her permanent look of good humour.

She went into the chapel first, according to custom. She said the First Glorious Mystery of the Rosary at Our Lady's altar ; she would get through the remaining four at odd times during the day. Then she said " Hail, holy Queen," and lighted a penny candle. Although she had no salary she was not penniless ; she drew the Old Age Pension now, for one thing. And Tom, suspicious of Dotey's status which his mother would never explain to him and which she said she " attended to " out of her housekeeping money, was always very generous to her at Christmas and Easter and on her birthday ; also she had a brother, a priest in Melbourne, who often remembered her with a little present ; and Hannah herself occasionally bestowed a pound or ten shillings of sudden largesse. So Dotey had a nest-egg for chapel money and bull's-eyes and with which to buy new flowers sometimes for her black hat.

She lighted the candle for her " special intention," which this morning was that this alarming business of Tom and his letter might come to nothing, and that Hannah, that " blessed saint," need not be upset about it.

Dotey genuflected deeply and with difficulty. Then she took holy water from the font, made the sign of the Cross and went out into the sunshine again.

She did her messages—to the Post Office first, and up the hill to Miss Doheny to know what was delaying her with the new chair-covers, in the name of God ? Then into the timber-yard to ask if Mr. Doran could spare Johnny to Mr. Tom for a few jobs of repair to be done next week. Darning wool, tapes, and butter muslin at Miss Conroy's. And in next door to old Hogan, to pay the newspaper bill, and while she was there, to treat herself to a quarter-pound of bull's-eyes, extra strong, and threepenceworth of cocoanut ice.

Then, with no-one in sight—it being, as Dotey had calculated, a nice quiet hour of the morning—she slipped up the
lane past McMahon the butcher, and in at a side-door of the
Royal Anglers', through the now unused wash-house and
across a dark corridor—into the snug.

Mrs. Cusack was alone there, at her usual table. She was
drinking tea, and had a novel propped against the teapot. It
was still *Gone With The Wind*, for she was a slow and thorough
reader.

" Good-morning to you, Miss Cregan," she said, but did
not raise her eyes until she had reached the end of a paragraph.
Almost alone in Drumaninch she always addressed Dotey
by her correct title of Miss Cregan. She thought less than
nothing of her, regarding her as " no class," but she understood
her weaknesses, and she liked to keep in touch with Waterpark
House, as with any other reasonably important house in the
neighbourhood. And she was the most discreet of publicans ;
she never mentioned the comings and goings of *habitués* of her
snug. So Dotey felt comfortable now, finding her alone—and
sank back in a creaking armchair with relief.

" Maggie May ! You'll require the usual, I take it, Miss
Cregan ? "

But although Dotey had taken the precaution of buying
strong bull's-eyes to eat on the way home, she suddenly felt
that the day was too hot for her favourite, port.

" No, not in this heat, Maggie May. I'll have a drop of gin
with peppermint this time, if you please."

Maggie May frowned. She disapproved of spirits on the
lips of ladies who set a good example by regular attendance
at the chapel. Port was quite another matter—an accepted
ladies' drink, even when taken in excess. However, she brought
a large gin and peppermint to where Dotey sat. The latter
paid for her drink and grasped it happily.

" Did I or didn't I see you at the rails yesterday at the eight
o'clock Mass ? " Maggie May asked severely.

Dotey nodded, looking surprised.

" That will do, Maggie May," said Mrs. Cusack, and the barmaid vanished.

" She's having one of her attacks—they take her religiously," said Mrs. Cusack. " 'Twill be an ease to me, I can tell you, when that one's periods are concluded and done with."

Dotey was somewhat shocked.

" The poor creature ! " she said charitably. " She never got rightly over the disappointment of the convent, I suppose ! " She took a good mouthful of gin, the mere idea of it spreading comfort through her already.

" And how are all above at Waterpark House ? " Mrs. Cusack asked in her suspicious way.

Dotey was on her guard.

" How would they be but splendid, Mrs. Cusack, and the weather the way it is and all ? "

" The foreign young lady, Mr. Tom's daughter, is still with ye, I notice."

" She is so. She makes great company for the children, God bless her." Dotey took another good mouthful of gin.

" She was a surprise to Mrs. Ned, I'll be bound—turning up like that with Mr. Tom's eyes looking out at you and his golden head of hair on her ? "

Mrs. Cusack had no love at all for Hannah Kernahan, " a draper's daughter from over her father's bit of a shop " who had assumed all the airs of a lady at Waterpark House, and carried them off so deceptively. She had deplored Tom Kernahan's infatuation for the obscure Miss O'Reilly, had rejoiced in his jilting of her—knowing from his drunken talk of the time the true run of it—and had resented the subsequent O'Reilly triumph of hooking Ned and Waterpark House. Hannah's detachment—during twenty-eight married years—from Drumaninch gossip, and her indifference to the existence of Helena Cusack, its *doyenne*, an indifference which amounted to not even knowing what the old publican looked like, had not softened the latter towards her. She liked the young Kernahans because they were " good stock and respectable people," but she wished no good to their mother.

" On the contrary, Mrs. Cusack, she was no surprise at all. All about her was known to Mrs. Ned from the hour of her birth, let me tell you. Only it was Ned himself—Lord have mercy on him !—that forbade all mention of the marriage. And would you blame him, the poor man ? With his brother allying himself with the lowest of the low, off the Parisian stage, if you'll believe me ! God help us, 'tis hard on the child to have had a mother of that class——"

Mrs. Cusack smiled slowly.

" Let me advise you, Miss Cregan, not to waste your fables on Helena Cusack. There's ignorant riff-raff in plenty round about here that has never heard tell of the *Comédie Française*, but I am not so placed. It's only last night the Major and myself were talking it over in this very room. He had observed the young lady down by the river one evening, walking with one of her cousins, and he was greatly struck with her. ' A thoroughbred, Helena,' says he ; ' blood stock in every line,' says he. But it's only what I had observed myself, of course, the moment I laid an eye on her."

" The poor Major, God help him ! Isn't it nice of him now to be noticing the girleen, and he so lonely there in his old bit of a shack ? " Dotey fidgeted with her empty glass, and glanced towards the bar.

" Maggie May ! " The barmaid reappeared.

" Once a man of the world, Miss Cregan, always a man of the world, shack or no shack. The Major has had his misfortunes and made his mistakes, and I thank God on my knees every night that Lady Octavia is spared the present sight of him—but he knows form when he sees it, Miss Cregan. And as he was explaining to me last night—and of course I recalled it instantly to memory as he spoke—the members of the *Comédie Française* in Paris are a most exclusive body. *Most* exclusive. Only ladies and gentlemen of the *highest* qualifications can get inside it at all. It has nothing at all to do with what is vulgarly

117

known as the stage, I need hardly say. It's like as if they were dedicated to be always giving private, command performances, if you understand me ? "

" You don't say ? " said Dotey. " Praise be to the Lord, I'd no idea at all there was a thing like that to do with the *stage*, Mrs. Cusack." She had hardly listened at all to what Mrs. Cusack was saying. She paid Maggie May now for her second drink and gave her a propitiatory smile which was ignored.

" Indeed, from what the Major was saying," Mrs. Cusack went on, " it seems as if Tom Kernahan was flying high for himself when he had the good fortune to marry where he did. You can bring me a drop of rum now, Maggie May— and the squeeze of a lemon in it, if you please."

" Well, of course you understand these things, Mrs. Cusack," Dotey said in conciliatory tones. " And indeed, as Hannah herself says, the child is a great credit to her parents, a very great credit, God help her, actress and all though she is ! "

" The highest in the land are actresses," said Mrs. Cusack. She glanced up with reverence at the signed photograph of Edward VII. " No less a gentleman than His Majesty there honoured many of them with his friendship, Miss Cregan— to my certain knowledge."

Dotey nodded with vague tolerance at the photograph.

" Did he now, the creature ? " She was feeling relaxed, and had half-forgotten her worry of Tom and his midnight letter.

And then Mrs. Cusack—no doubt in order to annoy and to see where the wind sat at Waterpark—said something which brought all the worry back.

" We were saying here last night, the Major and myself, wouldn't it be a nice, romantic thing now if young Tom and his French cousin were to make a match of it ? "

Dotey gave a bound, spilling some gin and setting up a creaking in her chair.

" Make a match of it, Mrs. Cusack ? And they first cousins, God help them ? Sure why now in the name of mercy would

118

anyone be thinking of a wicked, foolish thing like that for the poor children ? " She was very much shaken. It seemed extraordinarily ominous to her that Mrs. Cusack should be joking in the snug about her own great new anxiety, which she believed she shared with no-one living as yet.

" First cousins marry every day of the week in high society, Miss Cregan. All the royal families of Europe were founded by the marriages of first cousins. And come to that, the kings of Egypt married their own sisters ! "

" Well, may God forgive them, Mrs. Cusack, and that's all I'll say to that," said Dotey. " But I'm astonished at the Major, so I am, to be thinking up such foolishness, poor man ! "

" No foolishness at all, I thank you. Tom Kernahan should be taking a wife now, so he should—and he's made it plain that there's none around here that he's losing his reason over —let them hope what they like. And as the Major said, there's nothing like a bit of strangeness for getting a man shaken up. Oh no—there's little foolishness in what I'm after saying. You mark my words, Miss Cregan. Helen Cusack isn't one to make mistakes."

Dotey creaked herself out of her chair. Pleasure in her quiet drinks was gone from her ; Mrs. Cusack's idle talk had filled her with uneasiness. Perhaps there was " upset " ahead ; perhaps Tom would take a wife and Hannah would lose power, and she herself would be cast off, forgotten, overridden in the general post. There was no telling ever the selfishness of men —as she had heard Hannah say, and her mother before her. Perhaps so it was—and there was trouble coming.

She made her exit well. Her instinct for smoothness helped her to conceal her worry. She smiled and nodded, looking a picture of good humour.

" Well, well, we'll see. And 'tis well we know that you were ever wise, Mrs. Cusack. But this is a very queer guess you're after making, very queer entirely ! Ah well, God is good ! We'll see. But I can't stop talking any longer—I've idled away enough of my day as it is, may God forgive me ! "

She set off across the snug with her basket.

"Good-morning to you, Miss Cregan," said Mrs. Cusack, and she opened *Gone With the Wind* where the marker lay.

Dotey left the hotel as she had entered it, by the wash-house and the back lane. She entered McMahon's shop as she passed to utter a word of warning about to-morrow's shoulder of mutton, and so, leaving his doorway before turning into the street, was able to return Miss Toomey's greeting without anxiety. As Mrs. Kernahan's housekeeper she had a perfect right to go up the back lane to McMahon the butcher.

But she went home more perturbed than she had set out. It seemed as if she would *have* to drop a word to Hannah. May-be then it could be managed to send the French cousin off about her business—some tactful way or other, and no harm done. Trust Hannah to arrange that if it suited her! Make a match indeed! Is it with that thin stick of a foreigner, and she with her face painted so that you can't see it rightly? And sure what would *Tom* be wanting with a wife—a good quiet boy like him? Hadn't he all the comfort a mother's love could give him? Tch, tch—but the best of men are selfish, to be sure. Often enough I've heard it—from Hannah's mother, let alone from Hannah.

Dotey sighed. She felt sure of trouble now. An "upset" for Hannah. . . . She took a slab of pink cocoanut ice from her basket and ate it as she ruminated. That gin has me depressed, she pleaded with herself, anxious to be placid again and to enjoy her cocoanut ice. I had a right to stick to port, hot and all as the weather is. I never had the constitution for gin. And the way I am unsettled in my mind to-day—it's port I should have taken. There's nothing like a glass of port. I wonder how in the world ought I to warn Hannah? Of course not a word of the Major's talk, God help us! If she was to hear that they were match-making for Tom in the snug—in any case—Dotey almost smiled—it wouldn't suit her to hear that *I* was visiting Mrs. Cusack. Hannah has her own peculiar little ways, so she has—and sure what harm?

She's the best of good mothers, and it's only right that we should all try to please her and keep her from being upset. . . .

At a turn of the avenue where it forked by the ilex trees, Bernard appeared and stood in front of her, across her path. He was unshaved and unwashed and looked very tired. The poor old woman almost screamed. He gazed at her, seeming puzzled.

"What is it you want, woman ? " he asked gently. " Why are you eating ? What's your name ? "

Dotey tried to edge past him, smiling. She gave him a piece of cocoanut ice. He stared at it wonderingly, and then slowly crushed it up in his hand.

" I'm sorry," he said gently. " It's not your fault ; there's trouble on my mind, there's trouble coming—but of course it's not your doing. You're a helpless poor old woman."

He wandered past her, forgetting her. " *Sustinuit anima mea in verbo ejus* . . ." Dotey heard him say as she fled from him. She almost cantered up the steps. There were tears of panic in her eyes. Meeting Bernard was the last straw on this unlucky morning. And the way he was raving, the poor creature, you'd say he knew some way what was on her mind.

The Ninth Chapter   THE SUMMER'S FLOWER

THE sound of Tom's car going away from her ceased at last, but Angèle sat still on the top step of the jetty. It was an old disused landing-stage of the river, called Brady's Pier. In the letter he had pushed under her door Tom had told her that he would be there at ten o'clock, and would wait for her. " You have only to follow the river path southwards from the house for a mile and a half," he had written, " until you come to Brady's Pier. There's a burnt-out house in the trees near it, and a lane leading up from it on the left. But I'll be there— you won't get lost."

So she had gone to meet him and found him there, at ten o'clock. And now it was after midday, and he was gone, and she was betrothed to him, and all her future lay about her and at hand, within this bright, unpeopled stretch of quietness.

She did not consider it ; she did not look about her. She sat in careful composure, as if afraid that her heart might spill or crack.

I love him ; I love him enough, was the gist of her upper thought—repeating itself not at all in persuasion or argument, but simply in acceptant surprise.

She was innocent in love ; understanding it only vicariously, and through reflection. She did not realize yet how very operative and significant was the adverb " enough " with which she supported her new affirmation. She did not know that when the feeling broadly classified as " love " is strong it has to be accepted blind, and is only examinable by its sufferer, for better or worse, *after* such acceptance. Hitherto no promptings of her senses had been strong enough to darken her attentive eyes, and so she had never reached that moment of committal beyond which lie most of the miseries and deceptions as well as all the most natural happiness of human lives.

But now she was committed. She had pledged her love and faith, and if she was surprised by the peace that brimmed from a surrender so vast for her and so absurd, the surprise was only instinctive, for she was without experience. I love him enough. She did not know that this was almost never true, and that it was not became manifest to many lovers even within the very pleasure of the first embrace. Love can survive, a little or a long time, this lesson of its insufficiency— because it must, because self-love and self-respect insist ; because pleasure is strong, and compromise is an understood necessity, and because lovers learn to understand love cynically and yet value it. Love is too frequent an event to be frequently complete ; whether or not by direct experience it is probable that every living heart knows this and is resigned to it. Angèle, though fear of wasting a possibly precious thing had kept her watchful and virginal, knew it too, from observation and by the deductions of common sense—and if she had held back from feeling it was not because she expected to be granted perfect love. Merely she had had the young idea that she might be allowed the right of conscious choice, and to take the risks of delay and hesitation, more natural to her than those of hit or miss. Love need not be perfect, she had thought, but it might at least be allowed to be her own, rising in her unaided and unexplained, not merely suggested by the necessity or touchingness of others. It was not to be in her, she might have said, a *response* ; it was to be her free demand.

She was not conscious of these theories now. She did not know whether she had exacted love, or had it imposed upon her. She did not know her own desire from Tom's.

Last night she had stayed awake and stirring a long time. At first she sat in the wide, semi-circular window for which the room she slept in was incorrectly named " Round " ; she looked out at the river and quite simply felt happy—extremely and irrationally happy ; desirous love for Tom had been rising in her, both against and with her conscious will, throughout the day—and now at the end of it she knew at last that as with her so it was with him ; that he felt and answered her desire. Sheer pleasure filled her—and a little stupefied her. But she was not conscious of this. She was given up, for once, for the first time in her life, to one uncontaminated feeling.

She sat and stroked the shell from Carahone, and marvelled dreamily at the beating of her heart. She felt foolish, happy, excited, indifferent to thought. Only her senses apprehended these minutes, this phase—accepting the river outside, and the room about her, the smell and hush of the living house, the surface of the shell, the warmth of her heart—as if from memory, as if her father spoke of them ; and yet as they were, a whole moment, a proof of life. *Dans le trouble où je suis je ne puis rien pour moi*, she said, stroking her shell and smiling— and she did not know whether she or, long ago, her mother, said it. She said it again and again, listening to her mother

...he line's feet to the throb of the river. *Dans le*
... *je suis je ne puis rien pour moi.* The truth of that filled
... and made her smile.

... ...ught filtered back after a while, specific thought—of
To... She wondered if he was still in his mother's room ; and
thus came slowly towards reflection.

She did not think on *why* she was so suddenly and perhaps
oddly in love ; she did not ponder the pros and cons of Tom.
There he was, very simple, very quiet, as beautiful as Apollo
and Gary Cooper, and as good as gold. She had never thought
of a man like Tom, never expected to meet one. But now
she was in love with him. When she had stood beside him at
the supper-table waiting for Martin to go out of the room she
had undergone her first true pang of love—and as it wrung
and stabbed her had understood that if Tom did not speak now
to her need, answer it with expression of his, she would speak
herself, and beg his love.

She had heard people call sexual love a chemical reaction.
So be it. She knew nothing of chemical reactions, but this
visitation seemed as if to negative the things that she had
thought she knew about. All that she was or had believed or
desired herself to be seemed displaced now, dismissed. There
was this simple, sudden love—and that was all. The familiar
complications of herself, Angèle—the doubts, anxieties, emotions,
and ambitions of her particular self—were gone, it seemed.
For the first time in twenty-five years there was only one
inspiration, and no choice. It was certainly very strange.
Chemical reaction, if they liked—why worry with words ?
She ran her mouth along the smooth lip of the shell. *Dans le*
trouble où je suis je ne puis rien pour moi.

Nothing for herself. But something—perhaps much—for
him. Whatever he wanted. She did not really know what
that would be, for she didn't know him yet. She had never
talked to him alone—until to-night. But he said he wanted to
keep her here for ever. If he meant that, she would stay for ever.

She looked about her ; she thought of him in his mother's

room nearby, but would not acknowledge the cold centre of that thought. She was timid about people, and she disliked Tom's mother—but such tiny, everyday emotions were impalpable to-night. Still, thought was creeping back, and she acknowledged that what Tom desired now would be hard for him to get, and harder perhaps for him to enjoy. He had never strongly desired anything which excluded his mother from its pleasure, or removed her from first place in his life. Now—perhaps—he did.

Angèle's love stirred newly in her as she confronted this thought—stirred protectively with an especial movement of passion, and it occurred to her that she loved Tom so much already that were it now not she he wanted, but something or someone else as difficult of reach across his mother's guard, she would have to see him granted his desire, would die indeed to give it to him.

There would be trouble with Aunt Hannah ; if she stayed with Tom and married him, a life of trouble.

She had not wanted marriage—yet. She had nothing against it, save that, of her, it asked too much. Now, if this was to be marriage it asked not merely too much, but everything.

Angèle's mother had not wished her to be an actress ; indeed she had opposed her daughter's desire very strongly, all the more so when Angèle refused to enter the *Conservatoire* and become a *pensionnaire* of " *La Maison.*" She was hurt by that flouting of the tradition she adored. " But, Mother, it would be *nonsense* for me ! I'm steeped in it already. You *are* the *Comédie Française*—and thanks to you I start where the *pensionnaires* leave off. I'm going to be a missionary of tradition, Mother, in the vulgar stage ! "

The joke was tactful—but Jeanne Maury did not laugh. Yet when she saw her daughter play small parts in repertory or boulevard performances, she thought of it, and felt some professional reassurance—for she saw that familiarity with her own stiff, mannered school, derided now by the young, and

...ss of the historic theatre of France gave her child
...ity and a voice on the stage which, though they
...ill sometimes with the modern vulgarities she appeared
...marked her ; made her seem promisingly lonely and
suggestive, no matter how deftly she " threw away " bogus
lines.

So Jeanne gave in—but sadly.

" You'll marry. And then you won't know whether to be
actress or wife."

" You were both."

" I had to be," her mother said simply.

" You'd never have been just wife," said Angèle.

" It's a heart-breaking life—except for the very great."

" I intend to be very great, Mother."

" My child, so did we all."

Angèle knew better than to parry this uncomplaining statement with flattery. From babyhood she was familiar with the
shop-talk of actors, and she knew that peace of mind depended
for them not on their intention to be great, but on their certainty
that they *were* great. This belief seemed a necessary part of
the actor-quality—not found in at all the same form in other
kinds of artists. The latter can be assaulted from within, can
write or paint against the conviction that they are rotten writers,
rotten painters—but an actor may only be injured from without.
Everything may go wrong externally, and he will play for all
he is worth—but he must believe, he does uniformly believe
that he *is*, whatever his luck, a great actor. That faith is the
beginning of stage technique. Angèle knew this from observation—but she also knew, both amusedly and with blind emotion,
that she possessed it herself. She knew that she knew herself to
be a great actress—and though, loving the profession passionately, she sometimes shivered over the essential failure in it of
her courageous and talented mother, and shivered in greater
fear before more spectacular or more sordid failures she had
witnessed—yet she was *not* afraid. She would succeed. She
was a great actress.

"It's the only way to begin, Mother. One has to take the chance, after all. And you—you do admit I have talent, don't you ? "

"If I didn't think you had considerable talent, Angèle, I'd lock you up in a convent rather than let you appear even once on the stage." They both laughed. "Yes—I do truly see much talent in you, I regret to say. A talent I don't quite understand, or foresee, as yet. We shall see—if we live. There is something withheld, something muffled or muted, about your playing. I sometimes think this muffling, this muting, is a deliberate thing—an idea you are working out. Am I right, my darling ? Is there a theory ? " Jeanne's irony was very gentle, and did not hide her honest professional respect for her daughter's seriousness.

Angèle flushed with pleasure.

"Yes—there is an idea," she said.

"Left undeveloped, perhaps, by Eleanora Duse ? "

Angèle winced.

"I don't know ; I only saw her once, when I was a kid. It hadn't occurred to me to imitate anyone."

Jeanne stretched out her hand.

"Forgive me," she said. "You see, although I am your mother, darling, if I live to see you a great actress, I shall be very jealous indeed. I warn you now, Angèle ! "

Dear Mother. The "theory" about which Angèle was touchy was as much emotional as intellectual. Until she had collected some certainties about that personal life which was the chief concern of most playwrights, Angèle felt obliged to use her tentativeness, even to exploit her innocence, in interpretation. She could not make easy guesses ; she preferred to convey dilemma.

"It is necessary to be humble," her mother said once, in reproof. "If you are engaged to play a little rowdy, happy person, then *play* her, darling."

"But I don't *know* her—yet."

"In your sense you'll never know her. You have to be

modest, accept her from the playwright, consider her well, and *play* her."

"Yes—I see."

She would cease to be an actress, now. And she would cease to be French. Everything she knew and had been would go, and she would begin all over again. Like a pioneer, like an exile. She would live in this lonely, quiet place, with a handful of odd and ageing people ; in love with Tom. She would have Tom's children, and become what her father had refused to be, a Kernahan of Waterpark House. And when she died they would bury her in the stone tomb Jo had shown her, in the circular graveyard on the hill.

She heard a movement on the landing, and then saw a white envelope slide under her door. She crossed the room and picked it up. "Angèle" was written on it. She opened the envelope and read Tom's first letter to her.

" MY LOVE,
"I have to be at Mellick fair at seven o'clock in the morning. I will get away and meet you—if you can manage it—at ten o'clock at Brady's Pier, along the river. You must know it, I think. You've walked that way with Jo and Martin. You have only to follow the river path south-wards from the house for a mile and a half until you come to Brady's Pier. There's a burnt-out house in the trees near it, and a lane leading up from it on the left. But I'll be there—you won't get lost. I'll get there at ten, and I'll wait for you, Angèle.

"If you meant what you said to-night you will tell me again, and then all the future will be settled, and I will tell Mother of our engagement. I would come to you now, to make sure I am not dreaming like a madman, but I do not want your life in your own house to start with scandals and misunderstandings. So I must wait until to-morrow.

"I cannot write letters—indeed I don't know who could

write the things I am feeling now. Angèle—it is impossible that you could care about a dull country fellow like me ; it is impossible for me to hope that I could make you happy here. Yet, it *is* a good place to live in, and your father was born here. I can write no more to you, love. Whatever happens, I will love you all my life. Good-night now and God bless you.

"Том."

She had lived all night with the letter, moving through many readings of it from joy to fear, to deliberation, to re-assurance, and back to joy. It was a lover's letter, warm and strong, but it took her forward into to-morrow, into plans and conflicts, into formal acceptance of a future which amazed her. Thus it made her wakeful, and broke the first spell. But she went to sleep still holding it in her hand.

So she had gone to Brady's Pier, and seen him waiting for her there before he saw her. He was standing on the edge of the parapet, looking down into the water. He did not seem, as last night at her last glimpse of him, a radiant symbol of a boy in love ; he looked like a man with much to think about. His aspect made her want to hurry to him, and gave her also a sharp, new vision of their future situation ; they would be together, strangers and young, in this lonely life of his, sur-rounded by his watchful dependants, and his stiffly set traditions ; they would live with his mother ; they would live by this for ever crying river ; they would have fought hard to gain their perilous isolation in each other and would have given up much for a risk that would bind them for ever. And she would never really know what he thought of when he bent his head like that and stood so still ; and he would never know what she must not look back to, or how many pricking second thoughts she had, would often have, when as now she saw him waiting for her and felt this need to run to him.

Her heart leapt to him as she faced their dangerous prospect. I love him enough.

129

Then he turned and saw her, and face and stride and out-stretched hands confirmed her in desire.

She sat alone now where he had left her, and remembered him.

He had talked to her passionately, passionately pouring out his heart, astonishing her with the urgency and the grace of his love. He was enchanted with joy, and seemed indeed, as he had said he was, a man suddenly waking from long sleep. He made her laugh with his plans : if they were married at once—it could be done with special licence—they could get away to France and meet her people and see all the places she loved before this damned old war got going ; besides, September was his best month for being away. There was no sense in waiting, was there—if she meant it, if it was true ? He wasn't rich, indeed in a way he was poor—he would show her all the facts and figures—but he could afford a wife who would be content to live as they lived now, and things could be managed, settlements and things. About Mother and the others, he meant. Mother wouldn't like their being cousins, but she wanted him to be happy, and she was an angel. Angèle would see. Would she mind Dotey and Corney and having Martin and Jo use the place as usual ? If she did, something could be arranged. Mother, of course—but Mother will be very good to you, Angèle—she is to everyone—and above all, she'll be good to you.

He saw no difficulty on his own side that he couldn't handle. There might be a little surprise at first, and they might be called rash—and then about being cousins—Mother might worry—but all these things were nothing. Only psychological, after all.

Angèle smiled—but her longing for him grew, and made her agree with his broad, striding wisdom. After all, the way to achieve a difficult thing was to set it in motion.

No, nonsense—Norrie wouldn't be hurt. There'd never been a word of love between him and Norrie. He'd never been the least bit in love with her, and she was a rock of sense,

130

and not at all keen on getting married, in Tom's opinion. Dr. O'Byrne might have thought it a way of keeping Norrie near him—he was so devoted to her—but Norrie had heaps of men keen on her, and she never seemed to bother about any of them.

Angèle did not smile at this. She did not think that he was being disingenuous, but she felt the shadow of Norrie.

He questioned her rapidly, closely, lovingly, about herself —about France and her mother and her cousins and her friends. Would she truly be able to make this sacrifice, and live this life? But the stage, her acting? Would it make her very unhappy? Perhaps something could be arranged——

Angèle smiled again. He was clearly head of his house, for all his gentleness, and accustomed to " arranging " things. But she felt, without mockery or resentment, that he truly thought her " acting " was a problem which might conceivably be settled by some local compromise, as a mania for bridge might be, or for playing in chamber music. She knew that he simply did not understand about being a professional actress by choice and gift—and once and for all as he spoke of it she accepted his dear blindness, and burnt her boats.

"No, Tom. Nothing is to be arranged. I want to marry you. Oh, love, I want to marry you, and nothing else."

The bright day blazed on them. At every word, in every smile, each found a new, rare beauty in the other. Deeply and innocently they drank up love and tasted the fever of promise. I love you, I love you, they said. My wife, my dear, my love. She taught him the line that still ran in her head from Racine, made him translate and repeat it. *Dans le trouble où je suis je ne puis rien pour moi*, he repeated carefully. He thought it over and said it again. He said it was bosh, that he was in no trouble and could do plenty. My love, my heart, she said.

When he embraced her for good-bye his eyes reminded her of her father's, and her own.

"I wonder what sort of children we'll have," she said.

"Nice children," he answered gently. " Slim, gentle little girls like you, with long, sweet faces."

"Oh Tom !"

"My love, my treasure !"

"We'll have sons, Tom."

He kissed her. She heard a lark singing very near them, and she felt his sharp song rising as if in her own breast.

And now, sitting alone, she heard the lark again. I'll sit here often, she thought, on this very step. I'll often take this walk, I expect, when I'm quite old. She heard a clock chime the hour and then strike one o'clock. Drumaninch stables, she thought ; I'm late. It seemed as if this had often happened before—that throughout her life she had often sat here dreaming, being roused by that far-away bell to realize that she was late. But still she sat in the sun and stared into the clear, deep water. I wonder what he was looking at, she wondered.

The Tenth Chapter   A WORD WITH DR. O'BYRNE

AT half-past three in the afternoon Dotey was much relieved to be asked by Hannah to take a note to Father Gregory at Drumaninch House. It had occurred to her that this might happen, and she welcomed it ; it would have been no easy pastime to sit the whole afternoon with Hannah, and her mouth drawn in like that and she on the verge of being " upset," the creature.

So Dotey got ready with alacrity.

Hannah smiled as she gave her the letter.

" And don't spend the *whole* evening gossiping with Brother Nicodemus," she said good-humouredly.

" Indeed and I won't, the poor hard-working man," said Dotey. But she knew very well that Brother Nicodemus, the porter, would insist on giving her tea in St. Joseph's, after her walk—and tea in the monastery parlour was Dotey's idea of a *good* tea. And maybe before she left the Father Bursar would look in for a word, and press her to a glass of port. It was an ease to her anyhow to get away from Hannah for a spell—for when her mouth was that way, there was no knowing how to please her—for all that she'd smile away at you the same as ever.

It was an ease to Hannah to have the drawing-room to herself.

What Dotey had said to her an hour ago amounted really to very little—and at that, what was Dotey but a fool ? The only thing was that she wasn't a tale-bearer, or a trouble-maker—and certainly she was without imaginative power. She never noticed other people's behaviour much either, or worried one with surmises or forebodings. Still, what did it all amount to ? That, returning from the lavatory last night she had seen, or thought she saw, *Tom* outside the French girl's door, and putting a letter under it. And that, on top of that, this morning outside the chapel she had a word with poor Maggie May of the Royal Anglers'—and what had that half-mad ex-nun to say but that the Major and Mrs. Cusack were wondering would Tom Kernahan make a match of it with his cousin.

The little circular embroidery frame lay idle on Hannah Kernahan's lap ; she stared out of the window and the light from the sky and the river poured upon her. It made her look pale, and paled the deep blue of her eyes.

She wanted to think, but knew that she was not able to think effectively yet. However, an hour or two alone was all she needed. Self-confidence was by no means gravely injured—only challenged at an unguarded moment. She would think—and settle things according to her will. Meantime she knew she was undergoing an emotional shock. But she did know it—and that gave her caution.

She was glad now that she had committed nothing of this curious nonsense of Dotey's to paper, in her note to Father Gregory. She had actually been tempted to set it all down—and perhaps if her hand had not shaken as she wrote she might have done so. Thank God she had said no more than that she must see him to-night, and have his saintly advice in a little family anxiety. He would come running to her on that, and be of the greatest possible help; he was a man of deep and saintly understanding. But in any case, when she had got herself in hand, and was over the shock, she would need no help from anyone.

Could it have been Martin that Dotey saw? Martin made no secret of his fancy for Angèle—and she was the type he liked, high-browish, and a bit fast. Not of course that even Martin could ever be really fast with a girl, or like that sort of thing, for all his nonsensical talk. (Hannah, who had not liked her own experience of sexual love, believed or hoped, as do some women in her case, that her children were "above it.") But he did *like* Angèle, and Hannah had seen no harm in his amusing himself with her—in a gentlemanly way. And indeed, for all her lipstick and her French ways, no-one could say that Angèle overstepped the mark, in word or action. So far as could be observed. Perhaps it *was* Martin—he was much given to the pen, after all.

But no; even Dotey could not mistake Martin five foot nine and very heavy-shouldered, like his father, for Tom, six foot and lightly, perfectly made.

What *was* the matter? What threat was this she had not noticed coming? What in God's name had happened, that made the besotted gossips at Mrs. Cusack's link her eldest son's name with *anyone*—let alone with this unlucky visitant from the bitter, bitter past?

Hannah closed her eyes for a minute. Emotion seemed to sway and lap within her like a sea, and made her dizzy. Tom, Tom. What was this danger that threatened him, and so threatened her, and all her care of him, all her understanding, all their quiet, united, harmonious, loving life?

But she was here, and she was warned. She had the knowledge of life that he had not. It would be all right. She would get at the facts of this thing, and protect him, as a mother should, as indeed only a mother could. She would pull herself together presently, and think. It would be all right. She kept her eyes closed, and thought with passion of the long, quiet years of devotion that bound Tom's life with hers ; that justified and pacified a heart which no other relationship had ever fed.

The door of the outer drawing-room opened.

" The Doctor to see you, ma'am," said Delia.

As Hannah rose to greet Dr. O'Byrne all her instincts snapped together in acceptance of an unusual situation. This man was busy, and no great admirer of hers ; he had not been summoned professionally and was not a dropper-in. His presence here now must surely mean that his quick intuition had picked up something of this new possibility which threatened an unvoiced desire of his own.

" Dr. O'Byrne ! How surprising—and how pleasant."

" The first part anyhow, I'll be bound, Mrs. Kernahan. And I'm glad to find you alone."

The Doctor looked about him with interest and after his hostess had seated herself in her armchair in the window, he chose a chair and sat down facing her.

" You'll drink tea with me ? " said Hannah.

" Well, if it's your custom, lady——"

" It is, I fear. Dotey and I could never get through the afternoon awake without our four-o'clock cup ! "

" Does you no harm, except that no doubt Dotey eats too many cakes with it. This is a great view you have here, and no mistake. I don't know a better placed house in a radius of ten miles, I think."

" This side *is* very good—but the front aspect is rather barracky, I always think. I can't imagine why nearly all hall doors face north or north-east."

" To keep out the rain, I suppose. And then we all go and live at the back window, for fear we'd miss a drop of it."

Delia came clanking in with a tea-tray which she set on a little table near Hannah. While she was in the room Dr. O'Byrne looked coolly about him. He nodded towards a crowded china cabinet against one wall.

" Some of that Dresden there is very fine," he said. " I

remember it from when I was a boy—and it licks a lot of Corney's collecting into a cocked hat."

Hannah smiled tolerantly.

" I agree with you. We grow more and more miscellaneous here, as you can see. But Corney does occasionally bring home a plum. Sugar, Dr. O'Byrne ? "

" One lump, if you please. And very little milk. Thank you—that's fine."

Delia had closed the door of the outer drawing-room now, and the two were alone.

Dr. O'Byrne drank some tea ; then he folded a thin piece of bread-and-butter, bit at it, and smiled reflectively.

" I've come to see you on a classic kind of errand, ma'am," he said, " but one that has fallen into disuse of late in these parts."

Hannah looked all innocence.

" Yes ? "

" May I speak with the privilege of one whose father as well as himself was friend and physician to this house throughout a long life ? "

" But of course, Dr. O'Byrne. Your preamble makes me very curious indeed ! "

" Does it ? " asked the Doctor. " Mind you now, I'd have thought you'd be there before me with my simple idea." He paused. " I was wondering whether there was any way in which—without annoying the young people—you and I might help Tom and Norrie to come to the point, and get married. That's all. I thought I'd like to talk it over with you."

Hannah allowed herself a little start and glance of surprise, but she knew it would seem both silly and offensive to overdo astonishment at what had been said. Over the years, while always refusing outward acknowledgment, she had seen this proposition draw inevitably nearer ; she knew that she would loathe it when it came, and that she would play against it as long as she could, for postponement, for indecision, for the long finger. But not to the O'Byrnes direct, of course—that would be impolitic, stupid. Norrie was a good catch and a good girl—and if, one day, Tom needed a wife, what better could he have than this sensible, nice girl whom he had known almost as a sister from childhood ? No dangerous high feeling, no romantic nonsense to break his heart. But *did* he need a wife at all ? Would marriage be worth all its risks to him ? And anyhow, where was the hurry ?

It was curious, however, and alarming, that Dr. O'Byrne should bring the matter on to the carpet to-day of all days. Hannah braced herself for manœuvre.

"Forgive me," she said gently. "But isn't what you're suggesting—a little dangerous ? "

Dr. O'Byrne almost nodded his head as he listened to this delicate little speech—so exactly did it tell him what he had already told himself very often about this woman. She's certainly a great fly in the ointment, he reflected now with anxiety. I could hardly choose a worse mother-in-law for my girl. And she's only about fifty, so far as I recall, and she hasn't a thing wrong with her. Superb organic health. Nothing to stop her hanging on in vigour into the nineties. Upon my word, I think Norrie will need the heart of a lion to face it—but sure, that's what the child has ! The heart of a lion, and it's set on Tom Kernahan. I suppose I'm mad to want her to have what she wants, against odds like this. But no human life can be perfect. And she's the faithful kind ; there'd be no getting her to take a fancy elsewhere at this date, I fear. But it's no joke—setting herself up for life against as selfish a case of mother-love as has ever come to my knowledge, so help me !

The Doctor was somewhat disturbed to-day from his habit of broad, suave calm. And that was why he was here, drinking tea with Hannah Kernahan.

Driving back from Carahone last night he had not paid much attention to Corney's chatter of old times and vanished friends, for his mind had suddenly become fixed on the two young people in front. Tom was driving, and they were very

137

quiet ; not that they were ever exactly noisy together, but this quietness seemed excessive, at the end of a happy day ; it struck the Doctor as awkward and somehow uneasy—he thought that the line of Norrie's shoulders sloped a little dejectedly and once or twice he saw her face turn, without anything said, towards Tom, who did not look at her. Her profile then gave her father an impression of sadness.

When they got home, she increased this impression by saying that she wanted no supper, and only to go straight to bed. He forced her to come and drink some milk in his study while he had a whisky and soda. There were sandwiches on a tray and he made great pretence of appetite for them, but Norrie wouldn't touch them. He switched on all the lights and eyed her shrewdly. She looked very normal—in his opinion, very attractive. She smiled at him ; and made the jokes he liked to hear from her, about his golf and in general about the day's events. And as he responded and searched her face in vain for abnormal signs, irrationally he felt his heart wrung for her. She's depressed with him, he thought. She wants him to declare himself ; she wants to be his wife now, and sure of his love ; she's had enough of waiting round. And something's hurt her to-day, by God ! It couldn't be any nonsense about the blonde girl, could it ? But there's *nothing* there ! *She's* Martin's pigeon—and anyway, she's a first cousin.

But as he watched his beloved daughter drink her milk, and afterwards glance through his appointment book and see that everything was ready for him on his desk for the morning, his sense of paternal anxiety deepened, and he kept on being worried—which he thought very absurd—by stray, formless thoughts of the fair-haired Kernahan cousin at the picnic.

He shook himself back to common sense. We'll manage things, he told himself authoritatively. I've been selfish about her—but she'll have what she wants now, before she's much older, so help me !

She turned from his desk and smiled at him, covering a yawn.

"Everything seems all right," she said. "I'll go to bed, I think."

He looked hard at her when he answered.

"I wonder what in the world I'll do when you go off and leave me one of these days," he said.

Her eyes widened and darkened.

"Perhaps I won't leave you," she said softly. And then with a further drop of her voice : "Perhaps I'll be left."

He took that up at once, deliberately.

"What do you mean by that, you nonsensical girl ? " he asked with careful gaiety.

"Oh, nothing ! " she said. "Good-night, Father."

"Is that the way you say good-night to me ? "

She came to him and kissed his cheek, and he saw that her eyes had tears in them.

He stroked her head gently.

"Good-night, and God bless you," he said. She did not answer him, and he knew by her shoulders as she left the room that she was crying.

Such a thing was quite unlike her ; it alarmed him and it outraged his heart.

So here he sat sixteen hours later in Waterpark House, about to make practical assault on her happiness for her, yet daunted by the exactions he foresaw in it.

Pondering his next move, he decided to go on as he had begun—to keep to the masculine and direct, and so far as he went in plain statement, to say only what he saw to be true ; to roughride the feminine guile of his opponent, but genially and while seeming to accept as natural and genuine the facet of herself which she was about to present to him.

He smiled. It would be an amusing battle, and though it might be months yet before he won it, it would be waged in a dear cause, and was worth all skill and care.

"Dangerous ? " He allowed his look of innocence to deepen a shade to bewilderment. "Enlighten me, dear lady."

"But need I, Dr. O'Byrne ? All I mean is that these children have not opened their hearts to us, but they have both, so far as I know, been free to reveal them to each other. They are grown-up and sensible, and by circumstances thrown frequently together. Yet what you are so good as to seem to be setting your heart on—and I do see that it might be a very suitable thing—does not happen. So what is there possibly that we outsiders *could* do that would not be both dangerous and—may I say it ?—perhaps a little impertinent ? "

Dr. O'Byrne waved a deprecatory hand to and fro against this feminine mincing.

" I'm often 'impertinent,' as you call it. I have to be. If it's impertinent of me to have a word with Tom about his future plans, I'll risk it and sleep easy."

Hannah winced, she hoped imperceptibly.

" Oh, I know he's your son," the Doctor went on, thereby letting her see that he had caught her reaction, " but I did give him the first slap that knocked the breath of life into him—with this very hand ! "

Hannah disliked this piece of obstetrical reminiscence, and smiled hardly at all. She gazed out at the river, and when she spoke did so with her eyes still on the horizon, and as if choosing her words with great regard for Dr. O'Byrne's feelings.

" You can talk to Tom about anything under the sun, naturally—almost as his father might. You have always been very kind to my children, and they all trust you, as they should. But—truly it is very difficult for me to say this !—to ask his intentions, in the old phrase, of a young man who has given no indication of having any——"

" Tom is a suggestible chap. It's my belief that he has always by nature had stronger 'intentions' towards Norrie than those most nearly influencing him have allowed him to recognize."

It was a straight hit, suddenly decided upon. Bar infuriating her, the Doctor thought, it will be as well if someone begins to let her see that her mother-act is not entirely admirable. If

Norrie is to be able for her at all, I must do some undermining first.

"If you mean that *I* have ever sought to influence Tom *away* from the pursuits or affections normal to his age——" Hannah laughed outright—" well, no-one has ever called you a fool, Dr. O'Byrne, and I won't be so rude—but you know, you really mustn't rush in where angels fear to tread."

"Holy ground ? "

She laughed again.

"Better that than a psycho-analyst's puddle—I *have* heard, you know, of the messes some interferers try to make nowadays of simple, natural things."

"Messes older than Sophocles, lady ; as old as Egypt, or Genesis ; and none the healthier for having temples built above them, may I say ? "

"I don't understand that bit," she said, and turned her very blue eyes on him now in a hard, cold look. "What's it got to do with Tom's seeming reluctance to propose to Norrie ? "

"If you think to get me on my high horse—spare yourself the trouble, ma'am. I am much too seriously concerned for these two young people to indulge in tantrums. And I didn't come here to worry or upset you, but merely to let you know, by way of courtesy, that I intend to have a word with Tom."

"It seems, for your own point of view, an unwise move."

"Oh no, it isn't. And I have a line of talk for him, as the Americans say, that isn't the very least bit Freudian, I assure you."

"I'm glad to hear that," Hannah said ironically. "Tom is an unusually good—and innocent—person."

"Aye—he's innocent."

There was a pause.

"What is your ' line of talk' ? " Hannah asked.

"When Tom has thought, off and on, about marrying Norrie, two things have sheered him away. We'll leave the first alone. The second, which he has used to cover a multitude of neuroses, is that he is hard-up, has inherited mortgages and obligations with this big place, as well as his father's record for carelessness and bad luck, as well as a fair collection, round his neck, of relatives and dependants. In short, he tells himself that he is a rather overloaded hard-up, and that Norrie is most certainly a bit of an heiress. And that settles it, he thinks. I know that, thanks to his seriousness and good sense, his burdens are lessening here with every year. He has learnt, from you, the very fine and honourable lesson of living simply, working hard, and paying his way. By keeping your own expenditure down you have managed, the two of you, to wipe out much of the insolvent confusion you were landed with at Ned's death. You've made a very fine thing of Tom's natural integrity, Mrs. Kernahan—as everyone recognizes. You've got him out of the worst of his troubles by its means. And of course Jo and Martin practically looked after their own academic careers, and will soon be no kind of liability at all. One way and another, as I say, things are easing up at Waterpark House. But the Bank still has a much bigger stake in the place than you'd like. You are unusually clear-sighted about money and business ; I remember when you were left bewildered at Ned's death, you talked things over a bit with me, and I was much struck then with your quick grasp, and your extreme sense of honesty. Outraged honesty, it seemed then. I remember I thought you were a bit *too* proud, a bit *too* honest. The Kernahans were very well known here, you see, and the countryside was used to long credit and to easy methods. But still, you were as you were—and the years have justified you—even if they *have* been a bit hard on Tom."

Hannah looked at him sharply, and he paused for her comment, but she made none.

" Anyway, you kept him on the self-respecting road—and he's making a go of it. It'd be the damnedest hard luck if he didn't, faith ! But now he's rising twenty-eight. He's never had a fling, or much fun. That doesn't seem to bother him. But what he's ripe for, there's no doubt, is a wife and a family. If he had children or the near promise of them now, he'd be rewarded for everything, and he wouldn't call the Queen his aunt!"

"He has every opportunity to seek that reward, Dr. O'Byrne."

"I wonder! I wonder if you realize how deeply *you* influence him? I'm sure Tom thinks that a mortgaged man is not an eligible man——"

"Well, if he does—is that so wrong? And is marriage such a certainly happy thing as to be worth jeopardizing the restraints and ambitions of years, with its almost inevitable re-establishment of debts and dishonours?"

The Doctor watched her through this speech with an interested smile.

"You see?" he said. "You have disciplined him only too well. He knows, from you, that he is not an eligible man."

"I hope he knows, from his own heart, that a poor man does not seek to solve his problems by proposing marriage to a rich girl."

"No doubt he does—and in a general way he's right. But we're still a long way from what I'm going to say to him."

The Doctor put his cup back on the tray.

"No, thank you—no more tea. But would it bother you if I smoked?"

"Not at all. I believe there should be cigarettes of some kind in that box——"

"Thank you very much, but I have my own." He opened a cigarette-case and held it out to Hannah, who shook her head; then he chose and lighted a cigarette.

"I think a good deal about marriage, Mrs. Kernahan. As the father of six children I have to—though I don't fool myself with too much hoping that any of them will be guided by my reflections when they choose to settle down. Still, I'd like them to be happy—whether they deserve it or not; but Norrie does deserve it. Of that I'm quite sure." He paused and drew on his cigarette, watching his hostess, who kept an expression of kind attention on her face. "Norrie thought of being a

doctor when she left school—and sometimes I've regretted that
I was selfish enough to let her decide to stay at home with me
instead. She'd have made a good doctor—a damn sight better,
it seems to me, than either of her brothers look like making, for
all that they're so expensive and so sociable up there in University
College. They're going to be too smart for my practice—and
that's a mistake that Norrie wouldn't have made. Anyway
there it is—I kept her at home, and if she's ever been sorry
about that, she hasn't said so. She hasn't been idle—she practically runs the whole show for me : secretary, bailiff, farm-hand,
gardener, chauffeur—and the best of companions, thrown in.
In fact, Mrs. Kernahan, she's very highly trained to be a country-
man's wife ! "

They both laughed.

" She's a most accomplished creature—we all know that,"
said Hannah. " And she's a dear, sweet girl. And if Tom
needed and could afford a wife, obviously there is no-one in
the running with her. But——"

" Tom *can* afford a wife now—*if* she's the right one. And
if Norrie hadn't a penny, she'd be the right one, in my humble
opinion. But I've settled ten thousand pounds on her. There'll
be some other odds and ends for her to pick up, it may be, at
my death—but she will have ten thousand anyhow to take to
her husband——"

The amount of Norrie's fortune surprised Hannah. She
was intelligent about money, and she knew Dr. O'Byrne to be
very capable indeed in its management ; he had inherited a
useful fortune from his father, much of it invested in house
property in Mellick which he had nursed and managed to
good effect ; he was known to have made some very shrewd
moves in the stock market ; also he farmed, rather as a hobby
and on a small scale, but successfully ; and he had a good type
of sound country practice, to which he gave scrupulous attention. He lived well but without ostentation, and his wife had
apparently no use whatever for even the simplest pleasures of
prosperity. So he was rightly regarded as a man of solid

estate—but he had six children, of whom Norrie was the eldest ; and three of these were sons, and likely to prove expensive. A *dot* of ten thousand pounds was therefore a somewhat surprising figure, and revelatory of much.

Hannah was not avaricious. She was close-fisted about expenditure, but more in reaction from the untidy open-handedness of her people-in-law than for any deeper reason ; for in fact she disliked to seem to haggle—but also she loathed the slur to self-esteem which she felt, the weakening of power, in inability to pay at once for what she required. This pride was so native to her as to make extravagance impossible, and no temptation whatever. Also, indifference to everything and everyone not directly or very nearly connected with herself made her inhospitable—not because she was mean, but because she was cold towards whatever was not the direct concern of Waterpark House. Temperamentally she wanted nothing that she could not own, rule, and absorb—and as she was very sane, she would never try to grasp too large a kingdom. She chose to have only what she could hold without risk of indignity or loss of face. So her personal tastes were simple, and she was austere in habit and example. She had none of the obvious temptations, and she lived, in fact, in a kind of passion of privacy, requiring only for her happiness the fantasy she had made of herself, and the belief of her modest entourage in that fantasy—above all, the belief in it of her son Tom, who was both its source and its proof.

Dr. O'Byrne, who often pondered her enigmatic-seeming character, and considered her cold-hearted and egotistical, believed that also she was greedy. He was a fair psychologist and had a wide experience of human character ; but he worked on broad principles, traditional and masculine, and was unable to perceive how deep and narrow was the single stream of this woman's feeling. He believed her to be more calculable than she was, more like other smug and egotistical mothers. He disliked and feared what he saw—but he saw a type, not an individual.

So he thought that ten thousand pounds for her beloved

son was a perfect weapon against this calculating mother. And because she was a very sane woman, and *did* love her son, it was a very good weapon ; she felt its force and it shook her. And also on the very impact of the idea she realized its threat to herself. Whoever brought such benefit and power here, into Tom's home, and brought it to him with love, would be strongly armed indeed to fight the authority of established love. Money, a wife ; a great widening of view down vistas she could not share ; a change of perspective, allegiance to boons not of her bestowing and authority she could only guess against in darkness ; a change of orientation and of heart. The end of a long reign ; the surrender of the only kingdom she had ever won and held.

Yet she was sane, and knew that some day Tom must marry, and that it would be the perfection of her great part in his life to hand him on graciously to life, to crown and bless their exacting years together ; to seem in fact to have pulled down from the sky for him the peace and continuity she had so notoriously fitted him to deserve. One day there must be all that—Hannah knew. When she had decided to face it—but not yet, not yet. Only when it *was* time, it had best be this, this familiar and practical solution. For Norrie in herself was nothing—just a simple, dutiful girl, almost a sister ; manageable, undisturbing. Bearing only the one obvious and calculable arm—money.

Hannah smiled a little as, for the first time, she permitted her imagination to salute a possible change of the *status quo* in her house. Better the devil we know, she thought ironically, though without allowing herself to name any names. But better take—though without hurry still—an easy, manageable way of dismissing before they form themselves those threats from nowhere which gossips and old women are deft with and against which it is admittedly difficult to manœuvre ; better dispel for ever those shadows that cannot be captured or examined. For men, the best of them and the most innocent, become inscrutable in emotion, in sensuality.

She bit on her lower lip. Let it be Norrie then—eventually. Dr. O'Byrne watched her, but was without a clue to her thoughts. She smiled at him.

"Ten thousand pounds is a great deal of money. I think it would make your proposition almost hopeless in Tom's eyes."

"That's why I want to talk to him. I'll tell him about the money, and let him work off his reactions of embarrassment, or whatever it is that's fussing him. And then I'll point out to him that he has made a special pal and confidante of Norrie— for years now they've ridden the land together and taken each other's advice about cattle and bloodstock and prices and every damn thing. He's made her fond of him and trained himself to rely on her—and he has no right now, after so long, to penalize her for all that, just because she has some capital that would be useful to them both, if invested in Waterpark. For my part, I want to see Norrie's money used to promote her happiness, and that of her children—and I regard Waterpark as her best investment, every way you view it. She loves and knows the whole neighbourhood ; she wants to live and die in these parts—and if, say, she is at present a bit more in love with Tom than he thinks he is with her—that doesn't worry me. Knowing her character I know what she'll become in his eyes in marriage—what she must become to any decent man. And I know no better man than Tom. I'm prepared to stake a lot on my conviction that no marriage could be more happily or safely founded than theirs will be. And in the world as it is, and the worse world that's coming any minute, it's something to foresee the safe realities of human happiness invested somewhere. I believe you must agree with me about that, ma'am. And I believe that I could put the case to Tom in a way that would not offend him, and would make him see that he has wasted enough of his youth now, and should think about being happy."

Hannah winced again and the Doctor noticed the movement.

"What's the matter with you ?" he said amusedly. "Don't

you face life at all here in your watch tower? Don't you know that a man *must* have the natural gratifications that no maternal piety can blind him to?"

"Of course I know. And Tom has always been—only too much perhaps—his own master. Simply, I know his scruples about thinking of marriage while in debt. However—you think you can talk him out of that! And, indeed, I am very much touched that you should trust him as you do, and feel him worthy to be Norrie's husband. There is certainly no higher compliment you could pay any man, Dr. O'Byrne."

"Then I may talk to him one of these days?"

"I still don't see why you thought it necessary to ask *my* permission."

"I didn't, lady. What I'm after is your *co-operation*. For, rightly or wrongly, that son of yours will never do anything, I believe, that isn't sanctioned by you. No use blaming him for that—or blaming you either, I suppose. It's just the defect of a too great quality in you both—and it has to be reckoned with."

"I don't understand you," Hannah said coldly. The Doctor chuckled. He was going to have fun, he thought, training this mettlesome creature a bit before Norrie had to try her mouth. Silence was prolonged between them, somewhat awkwardly. Hannah took up her embroidery frame, and as she chose a stitch and began it she thought again of Angèle. Thought of her with a kind of pity—poor rootless, wandering waif; lonely, struggling actress, part of the dangerous, crude world outside Eire—to which presumably she would return.

"I wonder what prompted you to this decisiveness about Tom and Norrie—just now?" she asked the Doctor idly.

"That's delicate ground," he said.

She raised her brows. Was it possible that he too, this sensible man, entertained, like old Dotey and the half-mad barmaid, some baseless idea about Tom and this stray cousin, this Angèle?

"In plain words, ma'am, I cut in to-day because I know that, for all your past fame as a breaker of male hearts, there is one thing you know nothing about, and will have no truck with—and that is what these kids call ' sex appeal.' "

Hannah looked at him blankly.

" You have had the very twentieth-century *essence* of it loose in your house for a week now—without noticing her any more than if she was a white mouse, my God ! " He laughed and lighted another cigarette.

" But what on earth is this ? Forgive me, but if you are talking about my niece, Angèle, what you've said is in very bad taste, I think."

" She wouldn't think so. Not that there's a bit of harm in her. Indeed, she is an unusually nice kid—as intelligent and gracious and easy as any girl needs to be. But she's *attractive*, lady, in a way that is very, very dangerous. Believe me."

Hannah stitched carefully.

" We find her charming here—and of course she has for us the novelty of all exotics. But—your tone is, well, a little distasteful to me, Dr. O'Byrne."

He shrugged.

" You have two fine sons, ma'am ; and one of them, Martin, need be no trouble to you, about girls and so on. He's gone his own way, he knows what he wants and he'll be all right. But the other is defenceless, and you have chosen, at your own risk, to have him so. So be it. But Angèle is a proposition. Besides having the sort of Italian Primitive figure that her whole generation has gone mad about, God help them ! she's attractive in the say of suggesting that she would be exotic and distinguished anywhere. Not just here, but anywhere. She's variable, and quiet, and she suggests emotional force that hasn't been released. She's a very great change from bread and butter ; in fact, you might say she's caviar—but people take to caviar, when they can get it ! "

" You're very fanciful."

" I'm nothing of the sort. At the picnic yesterday I watched

149

all those kids—and everything was as smooth and nice as a nice school outing. But at the end of it, going to bed, I had only two fixed impressions—that my daughter Norrie was feeling suddenly and unreasonably unhappy—and that the young French cousin stayed in the mind, as a sort of question-mark. I suppose she is, really, and without her particularly knowing it—what her relatives in Paris would call " *troublante*." That's all—and it's little enough. But if you've made your son have high standards, if you've made him live without crude pleasures and substituting God knows what sort of dreams for common experience—then don't go sound asleep, ma'am, when something really unusual in the female line turns up ! That's all I mean—about sex appeal ! " He laughed outright.

" How very absurd ! " Hannah said icily. " And most unfair to Angèle—who has done no more than flirt a very little, quite prettily and simply, with Martin ! "

" Ah, my good woman, Martin's *mad* about her ! Flirt indeed ! But that's neither here nor there—and they'll do each other no harm. And you mistake me *entirely* if you think I'm censuring Angèle. I've nothing whatever against her. I think she's a charmer, and a credit to the Kernahans ! Oh no, my position is quite simple. I want Tom for Norrie and Norrie for Tom. I think that would be the best thing for them both. And that apart, I think Tom would be better off now without going through the hell of a romantic passion—cutting his teeth on all that at twenty-eight is lunacy ! And *marriage* of a Kernahan to a first cousin would also be a bad thing, in my view."

Hannah's heart was pounding. She was frightened and miserable. But she gave no sign.

" Marriage ! Romantic passion ! But what *is* all this fantasy? The two in question have hardly looked at each other, to my certain knowledge ! "

" Maybe. And all the better. Only—don't let them start looking, in that case. I'm just trying to explain this thing, sex appeal, to you, ma'am. It's an awkward quantity to handle, always has been. And Tom, you'll admit, hasn't the training."

Hannah shivered. When the Doctor looked at her he was surprised to see that she looked suddenly as if extremely exhausted. Her eyes seemed sunken, and her face was very white. What a curious creature she is, he thought, in bewilderment and with some pity. I believe I've really hurt her with my exaggerated talk about the niece. And as for her sons—well, her innocence is pitiful. What *sort* of a fellow was Ned ? What do men and women make of their natural relationships ?

"Ah forgive me," he said. "Sure I'm only half-joking. And I think the world of Angèle. Only, keep your eye on Tom for me—I want him for Norrie. And if I've made a fool of myself or seemed offensive—well, I'm the family doctor, and a rough-spoken individual always."

He stood up and patted her hand.

"Don't get up. I know my own way out. I'm sorry if I've tired you."

"Not at all. I *am* a bit old-fashioned and idiotic—you must forgive me. And I am very much touched at your desire to have Tom for your son-in-law. Truly I am. Perhaps you'll let me know if you ever *do* talk to him ? "

The Doctor felt a little pang of triumph. I'm winning, he thought. I frightened her all right with that talk about the exotic cousin. Perhaps I was a bit *too* inventive—but there's nothing like a good fright sometimes to get things going. And I still think there's something in my idea about her being a menace. I can't say I *saw* any danger yesterday—but Norrie's not moody, and she's nobody's fool.

"To be sure I will. And thank you for being so patient with me in a difficult matter. I have their happiness at heart."

"I know that. Tom's happiness is, I confess, almost my one earthly concern."

The Doctor frowned a little.

"Easy, easy," he said. "No son can bear that kind of load, you know."

Her eyes were cold again.

"Good-bye, Dr. O'Byrne. Give my love to Norrie."

"I'll do that. Good-bye—I must hurry now. There's no legitimate room in my book for calls of this kind!"

He smiled again, and made his way across the double drawing-room, the chandeliers and bric-à-brac ringing to his heavy stride.

When he was gone Hannah looked about her and out over the garden and the river—but blindly. She raised her hand and pushed back her light, silvery hair from her brows as if it oppressed her; there was sweat on her forehead, she noticed with astonishment. Romantic passion. Her lips curled disgustedly as her mind echoed the phrase. She supposed that that was what she had suffered in her absurdity once, for the father of this wretched girl, this cousin, this "caviar" whose nameless threat had suddenly thrust itself upon a normal, quiet day. Her folly would not be repeated in her son. He would not be humiliated as she had been—nor she be robbed of him by Tom Kernahan's daughter. She had endured all that she proposed to from that source. She was yielding nothing to his child.

She laughed suddenly at herself. What *was* all this theatre? A fable from poor old Dotey; a manœuvre from Dr. O'Byrne to hook Tom at last if he could—and here between them they had her almost in a fever! What was in the air to-day, to give such weight to the imaginings of fools and match-makers?

Tom should be home soon. He'd be tired. The fair all the morning; then that cattle sale at Rathdore, and then all the way up to Barnagh to see to the harvesting of the field of oats he'd bought. He'd be glad of supper, and to walk by the river afterwards and tell her all the business of the day.

Jo and Angèle and John-Jo's little girl were coming over the top of the Orchard Field, dragging big baskets. They had gone—Hannah remembered now—to gather plums. The Victorias from those trees were very fine this year. Hannah watched the little far-away group, and smiled at Dr. O'Byrne's romancing. Caviar? Poor, thin, defenceless girl, with her

152

living to earn, and a face as white as chalk. She looked like anyone at all this minute—indeed from here you'd hardly know her from John-Jo's Pegeen—a pair of leggy gawks.

Hannah laughed in soft contempt, and once again picked up her embroidery frame.

WHEN Dotey returned to the drawing-room at half-past six she was feeling well, having been given an excellent tea by Brother Nicodemus, and later two glasses of port by Father Bursar. Still, she had annoying news for Hannah—that Father Gregory had been called suddenly by telephone to the sick bed of his old friend, Lady Macnamara, and had taken the three o'clock train for Cork. Lady Macnamara was the one flaw in Hannah's spiritual friendship with Father Gregory, and Dotey did not relish naming her name to-day, when there was enough " upset " in the air already. It was a relief therefore to find the embroidery frame in use, and a bright, normal look of serenity in Hannah's eyes.

Dotey delivered her message, and concluded it, characteristically, with an untrue palliative.

" 'Tis the way he had to go, the poor man, Brother Nicodemus said. Some business of her will and the Order, that Father Prior put on him as an obedience, it seems. Nicodemus said you'd have to pity him, flying off like that and he still exhausted, God help him, from the big mission in Mullingar."

Hannah smiled absent-mindedly.

" It's all right," she said. " My business with him will keep."

Dotey sank into her basket-chair, put on a pair of silver-rimmed spectacles, took a pillow-slip from the pile of linen on her work-table and began to darn it. She reeked of peppermint.

" My indigestion is at me again," she said patiently. " It's a torment, so it is."

Corney came into the room and towards the two ladies in the window. He lighted a cigarette.

" Where's Tom ? " he asked idly.

" He isn't home from Barnagh yet," Hannah replied.

" Oh yes, he is," said Corney. " I was talking with Bernard now in the Big Yard and he drove the car in and went away towards the house. I was wanting to ask him what Mellick Fair was like."

" Then I expect he's in his room," Hannah said, and Dotey knew better than to look at her, however cautiously. Tom never went to his room, never did anything on his evening return to the house, before he came to the drawing-room to find his mother and tell her about the day.

Hannah turned her head after she had spoken, and saw him coming slowly through the rough grass that sloped from the haha to the river. He had evidently made a *détour* on his way from the Big Yard. He seemed in no hurry now ; his head was up, his eyes were on the house, but he walked as if dreaming, and he seemed to smile. As he came nearer Hannah waved to him through the open window, and realized as she did so that her action did not attract his attention, for his smiling eyes were focused higher than the drawing-room ; they were on the window above it—the window of the Round Room. His features did not change as if to salute anyone he saw there—so evidently no face appeared above—but as he came on his way without hurry he continued to dream and smile.

" There he is," said Corney.

Hannah leant forward and waved again.

" Hello, son ! " she said, determined to bring his eyes to her before Corney or Dotey noticed how far away they had been. But she was startled by the anxiety she heard in her own voice. And as she waited for his response she prayed for calm, for self-control.

His eyes and smile were hers when she spoke.

154

"Hullo, Mother!"

He jumped the haha, came nearer through the rose-bushes, and beckoned to her.

"Come down here a minute, Mother? I want to talk to you."

"All right, son."

Hannah laughed down to him with all the charm and grace she knew, put aside her embroidery frame, and went to join him, by the wrought-iron steps which led to the garden from the window of the outer drawing-room. "Oh God, direct me," she prayed as she went. "Oh God, oh God, direct me."

Corney strolled across the room and began to play with a row of china mandarins who could nod their heads when coaxed.

"Would you say there was anything the matter with Hannah, Dotey?" he asked.

Dotey affected a surprise which made her chair creak loudly.

"Glory be to God, and what *could* be the matter with her, Corney?"

"I don't know, faith. Only there's something in the air of this place to-day—and what was O'Byrne doing here an hour and more? I sometimes think that I'm a bit psychic, Dotey."

"Well, if you are may God forgive you," said Dotey calmly, "and let you keep it to yourself, Corney, for it is the power of darkness, as well you know."

As Hannah went down the steps and over the grass towards Tom, her intuition flew ahead of her, stumbling and disconnected. All the absurd indications of the day were about to be proved now, she told herself. Her foolish, innocent son was about to confide in her, to say—for the first time in his life—that he thought he was falling in love, and as it happened somewhat unsuitably, with his cousin Angèle. He was going to seek her advice, her sympathy now—as in a thousand lesser matters. They would discuss the difficulties of cousinship, of contrasted upbringing, and of money, no doubt. And Tom would want to know what she thought of his chances, and what she thought of Angèle.

Hannah underwent a pang of fierce pity for her son ; also she was visited by an inspirational decision as to her own conduct, whatever might lie immediatcly ahead.

Tom took her arm and they began to pace the path between the rose-bushes. The air was sweet and warm. Lavender and mignonette brushed untidily forward against Hannah's dress. She bent and plucked a sprig of mignonette, and smelt it.

"Thanks for coming out here," Tom said. "I want to talk to you quite alone for a minute. How are you ? How has the day been ? "

"Nice and quiet, son. Very hot. And Dr. O'Byrne came to tea—rather surprisingly."

She said this on purpose—to watch for some query or cloud on his face. But he gave the news no attention. "How was *your* day ? " she went on. "Tiring ? "

"Tiring·! " She was startled by the way he laughed. "Lord, I don't know ! Oh, I hardly noticed the day at all ! "

She smiled at him cautiously.

"How very odd ! " she said.

"Mother," he said, and stopped in the path and took her two hands in his. "Mother, I don't know how I've waited all these hours to tell you. Angèle is going to marry me. She'll marry me at once, she says. I'm engaged to her, Mother. We're going to be married. I—I don't know how to say what I feel ! Oh, Mother—I didn't know it was possible to be as happy as this."

His hands crushed his mother's against each other very hurtfully, and crushed the mignonette between them. Its perfume rose with curious force to Hannah—old-fashioned and bitterly familiar, associated not so much with this careless, open garden, as with the narrow walled-in strip of greenery which ran behind her father's shop in Mellick and was all she had known in youth whereon to found her resolute dreams of a life of space and privacy and romance and power. Always there had been mignonette in that overlooked patch where even to attempt the fantasies of childhood was an exasperation of pride, and where later to sit and receive the courtship of a Kernahan of Waterpark had been an inextricable maze of humiliation and pleasure.

The perfume was bitter and she shuddered against it ; she hated it as if it were in fact one of those passions or resolutions of long ago which had so flatly failed her and in doing so had brought about this moment of stinging epilogue.

Slowly the immediate shock impressed itself again, and the cloud of conjuring memory it had raised receded, and she re-apprehended that her sentimental intuitions had been ludicrously at fault. There was no question here, no appeal and no debate. Tom had taken and won the girl ; all that he asked of her, his mother, was the fatuous smile of felicitation—and to join him in marvelling that one day had revealed to him a happiness which all her life of love could not have hinted at, and which had carried him at its first touch not merely beyond need but beyond recollection of an intimacy and mutual kindness that had been the towering certainty of years.

She tried to wrench her hands out of her son's, but he held on to them, still talking feverishly.

" Oh, Mother, Mother ! Speak to me ! Say you're glad ! How could you not be, Mother darling ? Oh, we'll all be so happy here, Mother, when I'm married to Angèle . . ."

Her head was bent ; her eyes were on their hands, hers and Tom's, and on the brown-green sprig of mignonette. Ludicrous, ungrateful, clumsy, she thought of the words he was saying, and found herself marvelling in a kind of desolation, a kind of pity, at his ingenuousness. She gave up trying to pull her hands away, deciding that it was no more now than it had ever been her rôle to tussle with him. There had never been contention of the lightest kind between her and Tom.

That thought gave her her cue, and steadied her in the nick of time. A minute or more ago as she came down the steps to him believing the situation to be a vague one, of yearning and half-love, she had seen what her conduct must be. She must be whatever he most required, most anxiously expected her to be. She must be what he knew—mother, perfect, unfailing. More than ever now. He was committed, he was loved and in love. Hannah almost smiled. He knew nothing, exactly nothing, of all that. There were traps and catches everywhere ahead : anxieties, shocks, misunderstandings, disappointments ; and he was riding blind, he was defenceless, as Dr. Byrne had said. " If you've made him live without crude pleasures and substituting God knows what sort of dreams for common experience——" Hannah almost smiled again, as she apprehended the strength of her position. I'll be there, she thought, and I don't change or fail him. " Crude pleasures " were the most unmanageable things in life.

Tears swam into her eyes—she could not have said why. She wept seldom, and then as a rule for undefined causes, for humiliation perhaps, or pride or anger or simple weariness. She did not weep for grief.

Instinctively now she raised her head and looked at Tom, as if to speak to him. The tears were flowing—and would move and please him. He would understand tears, in moderation, for the first impact of his news.

He did understand—in his terms. She saw his look of radiant absorption deepen to loving awareness of her, to concern and tender gratitude. He was hers again for the moment, seeing what he knew best, her face, and seeing it express all that he counted on.

" No, no, you mustn't cry, Mother darling ! "

" I know I mustn't. I'm *not* crying, really. But—to see you so happy, son ! Oh, it's a difficult, unexpected thing—forgive me for being so silly ! But if it's what you want, if it's your happiness—then it's mine too. You know that, Tom."

" Yes, I know, I know. You're perfect, perfect always." He bent and kissed her forehead. He thought he had never seen her beautiful face so beautiful as now, tear-wet and smiling at him. His whole heart praised her and adored her. " You're so unselfish," he said, "so understanding, Mother! Oh, you're an angel! I told Angèle you were!"

She laughed at him, drew her hands away and dried her eyes.

"Poor Angèle! Any mother-in-law is bad enough, but one that's represented as an *angel*——"

"Ah—but she's an angel too!"

"How fortunate you are, my son!" Hannah teased him softly. She let her hand run over his face and hair in a quick caress. "God bless you, and keep you happy always," she said.

"Thank you, Mother." They walked on a step or two in silence. "I must find Angèle now and tell her you know—and you must bless her too," Tom said.

Hannah smiled at him.

She was thinking of all the difficulties immediately ahead of him, but saw no need to mention them.

She reflected as they turned towards the house that this brief and astonishing conversation, lasting three or four minutes, left her feeling powerful and calm, rather than frantic, as it should have rendered her. Things never were as formidable in fact as in imagination, she reflected. I am glad now, actually glad, that this totally unforeseen piece of folly has come to pass in this way. I even feel grateful to Dr. O'Byrne for much of his impertinence. She wondered where Martin was and how he would view this fantastic turn of events. And, smiling again at Tom, she was visited by another pang of compassion for him—but it melted into a sensation of power. I'll be here, she thought calmly; I'll see him through. As she went up the iron steps to the drawing-room, it crossed Hannah's mind that she no longer, in the adjustments the moment asked for, saw Angèle as a person at all, but only as a sign, an *x* standing for a quantity in Tom that she must discover and reckon with. I can't recall a feature of her face at this minute, Hannah reflected with satisfaction.

Jo reassured herself as she watched her mother and Tom come across the outer drawing-room together. Coming into the room while Corney was still insisting to Dotey about his psychic power, she had agreed with him more fully than she pretended that there was "something in the air." Certainly Angèle had been like a creature drugged, or sleep-walking, or perhaps in fever, all the afternoon. She had been sweet and absurd with John-Jo's children under the plum trees, but had seemed insistent on their close company all the time, talking to and of them, picking plums with crazy industry sometimes, and when she fell idle keeping the talk and the jokes on childish things and on improbabilities in a way Jo had never perceived before. She seemed as if afloat in spirit and yet, every now and then, as if on guard. At times Jo thought she looked very sad, and her eyes went as dark blue as night in her white face, but she would not linger on such quiet moments, but kept returning to her fooling with Pegeen and Elly, until she had them quite hysterical and above themselves. The mood, in all its variations, was clearly a defence, Jo decided. Defence of what, against whom? Had there been some kind of show-down with Martin, and was this its immediate effect? Very different from his reaction, if so. Martin, who had stayed inconveniently and bad-temperedly in his room all the morning, had sulked like a demon at lunch, and, according to Corney, had taken a bus or a train into Mellick in the early afternoon. "I asked him to try to keep a civil tongue in his head," said Corney, "but he didn't seem to hear me. A bit of life around the town will calm him down. Maybe 'tis the way he's psychic too?" Jo thought it unlikely that drinking in Mellick would calm Martin down. And as she glanced out of the window and saw her mother and Tom in the garden below, she wondered uneasily if Tom, by any chance, could explain this new tension and mystery. Yesterday once or twice she had apprehended a sense of mutual awareness, she thought, between her cousin and her quiet elder brother—and had dismissed it as impossible nonsense. In any case, even if there was anything in it, they *couldn't* have formulated it yet; they had hardly seen each other, hardly spoken. Still, Jo wondered, and considered the two in the garden—and felt anxious, and called herself a fool.

But now as they came across the vast room to her she felt reassured. Certainly Tom did look unusually lighted up, a bit unreal even—but Mother was herself, pretty, bright-eyed, unperturbed. Whatever was afoot, to make her anxious, to make Martin insufferable and Corney psychic, whatever had made Angèle like a creature of air and water all the afternoon, had so far not impinged on Mother's peace of mind. So—it couldn't be, as yet at least, the idiotic improbability that had floated for a minute into Jo's mind.

Jo was dutiful and affectionate, and therefore resolute against some of the menaces of her intelligence. When she caught herself refusing to look closely at her mother's character, she explained this as a symptom of jealousy in herself against Hannah—because the latter was so pretty, because the boys adored her so much, because she had such social grace, so much tact and ease and such a fine austerity. But she knew it wasn't as easy as that. She knew that if she pressed home on certain aspects of her mother's character, she might come to a dangerous, unhappy judgment. She had no wish to judge her mother— she had indeed an unsatisfied desire simply to love her, as Tom did, but she knew she never could. In spite of all her care, however, she watched and noted her mother, as she did everyone, but here with an added because unadmitted alertness—and she had felt for a long time that the day on which Tom fell in love would be dark and dangerous. So she had never known whether to rejoice or grieve for her friend Norrie, who wanted Tom so honestly, and whom Tom did not yet want as much as he wanted to uphold the *status quo* of peace and pleasure with his mother. So when once or twice during yesterday and to-day she had wondered about Tom and Angèle, she had felt sharp anxiety which dutifulness would not allow her to examine.

But no—there might be " something in the air," as Corney said, but it wasn't troubling Mother.

Reasoning thus, Jo was quite as much amazed as Corney or Dotey by what happened next.

The door of the outer drawing-room opened and Angèle

came in. Tom turned and strode to meet her, both hands outstretched. Hannah stood in the archway between the two rooms and looked towards the two ; her face was composed and she was smiling gently.

"Angèle," Jo heard Tom say, "I have just told Mother. Come to her, dearest. Oh, Angèle!"

He drew her across the room to Hannah, who took her hands from Tom's into her own, and leant forward and kissed the girl's cheek.

"Yes, he has told me," Hannah said. "I hope that you will both be very happy always, Angèle."

Jo could hardly believe her ears, but through her astonishment it occurred to her, in spite of her practice of dutifulness, that her mother was giving a truly marvellous performance. *Nothing* could be better—more suitable, more attractive or more in character—than this restrained acceptance, this soft smile, this refusal alike of gush and of coldness. *No-one* could see falseness in Hannah at this supremely hard and unlooked-for moment, Jo decided—yet for half a split second and with a chilling shock of admiration, she thought she perceived it herself.

"Thank you, Aunt Hannah," Angèle was saying. "Oh, thank you very much. I'm—I'm sorry it's all seemed so very unexpected——"

Still holding the girl's hands, Hannah laughed first at her and then into Tom's eyes.

"How do you know it's so unexpected, children? In any case, why should love wait on the slow wits of the middle-aged?"

"What's this I hear?" Corney was exclaiming.

"Glory be to God!" said Dotey.

"Come, let's explain ourselves," said Hannah. And taking a hand of each she led Tom and Angèle forward to the three who waited in the big window.

"Yes, Corney," she said, laughing at him. "It's as you see. These two romantic creatures are in love, and intend to get

married." She held up her hand in light refusal to be inter-
rupted yet. " You can kiss the bride in a minute, Corney ! But
first, I want to ask you all—please, my dears," she appealed
directly again to Tom and Angèle, " to keep this great news
strictly within the family for a few days. . . . Will you ? There
are things about it which we must discuss a little—and I would
like a day or two of peace with the idea, before everyone breaks
in on it——"

" Oh, but Mother——" Tom began.

" Of course, Aunt Hannah," said Angèle, and Tom smiled
at her and gave in reluctantly. " It's a very little thing to ask.
We'll keep it as dark as ever you like." She did not feel entirely
at home with her aunt's curious graciousness, but she was on
her mettle to respond to it.

" Thank you, child," Hannah said. " I thought you'd
understand. We must try not to let even the servants know
the news, until we announce it formally."

" But we'll do that soon, Mother ? " Tom said pleadingly.
" You see——"

" I see, my son. I see your happy face ! " she said with
affectionate teasing.

But Corney was practically dancing round Angèle now, in
delighted astonishment, and Dotey, in a whirl of not entirely
reassured amazement, had heaved herself out of her basket-
chair, to offer pious and exclamatory congratulations.

Jo watched them all ; Angèle and Tom would know that
they had her goodwill—she need not hurry to express it. Her
surprise before this correct and official situation, so smoothly
conducted, had been immense, but already was giving place
to a wave of uncertain conjectures ; and to natural emotion,
as she considered the shining, wild happiness in Tom's face,
and the more veiled, more dreamy certainty of Angèle's. The
latter was looking superlatively beautiful, Jo thought—and
marvelled again at how her face could vary and surprise. She
had changed her clothes since returning from the plum-
gathering, and now wore a dress of very pale blue silk ; her

163

gold hair, brushed very flat and simply, shone like floss silk; her painted mouth seemed, as always in this room, too obstinately exotic. But the innocence and purity of her eyes, the intelligence of her high, wide brow, and the whole exaggerated grace of her seemed angelic in this moment, Jo thought, and of the nature of a dream. It was no wonder if Tom, the innocent dreamer, had come home to full desire in such a myth. But did he guess at all at the complications that lay behind that intelligent forehead, those candid, reflective eyes? any more than he guessed what might lie behind Mother's intelligence and seeming faultlessness? Jo smiled a little at the complicated scene, proceeding now with such innocent, domestic cheerfulness before her. And as she smiled, she felt tears rising to her eyes.

"Well, who'd have thought it?" Corney cried, as he skipped round Angèle and Tom, and pressed their hands and kissed their faces. "Who'd have thought it—if it wasn't myself?" The idea of this betrothal had never crossed his mind, but now it took him with sudden bright pleasure; it was a romantic event, it was strange, and it touched him. Moreover, he admired Angèle very much. "Good man, Tom! Well done indeed! I wouldn't doubt you, son!"

Dotey dried her eyes and hugged Angèle to her immense, warm person.

"Glory be to God!" she said. "His ways are wonderful—and sure didn't I always say that He had something good in store for you, Tom, and you the best son a mother ever had?" Dotey felt that this impromptu was somehow going wrong on her, and went on to adjust it. "But if the prayers of a saint like you, Hannah, wouldn't be heard for your children, what would the rest of us be doing praying at all at all?"

She embraced Tom as warmly as Angèle. No-one paid any attention to what she was saying, she noticed with relief. She couldn't make out what Hannah was thinking or feeling—but maybe after all she *was* as glad as she looked; maybe it was for the best. God was good; the Sacred Heart was never known to forsake the widow or the orphan.

"You're lovely, God bless you!" said Corney to Angèle.

"Ah, dear Uncle Corney!" said Angèle.

She could not escape from the sense of dream which had folded her all the afternoon; even now, when she beheld Tom again, and felt her heart and senses wrung for him, it was still as if each actual moment *just* failed to become real. All was afloat to-day, and merged out of reach with the far-away future in this house to which she was now given up—less real, indeed, all these jokes and embraces, than those years to come which she seemed to be living through to-day—and Tom, in his shining, reckless joy, even so, less real than the man with whom she would grow old here, with whom she felt already she had grown old.

Jo took her hand and brushed her cheek very quickly with her own.

"I'm glad—you know that," Jo said. "But I'm astonished too. I hope you'll both be as happy as you should be." She smiled at Tom, who came and kissed her, and put his arm about her, and then took Angèle's hand and held it to his lips.

"Oh, Jo! Isn't it marvellous? Isn't it amazing?" he said. "Are you delighted, Jo?"

Jo felt tears rising in her throat again, so she gave up the unsteady task of trying to formulate wishes for these two lovers who were dear to her.

"You're a rash pair," she said, and her eyes were kind and grave.

Hannah looked at her attentively. She did not often listen to Jo's unassertive comments on events.

"Why do you say that, Jo?" she asked lightly.

"Well—not for the usual reasons," Jo answered, withdrawing from her mother's attention.

"Don't be a skeleton at the feast, dear," Hannah pleaded.

Angèle stretched out a hand for Jo's.

"You couldn't ever be that!" she cried. "Oh, Jo, you're right. We're very rash!"

"We're not," said Tom. "We've got more sense than everyone else on earth, it seems to me!"

Corney was on his knees now in front of an old marqueterie cupboard. He had a tray of beautiful inlaid papier mâché beside him on the floor, and he was very carefully placing on it some very tall, fine-spun glasses with fluted stems.

"This is an *occasion*, so it is," he said. "And Jo, will you be so kind as to bring me a very fine, soft glass-cloth, like a good girl?"

Jo sped to obey him.

"Let you be sure it's *fine*!" he shouted.

"Glory be, but 'tis the way we ought to have something very nice entirely for supper on this night of nights, I'm thinking!" said Dotey, who approved of Corney's preparations, and was not merely fond of food, but a good housekeeper, who liked to meet situations with the dishes proper to them. She prepared to bustle off now to the kitchen, but Hannah shook her head.

"I'm sure supper is quite good, Dotey; it usually is. And we don't want the servants wondering what our festival is, you see. That's agreed, isn't it?" She appealed to Tom and Angèle, who smiled assent to her.

"Faith then, they'll have to wonder if they like," said Corney, getting up off his knees and then very carefully lifting his tray of glasses, "but I've a Heidsieck downstairs that's fit only for the table of His Holiness, you'd say—and we're drinking it this minute, Hannah, secret or no secret!"

"That's right, Uncle Corney!" said Tom.

Hannah laughed.

"Very well, Corney. Only try to get to and from the cellar without letting Mrs. O'Flynn know *all* our business, will you?"

Corney skipped towards the door.

"It is a well-known fact, Hannah," he said, "that *I'm* hardly on speaking terms with Mrs. O'Flynn!"

"Sit down, Angèle," Tom said to her.

She sat in the little Victorian chair near the window where she had sat during her first interview with Hannah six days earlier. Tom pulled up a stool and sat beside her, where Martin sat, she remembered, on that first evening.

"Where's Martin?" Tom said suddenly, as if lifting the name out of Angèle's thoughts.

"In Mellick, I think," said Jo, who had returned with a 'very fine" glass-cloth, and was polishing the trayful of glasses.

"Isn't it a shame for him now, the wanderer, not to be at home with us all for this great occasion?" said Dotey. "Praise be to God, but there's something very fidgety about that boy, so there is."

"Poor old Martin," Hannah said in a quiet voice, reflectively.

Jo glanced at her mother in surprise, and then at the affianced pair. But they were self-engrossed. Tom was looking at Angèle's left hand. Wherever will I find a ring fine enough for her hand? he was thinking. And Angèle was looking at Tom's bent head, and thinking of him, and of her mother, and of the far-away years—of childhood and of middle age.

Corney came back walking carefully, with a dusty, gold-necked bottle in each hand.

"Now!" he said. "Now we can drink to love and beauty! Ah, that's right, Jo—the glasses are ready." He had brought a napkin, too, and a wire-cutter. "I went past the kitchen like a fairy, Hannah, coming and going. Mrs. O'Flynn and Delia might be the Seven Sleepers, for all they know of *my* recent movements," he said delightedly. He lifted one of the glasses, spun it in his fingers against the light, and turned to Hannah.

"Do you remember these glasses?" he asked her.

"I do, Corney. You bought them for Tom's christen-ing——"

"Yes. I bought them for you and Ned to drink the health of your first son. From old Rubenstein I got them, in Eden Quay, in Dublin. Out of the Drumanglin sale, they were— and I remember the old fellow telling me that the first Lord Drumanglin—a Union peer, God forgive him!—brought them back from St. Petersburg in 1810, and that *he* bought them from a Romanoff, no less. So now, Angèle——" he came forward with his tray of brimming glasses—" are they good enough for this occasion, will you tell me ? "

" Well, nearly good enough, Corney," said Tom, as he handed champagne to his mother and to Angèle.

" Anything would be good enough for this occasion," Angèle said, speaking dreamily.

Jo laughed at her with understanding.

" Then you really are as happy as that ? "

" But why that tone of wonder, Jo ? " Hannah asked.

" Because I think happiness is much to be wondered at, Mother," Jo answered coolly.

" Ah, so do I," said Tom.

He drew himself up, very tall and fine, and lifted his full glass.

" I gave you her toast to drink the first night I saw her," he said to the others, " and now, with all my heart, I give you her name again : Angèle, who has promised to be my wife."

They lifted their glasses with him.

" Angèle," they said, and Hannah looked into his eyes as she said it.

" Angèle, who has promised to be your wife," said Corney softly.

Angèle stood up then and put her hand through Tom's arm.

" Thank you, oh thank you," she said. " I'll try to be a very good wife, I promise—and now, let's drink to that promise, and to Waterpark, and to you all ! "

" Hear, hear ! " said Corney.

They drank again.

And so the two were affianced—and Dotey marvelled, as she enjoyed her glass of wine, that a thing that in the morning had seemed a preposterous threat, a danger, and an impossibility, was now by evening a peaceful, quiet matter of fact, with every-one smiling and having tears in their eyes—in the most natural way in the world. Glory be to God, said Dotey to herself; His ways are wonderful—but what's come over Hannah at all at all? And she kept a baffled, unrewarded eye on the serene, pretty features of her mistress-cousin.

They gathered up the glasses and the bottles, and moved across the two great drawing-rooms towards supper.

"It's all right about the champagne, Mother," Jo said soothingly, "because it's Delia's night out—and I'm doing all the waiting. I'll wash the glasses in the upstairs pantry—and we can bury the bottles by moonlight, if you like!"

Hannah laughed.

"You'd make a good criminal, Jo," she said.

"And all she wants to be is a nun!" said Corney sadly.

"What higher call could she have, God bless her?" said Dotey.

"Oh, drop that topic," said Jo. "You're making Angèle look sad."

There were cold roast ducks on the sideboard, and very fine salads and dishes of fruit.

"Really, Dotey—I don't see what you were worrying about," said Hannah. "It all looks as if you have a prophetic soul, I think!"

"Maybe she's psychic, like myself," said Corney.

Tom made Angèle sit at his right hand to-night, and turned away from her unwillingly to the sideboard, to carve the ducks.

Everyone was lively at supper—made easy before the new situation by Corney's Heidsieck, and by Angèle's dreaminess, which—the formality of acceptance over now—seemed to refuse all overstressing of the emotional change she had imposed upon the house.

Hannah watched her, but without seeming to, so that even Dotey did not intercept the direction of her eyes.

"You must eat a good supper, Angèle," she said gently. "You're looking white—and a little tired, I think."

"I don't feel tired, Aunt Hannah."

"Well, you look a bit ' away ' then ! There are a thousand questions I want to ask you, naturally—but we can leave them all until to-morrow. For to-night, you must just eat well and rest, and go to bed early."

Jo, as she listened, caught herself actually wondering what her mother's real game was. She crushed the inadmissible, crude surmise with customary self-reproach.

Jo thought that this engagement, so golden, decorative, incalculable, and romantic, was a mistake. But she did not on the whole regard what people call mistakes as very significant, or worth avoiding. Most human actions which she had considered, either in history or in actual life—except perhaps the actions of some of the most intelligent among the saints— could be made, in one light or another, to look like mistakes. It seemed to Jo that almost any major decision in any life was hazardous—and that that fact was of no importance. Importance came from within, and informed events only through the natures of their participants. Angèle might be unhappy in a lonely place like this, with a difficult mother-in-law and other difficulties ; or, she might be unhappy if she married a cad and was in London or Paris, or if she didn't marry at all, and just was battered about on the stage, successful, or half-successful, or a failure—she had, whatever her decisions, the power in her to be unhappy and to be unusual ; and circumstances, any kind, would only be the temporary servants of that power and of its development in her, for better and worse. Tom might be happy, here in his own place, having captured the love of his strange, golden-haired cousin ; but so he might be, Jo thought, with any good girl who would love him and love his home and love his children ; for he was very simple, and needed to be happy in conformity and in the known routine of things. *But*, by chance, the two had fallen into this romantic impasse ; by a trick of the senses and of their passing needs, each saw the other suddenly and illusorily as the one necessity in human life, and forgot all else, much more fixed, that they had known or taken for granted in themselves. Jo thought that they were making a mistake—but she inclined to think human love a mistake anyhow—and she regarded mistakes as inevitable here below, and as tests of what lay within. Lovers were brave, she conceded—and these two were very much braver than they knew. Bravery was more important than most things, she thought, because it established so many tests.

Tom looked at Angèle and tried to grasp, through a bright haze of joy, the reality of what he had brought to pass. He had dreamt and sung all day, it seemed to him—and now he longed to be alone with his girl again and in talk, in love, and touch, make sure of this evident, astounding thing. But he delighted too in the sweet formality of these family moments, this graceful, polite establishment of Angèle as his betrothed ; he was passionately grateful to his mother for it all—and looked at her too as he pondered his blazing content. Everything is all right now, he thought ; there's plenty of time for everything now.

"Aha !" said Corney. "I have it."

"Eureka !" said Hannah. "What is it, Corney ?"

"It's a present for Angèle," he said. "I couldn't bear to-night to pass, child, without giving you a present—and sure there it is, staring at us ! The Grey Horse !"

Angèle looked up at the picture over the fireplace.

"But it's yours, Uncle Corney ! You love it very much."

"That's why. You like it still, don't you ?"

"I like it more all the time."

"There then ! What could be better ?"

"Oh—no !"

"Oh yes, I say !" said Corney.

"Well—later on perhaps—for a wedding present——"

"Angèle," said Tom, "he's dying to give it to you——"

"Wedding present indeed *not* !" said Corney. "I'm going to take *trouble* over the wedding present ! I'm going to comb Ireland, so I am, for something good enough for the *wedding* present ! But to-night, for your engagement, I'm giving you the Grey Horse. It isn't a Géricault, Martin says—but I'm not

171

so sure ! Anyway, you always look at it, I've noticed, Angèle —so now it's yours——"

Angèle looked at him gratefully. His tired, affectionate eyes reminded her of her father.

"Well, it's *ours*, Uncle Corney. It'll be there, and we can both look at it. I always do, when I sit here—I love it."

"No, child, it's yours. Move it, or do what you like with it. You'll be making changes anyway—you won't want all these rooms as they are now, I expect——"

Tom moved uneasily without knowing that he did so— and his eyes met his mother's. But she looked at him very contentedly. She did not seem to be listening to Corney.

Angèle answered him straight out of her true thoughts.

"I love the house," she said. "I should hate to see anything moved in it."

Tom smiled, but Hannah still seemed inattentive to the talk.

Angèle looked at the drooping roses on the table, and looked at the plums and the pears in the old, stitched Worcester dishes. What could be better ? she thought. What would I do if I had to marry someone—raw ? Someone who was just standing there alone—with whom I had to go into a little empty house, a little bungalow or something ? Say Tom were like that—Tom, himself, just as he is—but not here. Not a cousin, not a whole person, with a whole difficult web and history of life around him, visibly ? What would I make of him if he were just a chance acquaintance, by himself ?

She met his eyes, and felt her own burn with response. No matter, stop debating—her heart said. You would want him on any terms ; there is peace in his every look for you ; he is your peace.

"The Grey Horse reminds me of you," she said suddenly to him ; "that's why I've looked at it so much, I suppose."

He laughed delightedly.

"But it isn't a bit like a horse, you know ! "

"And neither are you, son," said Hannah.

"So everyone's proved right," said Jo.

172

" Are you drunk, Jo ? " Angèle asked her.

" Tch, tch, what next will we hear ? " asked Dotey. " Is it Jo to be drunk, praise be to God ! "

When supper was over, and as everyone crossed the hall, Tom took Angèle's hand in his.

" Come out, love," he said softly. " Come up to the upper yard, and I'll show you what horses really look like."

Dotey was careful once again not to look at Hannah. Always hitherto when Tom went out after supper he asked his mother to accompany him. But Hannah was already on the drawing-room threshold, and smiling over her shoulder at the young people.

" Perhaps you ought to have a coat, Angèle ? No ? Well, don't let her catch cold, Tom, like a good boy."

The affianced two went through the open door and down the steps hand in hand.

Corney stood and watched them out of sight.

" I don't know where you'd see a better-looking pair," he said to Jo, who stood beside him. Dotey had followed Hannah to the drawing-room. " I suppose I mustn't mention the matter even to Bernard, would you say ? "

" Better not, Uncle Corney."

" But what's the sense in all the mystery, will you tell me ? "

" Well—they're first cousins. It isn't really a very good plan, you know——"

" Yah, nonsense ! In all the best continental families it's nothing but cousins marrying—right and left ! And sure anyway, if they're going to do it, they're going to do it—so what's the good of the rest of us humming and hawing ? "

" Still—better not tell Bernard."

" I suppose not. Though it would cheer him up, the poor fellow, in my opinion. Cheer anyone up to see two like them in love. Ah well, is there a drop of the champagne left for me to take round to him anyway ? "

Corney went back to the dining-room.

I ought to be clearing away supper, Jo thought. But she stayed on the steps outside the hall door, and surveyed the brilliant evening. The evening star was riding up the sky beyond the river ; the air smelt sweetly of stocks and tobacco flower ; bats wheeled about the house.

Jo was reminded—she did not know why—of the Convent of *Sainte Fontaine*, near Bruges. It was the novitiate house of the Order of *Sainte Famille*, by which she had been educated, and which it was her purpose to join. She had not become a nun upon leaving school because, as she was particularly intelligent, it was felt that she would be more useful to the Order if she took a university degree, and she had preferred, if doing that at all, to do it as a lay person, and not nervously and crampedly, as a novice in a religious habit. She had distinguished herself academically—taking a double First in Romance Philosophy and Mediæval History ; in June she had presented her M.A. thesis on " Humanism and the Benedictine Rule," and on its merits was offered a travelling studentship which would permit her to work for a doctorate in any European university. Martin, who had read law and modern history, had just completed such a studentship and was now finally assembling a work he was about to present as doctorate thesis to the Sorbonne. He was the darling, it seemed to Jo, of his faculty, and would no doubt be offered further years of unhampered study abroad—if the war did not intervene. And if it did, no doubt a lectureship would be founded for him, if he cared to take it. Jo believed that she could have a similar prolongation of freedom and sweet study—in any case, here were the first two years of it explicitly offered to her. She could not make up her mind what to do but she was certain that she must ultimately be a nun. The more she dawdled in the world, the more its vanity and, for her, its pointlessness, impressed her. Yet freedom and indecision were sweet, and to study and read and dream as she chose were an ever-increasing pleasure, and not yet to have taken vows was sweet. But—she believed that to postpone effort and conflict was

174

almost to refuse them, and she thought poorly of a vocation to God's service which withheld the happiest, the youngest years. She had set out resolutely on university life, pure in her desire to make herself a more useful instrument for God's service—and she still saw no other service worth her soul's attention. But she had been seduced somewhat by the leisures and delights of study; and she knew that her brothers hated the idea of her religious calling, and that Martin particularly desired her to take this studentship offer—believing, no doubt, that two years of freedom in Europe and among books would deflect her finally from the religious life.

She did not think they would; but she was tempted by them, nevertheless. She had spent most of her university vacations abroad, and she knew that she was greatly tempted now to go and live in Paris, and become a doctor of the Sorbonne, and waive the question of the religious life. Yet—just because she *was* so tempted, she saw how real was the persistent claim upon her life—and she appreciated its rightness, the persistent purity and detachment of its exaction in a world of increasing savagery and vulgarity and personal passion.

And she had visited *Sainte Fontaine*—and knew that the best part of her soul was waiting for her there, had gone ahead of her to that out-of-date, cold, mediæval centre of discipline and rigidity and elimination. No vulgarity within those cold, high, echoing walls; no personal passion. And if war came—all the more reason for the anachronism of Sainte Fontaine—and perhaps all the more danger and difficulty in getting there.

Jo smiled. Perhaps she would have to be brave, as she saw those two lovers to be. Tom and Angèle. Perhaps she would have to prove her contempt for debate about personal decisions, personal fate.

Corney trotted past her, down the steps and round the corner by the yew tree, bearing a champagne bottle and two glasses.

I wonder what he talks about to Bernard? she thought. What an ineffectual, busy, happy life he has!

A motor horn sounded imperiously in the drive, and a second later a car flashed into view. It was Hugh's bright blue Frazer-Nash, with Hugh and Martin seated in it. It drew up noisily below the steps.

" Hello ! "

" Hello, Jo," said Hugh, as he scrambled out of the car. Martin got out too, looking wild and tired. " I thought you wouldn't mind my looking in for a minute—picked Martin up in Mellick. How's everyone since yesterday ? "

" Very well, I believe, Hugh," said Jo, and smiled as she heard an echo of her mother in her own tones. She looked with some anxiety at Martin.

Hugh lifted a large box of chocolates out of the car.

" Thought you might like a few," he said.

Jo laughed.

" Oh, thank you, Hugh," she said feebly.

Martin looked all about him questioningly and then at Jo.

" What is it ? " he said. " What's up ? "

Jo decided she had better tell him. He had been drinking, and had better hear it from her than from others. So she spoke French to him. Hugh's acquaintance with it, gathered at Clongowes, was quite unequal to the naturally spoken tongue.

" *Chose assez étonnante*," she said. " *Les fiançailles de ton frère avec Angèle.*"

Hugh was unwrapping the chocolate box.

" Why all the French, Jo ? Come off it ! "

Martin sat down on the top step, and Jo could not see his face.

" *Tu dis ?* " he said.

" *Tu m'as entendu.*"

" *Oui, en effet.*"

Hugh offered Jo the exposed chocolates.

" No, don't have that—it's a nut centre, you won't like it. *That's* a marzipan, I think."

Jo bit through a chocolate.

" There are *two* good pictures on in Mellick, Jo, this week--

176

you can have your choice, but you must come to one of them. Perhaps we could all go, your cousin and all——"

"*Est-ce vrai ? Est-ce vraiment vrai ?*"

"*Je ne plaisante pas, Martin.*"

"*Bien entendu.*"

"What's up with you two ? Martin's had a few, I think, Jo—but that's no reason why *you* should talk French, is it ?"

"Sorry, Hugh." Jo sat on the parapet by the steps. "Sit down, won't you ?" she said.

"You wouldn't care to come for a spin ? Just up to the lake and back ?" Hugh asked.

"No, thank you, Hugh. I'm a bit tired."

"Do you good—the fresh air."

Martin turned his face to Jo, and she was shocked by its whiteness. He did not look at all drunk.

"*Et Madame Mère ?*" he asked.

"*Tout à fait aimable. Explique ça comme tu peux — mais on a bu du Heidsieck ; on a fait tout ce qu'il y a de comme il faut ; on a été très étonné et maintenant c'est fait accompli, mais — tu comprends — pour le moment un secret de famille.*"

Martin laughed.

"*Naturellement,*" he said. "*Mais, ça ne change rien.*"

"Poor old Martin," said Hugh. "He's worrying about this war that's coming, I think."

"I heard to-day," said Martin, "that the Nazis are going to march into Poland on 31st—that's Thursday, isn't it ? Three days to go, boys, and then *Der Tag* ! "

"I really don't think that anyone in Mellick can know what the Nazis are going to do on 31st," said Jo.

"Who cares anyway ?" said Hugh. "Blast those old Nazis ! "

"France will fight," Martin went on, dreamily. "Daladier means to, I think."

"How soon will it really start ?" Jo asked.

"It won't start at all," said Hugh. "Cheer up, the two of you. Have a chocolate, Jo."

177

" ' *Oisive jeunesse.*' "

" '*A tout asservie,*' " said Martin, and laid himself out flat along the top step. " I feel a bit sick, Jo."

" Why do you go drinking like that ? "

> " ' *Par délicatesse.*
> *J'ai perdu ma vie.*
> *Ah, que le temps vienne*
> *Où les cœurs s'éprennent.*' "

Hugh stared at him.

" Could you translate that, Hugh ? " Jo asked, smiling.

Hugh stared at her. Suddenly he wished he could translate it—whatever the stuff was. He was stupid and jovial and ordinary—but he was sensitive to Jo, and indeed in general to the feelings of those he was familiar with. And he felt emotion and alarm about him, and plainly saw shock in Martin's face—and all of this seemed to him, because he loved her, to reach back to Jo, and make her more valuable, and his need of her more imperious, than ever. So he wished to enter into her mood and Martin's—and knew he could not, and that they were off on some high-hat racket, and he'd only make a fool of himself by joining in.

" I hardly know any French, Jo," he said nervously.

Jo suddenly felt in sympathy with him, and unequal to Martin and the family situation. She had broken the news—she could do no more.

" I think I'd like to go up to the lake," she said.

" Ah, good ! " said Hugh, all happy again. He rushed her down to the car. As the engine roared and they moved off, Martin opened his eyes again, and sat up. He stared about him.

> " ' *O mille veuvages*
> *De la si pauvre âme*——'

" Blast him ! Blast him ! " he said.

Hannah came out of the house and stood beside him.

" Hello, Martin ! "

" Ah ! *Madame Mère !* "

She touched his hair lightly, and he leant his head against her.

" Is it true, what Jo tells me ? Are they engaged ? "

" Well, they've announced it to us."

" Ah ! "

Silence fell.

" There's hell's own trouble going on in Danzig, Mother."

" Danzig's a long way from Drumaninch, my son."

Certainly it seemed a long way, he conceded wearily, as he looked about him at the familiar view.

" Jo and Hugh have gone up to the lake," he said.

Hannah stroked his hair.

" Poor old Twenty-Two Misfortunes ! Do you think Jo will marry him, Mother ? "

" I don't. Do you ? Aren't you hungry ? "

" I believe I am."

" Come in ; I'll find you some supper."

They went indoors together.

The Twelfth Chapter   WHILE THERE'S TIME

IN the days immediately succeeding Tom's engagement to Angèle, Hannah allowed herself to be much occupied with her customary duties, and did not at once encourage either of the lovers to discuss the future with her. Whenever Dotey or Corney made allusion to the new state of affairs, she smiled benevolently ; her eyes were, as they had always been, particularly gentle when they rested on Tom, and speculative, though not at all unkind—Jo thought—when she looked at Angèle. But she was busy—and elusive.

Although Hannah took almost no share in the physical labours of Waterpark House, she was not an idle woman. She did not care for dusting, bed-making or laying tables—

but she was the mistress of her house and every inch its Clerk of the Works. She attended personally to all the bills, shopping lists, and wages of Waterpark, in and out of doors ; she knew where every penny went, and, though not quite as exactly as she believed—since Dotey had her own cunning—what every cupboard held ; she dealt with all Tom's correspondence, managed his Income Tax, his banking and all Government forms, inquiries, and applications ; she sat on committees in Mellick—St. Vincent de Paul and the Legion of Mary ; she attended personally to certain private charities which were a tradition of Waterpark ; she corresponded with scattered branches of her family ; she gardened a little ; she embroidered and did fine sewing, and she read two newspapers every day, quickly and attentively.

She made something of a bulwark of these normal occupations now, and seemed engrossed in them. But she was in fact very watchful of all the moods and movements about her. She felt much restlessness in the air, but had no desire to force the situation forward, or to examine the causes of restlessness. She half-wished Father Gregory would return from Cork ; she would be glad of his views on marriage within the forbidden degrees of kindred, and on the Bishop's present policy as to dispensations for such marriages. But there was no hurry ; and time was always a good cure for such emotional stirs as she apprehended through the household. She was surprised at her own calm before a situation which she had for years prefigured as certain to break her heart.

As she walked back from inspection of the kitchen garden late one afternoon, carrying a small basket of windfalls and a handful of dahlias, she reflected that now it was two whole days—yes, this was Wednesday—since Tom had announced his intention of marrying Angèle, and in that time she, his mother, had not had one minute of private conversation with him. This was contrary to all custom ; always in summer they walked in the garden together for twenty or thirty minutes before supper ; very often she strolled to the stables with him after supper ; and always, when everyone else was gone to bed, they either sat together at her desk in the breakfast-room for a business talk, or, if he was feeling lazy, they just stayed and gossiped awhile in the drawing-room before locking up and climbing the stairs together. But now he was bewitched —and all but invisible ; he followed Angèle about, and led her hither and thither ; he took her " walking the land " with him by day, and about his business round the country, using the gig or the Ford, instead of riding as he had preferred to ; and in the evenings he had this or that to show her along the river-path, or in the schoolroom, or in his beloved upper yard where the brood mares were.

As he sped in this perpetual chase of love, Hannah saw his eyes turned back to her sometimes, affectionately, but in certainty of her acceptance of his new allegiance ; very trusting, very bright in their gratitude. She did not always show that she saw this glance, for she thought that her seeming absent-minded, non-expectant, should make his forgoing of all their habits even easier for him. She wanted it to be easy for him, for the moment ; and she wanted to behave impeccably. So far she felt curiously amused, and touched in some ways, by the spectacle of Tom infatuated. But a little contemptuous too of simple masculinity, that could believe life was in fact as he now thought he was shaping it, and that he had only to smile backwards in salute to her flawless love as he ran after his new passion, leaving her empty, widowed, occupationless.

She turned the yew-tree corner towards the front of the house, and met Bernard. He had some newspapers in his hands ; he looked weary and quiet.

" Good-evening, Bernard," she said. " How are you to-day ? "

He half-smiled at her ; he seemed to know her.

" I'll pray for them," he said. " I see them going about like children, hand in hand, the two of them. I'll pray for them, ma'am ; I'll ask the Merciful Son of Man to spare them."

" Thank you, Bernard ; pray for us all."

But he had passed on as he spoke, not seeming to hear her answer.

Jo came round the curve of the drive on a bicycle; she jumped off as she drew near her mother.

"What had Bernard to say, Mother?"

"Promising to pray for us. Where've you been gallivanting?"

"Went up to see Norrie," Jo said off-handedly.

Hannah looked at her with quick approval. Jo's qualities of judgment and independence impressed her sometimes, and she saw the general arguments of kindness, loyalty, and good sense behind this casual move. Tom seemed to have forgotten for the moment that Norrie trod the earth—all the more reason therefore, Hannah understood, that Jo, who had been her friend from babyhood, should seek and remember her.

"You didn't tell her our—surprising family secret?"

"No. She's depressed though. I'll put my bike away."

Jo turned off by the corner of the house.

She had not told the family secret; that is, she had not said that Tom was affianced to Angèle and with his mother's consent, but she had replied as honestly as she could to an abrupt question of Norrie's—believing that she owed such honesty to one who was so sound and truthful.

"What's up with Tom?" Norrie had asked her suddenly, without any false brightness.

Jo had paused before answering—had done so deliberately, as if she were an actress, as if she were Angèle, she had thought ironically. But she wanted Norrie to understand that she had nothing very cheerful to reply to her.

"He's having a mad craze on Angèle," she had said, looking straight into Norrie's grave eyes.

"Ah!" Norrie paused. "I thought there was something like that on Sunday. It's sudden though."

"Yes. It's very sudden. And—unlike him, somehow."

"All the more reason why——" Norrie stopped.

"Yes, I agree," Jo said gravely.

182

" Then—you think it's serious ? "

" At present they both seem perfectly serious."

" But they're cousins. And your mother——"

" Oh yes—still—you know Tom. He doesn't do things he doesn't mean. It seems as if this is out of his power——"

" I know."

That was all that was said. But Jo knew that Norrie was grateful to her for the brief, painful interchange—and for herself, she felt that, whatever lay ahead, Norrie could not but be the better armed, in spirit and in outward bearing, for this indication of what might be coming. Family secret, thought Jo, as she pushed her bicycle into the coach-house. Poor Norrie. Mother and her family secrets. Tom and his nursery romanticism. Poor Norrie, she thought again—and then suddenly, involuntarily, but with a colder, deeper anxiety than she could have explained, poor Angèle.

As she thought of her cousin she saw her. She was coming through the archway from the upper yard, with Tom. They both waved and called out to her and she went towards them.

" Take this time-waster away from me, will you, Jo ? " said Tom. " Poor unfortunate Coffey is sitting waiting for me in the harness-room for the last hour, John-Jo tells me."

Coffey was a veterinary surgeon.

" We've been choosing a horse for me, Jo," said Angèle. " Down in the Lower Field. You know, where all those very wild horses are ! "

Tom laughed at her.

" I'm going to school a mount for her," he said to Jo. " Of course, I'll actually teach her to ride on one of the old reliables, Jupiter or Blackeye——"

" Well, neither of them will do her any harm," said Jo.

" But she's picked the trickiest colt in the place for her *own* mount," said Tom, beaming with a delight which Jo thought somewhat fatuous, as he turned away reluctantly towards the harness-room.

" Which colt did you pick ? " Jo asked Angèle.

"Oh, a very slim, bright-coloured one—a kind of red colour——"

"Chestnut," said Jo.

"Ah, chestnut—that's right. That's a nice name for a colour. He's got a pale mane, that blows about, and he has a white streak down his forehead, and he's very wild. I told Tom I'm going to call him Hippolyte—you know, Hippolyte, from *Phèdre*——"

"Why?"

"'*Mon superbe ennemi*,'" Angèle said gaily. "'*Athènes me montra mon superbe ennemi*.' That's why. It's the first line of verse I ever remember hearing—Mother chanting it when she was teaching herself *Phèdre*, and I was supposed to be asleep in my cot . . ."

Jo nodded.

"You're a great one for transferring things," she said. "You're very escapist, Angèle."

Angèle looked at her quickly and then looked away.

"Yes," she said. "I'm escapist. Or perhaps I'm only selective. After all, no life can contain everything you want— you've got to choose. And look at you, Jo——" she smiled and became gay again—" you're the greatest escapist of us all!"

"If I make a good job of being a nun, I won't have been——" said Jo reflectively.

"Go on——" said Angèle.

"Lord, no! Anyway it's complicated. But you—you've made your final choice now?"

Angèle paused and looked about her before she answered.

"I've fallen in love with Tom," she said gently.

"But—I'd have said three days ago that you were in love with France, with the theatre, and—you'll know what I mean by this—with yourself."

"Yes. But all those things, including the last——" she laughed—" are ideas. He is real."

"That's what I mean—that's what makes me wonder—for you."

184

Angèle took her cousin's arm and pressed it.

"Stop wondering. I've stopped. I want him, Jo, and I can't haggle. I'll take him decently on his own terms, or I'll leave him."

"You have nice instincts," said Jo, with loving irony, "but it seems to me you have to pay rather high for the satisfaction of following them."

"I don't know what all that means, you silly," said Angèle.

Jo did not say out loud that Norrie, for instance, had nice instincts too, but because she was quite simple nothing would be endangered for anyone by her being permitted to follow them. There is a great deal of waste in this new arrangement, thought Jo—but so there is in almost every human plan.

The two girls went up the front-door steps together and crossed the hall to the drawing-room.

Hannah was in her usual place in the big window. An English voice—that of a B.B.C. announcer—filled the room ; Martin lay in a dejected attitude in an armchair near the radio set.

"Ah ! We've missed the beginning of the news," said Jo. "Anything exciting ? "

Martin switched off the voice and stood up.

"Berlin is saying that the new British proposals about Poland have come too late," he said.

He looked at Angèle as he spoke. Since her engagement to Tom he had avoided all real conversation with her. On the night when he heard the news he went to bed after he had eaten supper alone, and spoke with no-one. The next morning he came down last to breakfast, said good-morning to Angèle and added : "I've heard your extraordinary news." He made no conventional wish or gesture of goodwill, and did not smile at her. He seemed to have no more to say about the situation, and he offered no comment of any kind to Tom. In the two intervening days, he had seemed to do some work, sitting about with large volumes and with note-books ; he listened to all the news bulletins, and went down to the village to drink sometimes ; when he spoke it was to no-one in particular, and almost exclusively about events in Europe.

He was not posing. The war which was at hand now had long plagued his imagination. He was familiar with parts of Europe and the history of its past three hundred years was the field of his intellectual interest, over which he proposed to work in his time, by his own lights, in peace. He was not ambitious, or attracted to domestic dreams ; he only wanted such success as would allow him to pursue his own interests peaceably, and his fair share of pleasure in life. He wanted to live with ideas, not with conventions, and he shrank somewhat from the pompous certainties of ideologists.

He was no Fascist, therefore ; and he feared that, in what was coming, although his Eire citizenship would probably give him a just immunity, he would feel himself pledged somehow to war—which he loathed ; which indeed, he confessed to himself, he dreaded quite selfishly, without reference to its general dreadfulness.

He had come home to Eire at the end of June, after an absence of twelve months abroad, the latter six spent in Italy, where, reading hard in the Vatican Library and fooling hard with women, he had tried to ignore the ultimate meaning of what had happened to Czecho-Slovakia in March, or on Good Friday in Albania ; what was happening every day in Germany, and all day and all night, year in and year out, in China. He told himself that in closing up his mind and his senses to all but their own tiny concerns, he was doing no worse than were his elders and betters everywhere.

He was tired when he got home, and he dropped back with gratitude into the beloved native air, and the peace of the place he was born in. It rested him to be with Tom and Jo again, for he loved them with the trust and certainty which was natural to their love for him. He was glad to see his mother too ; for though he knew that jealousy of Tom's place in her heart had long ago made him watchful against her, and though he believed he was no longer her fool, he admired her ;

and he knew that she still had some power over him which it half-pleased him to accept, and which in any case he felt not all his wits would ever help him to escape.

He liked being at home for awhile, with Corney and Dotey and all the well-known habits and oddities. And at first he liked very much the almost non-existence, from the point of view of Drumaninch, of contemporary Europe. It was fine to be simply unable to get hold of a *Corriere della Sera* or a *Berliner Tageblatt* or a *Journal des Débats*, and to know that even if one did exert oneself to buy a *Times* or a *Manchester Guardian* it would be a day old, quite useless. So he hardly glanced at the *Daily Express*, Irish edition, though sometimes, in sheer wonder, he read De Valera's official newspaper, *The Irish Press*. He listened, at first, very little indeed to radio news ; he slept, smoked, and read, assembled recent researches into order, and leisurely planned his next year's work, to be done for the most part in Paris, he hoped.

But his nerves told him that war, which should have come long ago perhaps, was certainly very near now ; and he grew restless and began to listen more and more to the news, and to curse the newspapers and buy any he could find, and to long for pleasure and delight, and to spend much time in the snug, and to think of France and his friends—in short, to grow afraid, and to feel persuaded against all escapes that there was no future, and nothing to be leisurely or dreamy about.

So whilst, like many another young man during that bright summer, he was trying to get himself to measure things precisely—fear and loss and right and wrong—and to say good-bye without excess of personal despair to all that life had seemed to be—Angèle appeared. He found her, unsought, in his mother's drawing-room, and falling at once a little in love with her, did not hesitate, in his need of illusion and distraction, to go on and fall further. By the end of the Sunday at Carahone he was crazy to possess her. War, war—all right, no doubt ; years of it, and everyone miserable ; and death, or worse, very likely. All right—but meantime—she is here. She has spun into my hand like a gold coin; she is real; she is the true thing. And perhaps, by God's grace, she isn't a virgin, and even if she is—and, to hell with war, let us wait till it comes, and who said I had to fight in it? I'm a citizen of Eire. She's lovely, she's lovely—she's the curious kind of thing one need never tire of——

But something struck him, at supper that Sunday midnight, in the face of his brother Tom; something brilliant and set in Tom's eyes, which was not to be dismissed as other vague hints and foreshadowings had been through the day—and something, then, that seemed responsive to that strangeness, in Angèle. He stood, holding a tray in the shadows, and he stared at them. They want each other, he said to himself in amazement. They want each other. I've lost her somehow.

Going upstairs he had remembered the little box he bought for her, and he went into her room and put it on her pillow. He stood a moment by her bed, chewing a piece of dillisk he had found in his pocket, and tasting the long day again. He wondered how many days or hours were left to Europe at that moment. *A Present From Carahone* he read on the little box, and then he switched off the light and went to his room.

Since then he had been miserable, and had brooded monotonously on war.

He looked at Angèle now, feeling wounded and exasperated.

"France is for it," he said to her. "Don't you mind, any more?"

Angèle was glad he had spoken to her directly again.

"I do mind," she said. "It would be absurd to try to say anything at all—I mind so much."

"It sits very easy on you, then."

She laughed at him.

"Oh Martin, don't be silly! How can *one* person start making scenes when the *whole world* is facing misery?"

"Am I making scenes?"

"No, no—you know that isn't what I meant."

"Don't be unkind, Martin," said Hannah. "Naturally,

Angèle, all this terrible news from Europe must be immensely distressing to you—and just now, of all times !"

Angèle smiled gratefully.

"Well, of course, Aunt Hannah, I *haven't* actually paid much attention to the news to-day or yesterday, I admit ; but I do want to listen to-night, if I may, at nine o'clock—I was saying so just now to Tom. Because—well, I suppose there's no desperate hurry about things and I don't want to bother people, but about our marriage—there would be some complications——"

Aunt Hannah listened sympathetically.

"Yes. Yes, I suppose there might be——" she said, as if receiving a new idea.

Martin laughed.

"I don't know what you mean by ' no desperate hurry,' " he said. "When do you think this war is starting, and do you want to get married before or after it ? "

Hannah stretched out a hand in a kind gesture towards Angèle, and then indicated to her the little Victorian chair near the window.

"Don't mind that rude, disgruntled boy," she said, and then smiled at him. "Sit there, Angèle, and tell us something of your plans, and Tom's. I've been waiting to hear them, you know."

Angèle sat down. She was surprised ; she had had an impression that Aunt Hannah was anxious to avoid discussion of plans, but had not liked to say so to Tom.

Jo, who had been seeming to read *The Irish Press*, glanced at her mother, and then went on seeming to read.

"You see, Aunt Hannah," said Angèle, "I am French—I mean I am officially a citizen of the French Republic."

"But—your father was an Irishman ? "

"Yes—but I was born in June 1914, and in January of that year Father had formally become a Frenchman. He was very glad later, Mother told me. He didn't want to serve in the Foreign Legion or anything—and he was able to enlist as a

Frenchman. So you see that by birth I am entirely French. In fact, when I was twenty-one, I registered as Angèle Maury——"

Hannah made a small sound of disapproval.

" Well, it was my stage name—and Father's people clearly took no interest in me, and it is simpler to have one name, you see——"

" You can't expect us to like you having spurned your father's name," Hannah said gently.

" Well—you didn't like my existence—and you can't expect me to like that."

" *Touché*," said Martin.

Hannah flicked a half-smile at him.

" I agree," she said. " Let us leave the awkward past ; it was mismanaged—and Angèle has—obviously—forgiven us."

" But, of course." There was a pause. " May we really talk about—about plans, Aunt Hannah ? "

" I've asked you to, child."

" As I'm a foreigner, Tom thinks there may be things like birth certificates and so on needed—and he wants me to see your lawyer, to-morrow if possible. You see, if there is going to be a war, we can't delay very much——"

Martin laughed softly.

" But, Angèle," said Hannah, " I haven't liked to bring this up—but there *must* be some delay. Clearly you and Tom have quite forgotten that you are within the forbidden degrees of kindred—and a dispensation will be necessary——"

" No, Aunt Hannah. We haven't forgotten. Tom is going to tell you about that to-night. He's seeing the Bishop to-morrow——"

Hannah started involuntarily.

" To-morrow ? "

" Yes. He rang the Bishop's secretary to-day when we were driving through Mellick, and got an appointment. He didn't say what he wanted to talk about—he wants your permission about that to-night, as you have asked us to keep it secret—but you see, there is very little time, really."

Hannah felt alarmed—and outraged. She had thought that the two foolish, dreaming lovers were still no more than foolishly dreaming ; she had felt calm and even amused. But it seemed that in fact there was very little time, as Angèle said. Many impetuous reactions to her own surprise assailed her ; yet when she spoke she believed that her tone was exactly as it had been.

" The trouble is," she said, " that whatever your hurry you cannot hurry the procedure for a marriage dispensation——"

She noticed Jo lift her head from the paper and look at her as she said this, which made her fear that perhaps something of her inward change of mood had escaped into her voice. However, Angèle's eyes, fixed on her, did not vary their polite, attentive look.

" Tom says he thinks you can," the girl said gently. " He says that since the Bishop has been a friend of the family always, and in view of the war situation, it could be rushed. He says that if the Bishop has a talk with me, and examines my credentials, the dispensation might be arranged through the Cardinal and the Papal Nuncio, without waiting for Rome—he said that you'd be able to advise us about that, Aunt Hannah, through Father Gregory perhaps."

Hannah laughed a little.

" Father Gregory is in Cork this week," she said.

Angèle's expression remained polite and attentive, but she, like Jo, had noticed a variation of tone in Hannah's voice once Tom's telephoning of the Bishop had been mentioned. In the two dreaming days just sped, softened and perhaps stupefied by the peace of being in love at last, charmed and made slack by Tom's engulfing tenderness, she had hardly allowed herself to consider the salty, consistent problem of his mother. She had listened to his eulogies of her, and had idly conceded in her heart that something at least of what she believed of Hannah must be true, and that anyway, if she was so very much, so exemplarily, a mother, she would be glad of his happiness, and make terms to concede it to him. But now, coming back to reality and talk of facts, she knew that all that was nonsense, that Tom's mother was her enemy, and that marriage with him on his terms embraced also this ordeal, of living for ever in rivalry, indeed, in an antagonism which could never be expressed, with one whose love for him would always be as unrelenting as it was egotistical.

She felt afraid, and shivered a little inwardly. But her spirit rose nevertheless to the immediate issue and she reminded herself that she was not an actress for nothing. And how Mother would have liked to tackle her, she thought with love, and almost smiled outright at the imaginary encounter.

" You certainly are in a hurry ! " Hannah went on lightly. " Ringing up the Bishop, no less ! When exactly, then, is this marriage to take place ? "

" But—as soon as possible, Aunt Hannah. That's what I'm trying to explain, you see. Because September is Tom's best month for going away, he says, and we want to go to Paris, to meet Uncle Emile and everyone—while there's time."

Hannah made no reply. Jo wondered what the dark, fixed look about her eyes indicated.

" There won't be time," said Martin.

Hannah turned her face towards him—a fraction too quickly, Jo thought.

" How do you mean, Martin ? " Angèle asked him.

" Well, the Nuncio couldn't marry you *to-morrow*, I take it ? " he said.

The two stared at each other.

" But—when does this war start ? " Angèle asked impatiently.

" You little fool—it's as good as started."

" It's been like that since before Munich," she said.

" Yes ; increasingly like that. But now—every vestige of ' appeasement ' rope has petered out. I tell you, seriously, that there is *no* escape now. It's a matter of hours, Angèle, for England—and France ! "

" France ! " Angèle said the word twice, as if considering its

192

quality. "France?" Then she spoke directly to Martin, and half apologetically : "One has lived so long now with this sense of danger—do you really mean that war is here at last?"

Martin threw up his hands.

"Does no-one in this house of sleepers listen to the news?" he asked.

"I do, sometimes," said Jo. "I think it's as bad as could be."

Angèle looked at her and then back to Martin, who stood up suddenly, and came nearer to her.

"Listen," he said. "Anyone who wants to see France again in the near future had better get packing—married or un-married."

See France again! Irrelevantly Angèle was visited by a crowd of memories of things which, war or peace, she could not ever see again : moments and lights from childhood, gone with the years and with her mother, gone with many renun-ciations which she had exacted of herself through the soft insistence of two days of love—yet imprisoned too in the word "France," returning now to illustrate it ; dead things from a commonplace childhood that was gone—but French, as it happened, and as it happened, her own ; her private possession as nothing which was not French could ever be.

She pulled herself away from the cloud of the past.

"France isn't ready for a war. Uncle Emile says . . ."

"And Uncle Emile is right. No civilized country is ready. All the same, we're having it."

"*We're* not having it, Martin. It's nothing whatever to do with us. A plague on both their houses."

No-one answered, but Angèle's eyes were on Hannah's face as if in some kind of inquiry, so the latter went on, in a friendly, explanatory tone : "Eire is certain to be neutral in this war, you see, Angèle. Absolutely neutral."

Angèle nodded.

"Neutral? Yes—I suppose so," she said absent-mindedly, and her eyes turned back to Martin's face.

"I've practically ignored the news since I've been in Ireland," she said to him apologetically. "Are you—are you making theatre, or is it really war this time, at once ? "

He nodded.

"No-one has declared it yet," said Jo.

"And if England likes to make a pretext out of a mere frontier dispute between Germany and Poland——"

Martin laughed outright.

"*Madame Mère* ! " he said, and then turned back to Angèle. "Honestly, you won't take Tom to Paris on any honeymoon ; you won't introduce him to Uncle Emile and the rest of them, Angèle. It'll be the hell of a time before you see France again. But after all——" he smiled at her coldly—" you've fallen in love. You can't have everything."

"She knows that, Martin," said Jo.

"And if she doesn't she'll find it out, like everyone else," said Hannah brightly.

Angèle had been looking away from them, towards the river. She turned anxious, clouded eyes upon them now.

"If I were a man I couldn't stay," she said, as if to herself.

"But luckily you're a girl," said Martin.

She gave a little cry, and pushed away the heavy fair hair from her forehead as if she felt hot or ill.

"Stop it, Martin ! " she said. "Let me alone ! Let me think ! "

"Why, Angèle ! " said Hannah with a cool, soft laugh, " I believe you're actually upset ? "

The absurd comment exasperated the girl as she felt sure it was intended to, but she braced herself to take it easily.

"If France is on the very brink of war——"

"But France always wins her wars—well, perhaps not always ! Still, it surprises me to see you look like this, child. Hitherto you've been so nice and placid, so unemotional——"

Jo put down her newspaper and decided to observe her mother closely.

"I'm not ' nice and placid,' Aunt Hannah ! "

"No ? What a pity then ! You made that impression on

me, I confess—demure and polite and unexcitable, you know—and I, well, I like it very much."

Angèle looked at her out of eyes which had grown cold and blank. This was rudeness scarcely veiled. This was a challenge of some kind. She could not see where the combat was to lie, or what its purpose was—after all, she was engaged to Tom, and her intention to marry him had been allowed—but whatever this enmity was, in the name of all she was, or meant to herself, she must face it and question it now—or lose her nerve for ever.

"You got me wrong," she said. "By what rules do you work out whether people are or are not emotional?"

"My dear child—but you mustn't take offence! Can't you bear a little teasing?"

"Not this kind, Aunt Hannah. Not in this house at this time, or from you."

Hannah smiled, put down her embroidery frame and leant towards Angèle. Her face was full of benevolent reasonableness; she looked her very prettiest, Martin thought.

"Surely you and I aren't going to be rude to each other? And over a mere nothing too! What on earth would Tom say? All I meant was that, for an actress from Paris, with such wonderful cosmetics and such a distinguished appearance, you were surprisingly—well—demure and, and adaptable—and that I found that rather nice."

"You're right in thinking that I'm adaptable, perhaps," said Angèle icily. She did not yet see why her aunt's absurd and amiable quips were driving her, each one further, into blazing anger. "If I were not, indeed, I'd have gone away from this house after your very first conversation with me, I think. But I stayed, because you made me curious and because I know Father would wish me to stay awhile, and because the others were kind to me. But if one decides to stay in a house where one is only half welcome, and under some cloud—then one doesn't make scenes, perhaps, or discourse overmuch on one's own concerns or feelings."

"So that stupid old muddle of the past still rankles," Hannah said, thoughtfully and kindly. "Poor Ned, how unwise he was—and I too, indeed ! But after all, Angèle, you've taken your own romantic revenge—now haven't you ?—by captivating Tom and carrying him off ? "

It was very graciously said. Jo marvelled at the imperturbable gentleness.

"I wouldn't have chosen such a—difficult—revenge," Angèle said slowly. "But there it is—I love him and he loves me. It's unlucky perhaps, but it's true."

"Unlucky ? " said Hannah.

"What do you mean by ' unlucky ' ? " Martin asked. "And why is your romantic revenge on the Kernahans so difficult ? "

"That's my affair," she said, and stood up and turned as if to leave the drawing-room.

But Martin blocked her path.

"Not altogether," he said. "You opened this conversation after all, and if there are difficulties, we're trying to help." His face was hard and his voice angry ; Jo marvelled that her mother did not interrupt or silence him, but the latter simply sat in her chair and observed the scene. "In the first days, last week," Martin went on, "you talked a great deal to me, for one, about France and your people and the theatre and your work—at Carahone on Sunday I remember we heard a French tune on a gramophone and you said it reminded you of how far away you were and I asked you if you minded, and you said you would if it were to be for long. That same day— only three days ago, Angèle !—you told me you'd loathe to be married. Well now—it's going to be for long, and you're going to be married ! No-one has forced these extraordinary changes on you, so far as I know—but if you ask us to discuss your difficulties with you, we're more than willing—aren't we, Mother ? "

"Martin, Martin ! " said Hannah. "This isn't a very graceful way to wear your heart on your sleeve ! "

Angèle turned to Jo.

196

"Why are they baiting me?" she asked. "What have I done?"

"Don't mind Martin," Jo answered. "He's just unhappy—about the war, and things."

"The war—yes. But the war is easy, for an Irishman," she said, turning cold eyes on Martin. "Either you're neutral, as you're told to be, or else you are free to go and take part in it."

"That is so," said Hannah smoothly, "and all the more easy, therefore, for a girl who marries an Irishman?"

Angèle did not answer. She stood and fidgeted with the lid of Dotey's mending basket. Jo thought she looked very unhappy.

"What are you thinking about?" said Martin.

"Fernand and Josèph; and Séraphine's son, Pierre—and, and others."

"Poor Angèle! Indeed, you must be feeling very anxious!" said Hannah.

"If I could only *talk* to you, Aunt Hannah; if you would let me be natural!"

"But isn't that what we are trying to do just now?"

"Oh—but all the time, I mean! From the beginning. I fell in love with Tom. I didn't mean to, and you didn't want me to—but there it is. You've been nice to me these days, so as not to hurt him—but you've never asked me a single question about myself, or my plans or my people at home or anything. You've never bothered about whether it means anything at all to me to give up everything and everyone, and live here in a strange country, in a house full of strangers, for love of Tom. It does mean a great deal to me, and it frightens me—but it's my bargain. And already after three days I love him so much, Aunt Hannah, that I can't imagine what it was like to be without him—and I know that I want with all my heart to stay with him, and keep my word, and make him happy."

"That is very exemplary of you, Angèle. I'm glad you realize, as every Catholic must, that marriage is a sanctified contract, and involves some sacrifice of self."

Angèle did not answer this piety.

" All I want from you, Aunt Hannah, is help about getting married quickly, at once ! Oh, don't make difficulties ! Don't you see, if Martin is right, if it's war any minute, we *must* get to France without a day's unnecessary delay ! "

" But—if war is declared, that would be impossible, Angèle!"

" No, no—not at first. We could get there somehow in the first confusion—I can plead urgent family affairs. Or we might get there before the war breaks out ! Once we're there, we can always get back, to a neutral country. Don't you see why I've tried to talk about plans—when Martin was so insistent that it really is war now ? "

" But—would it not be—selfish of you, Angèle, to drag Tom off into all the risks and discomforts of such a journey ? "

" Selfish ? He wants us to go, Aunt Hannah ! Oh, I don't want to be selfish—only, if it's war, I *must* see them all again, just once, at Rue d'Estrées. I must see Séraphine too, and there are things of Mother's I must bring back—and I must see how they all are, how the war is going to be for them, how they feel. I must get them to know Tom—so that they'll understand why I have to leave them at such a time, why I can't help it !—oh, don't you see ? If only you'd help me, Aunt Hannah ! If only you'd take an interest ! "

" But I do take an interest. How can I not—in such a problem for my son ? "

" It isn't a problem—for him. And it only means letting us announce the engagement and hurry things up—for my sake, because of the war. Don't you see—if I were the man, and he the girl, there'd be no problem. I'd just *have* to go, and stay away, for the duration ! "

" And you'd be glad to," said Martin. " You belong to France."

" I did—until I met Tom."

" Oh rot ! Romantic drivel ! We are what we áre born and bred and work in—not what we feel in our senses all of a sudden one summer night."

"We can be all of those things at once, I think," said Jo—"and that's the difficulty now."

"Tom's the difficulty," said Martin. "If it had been me she fell for on Sunday night, we could all sleep easy now."

"Martin—please!" said Hannah. "Angèle, my dear, sit down again. I know the news has upset you—but you are wrong if you feel that I am uninterested in your plans, or pessimistic about things. It was Martin, and only Martin, who threw cold water on your talk about the dispensation and so on. I know very little of these things—but perhaps, if Tom saw the Nuncio, and got a special licence or whatever it is——"

Angèle, looking very tired, had sat down obediently. She looked up now with some friendliness and hope in her face.

"Do you think——?" she asked.

"It's impossible, I swear," said Martin. "You won't see France again for a while, Angèle."

"I must," she said. "I can bear everything else, because I love him. But I must go home before all this begins."

She bent her head into her hands, and her shoulders shook.

"Angèle!" said Jo.

Martin stared at the bent gold head. Hannah clicked her tongue and smiled affectionately.

"Come, come, Angèle—you're tired, my dear."

The soft, crushed sobbing went on.

Tom entered the drawing-room and came striding towards them.

"Hello! Where's Angèle?"

Hannah smiled at him, and towards the pent-up girl.

"She's a little upset, Tom. The news from Europe is worrying—and Martin wasn't very kind——"

Tom turned an astounded face upon his brother, and then dropped on his knees beside Angèle, his arms around her.

"Love, love! Don't cry, I beg you! Oh Angèle, don't cry like that!"

She was crying uncontrollably now against his shoulder.

He held her close to him in warm, defensive love and stroked her hair. He turned his face on Martin again, more hard than astounded now.

" What have you done to her ? " he asked.

" What have *I* done ? Oh think again, you great complacent fool ! " said Martin, and turned and strode across the room and down the iron steps into the garden.

" Son, son—you must forgive him," said Hannah. " Leave it for now. I'll explain it all to you."

Angèle was making an effort to stop crying.

" Give me your handkerchief," she said to Tom. " I'm all right now ; I'm sorry."

He dried her eyes and stared in much distress at her.

" I've never seen you cry," he said. " Oh, love—what did he do to you ? "

Jo looked on with kind eyes, and in anxiety. She could read no more into the scene just over than that it had stirred up anger, and sown confusion. Was there a plan just in that ? Was Martin, in his foolish pain, a cat's-paw ? How like a child Angèle looked now, trying to smile with reddened eyes ! Good Lord, what a muddle human feelings were !

" There you see—it's all just nothing," said Hannah. " Just a tiny little emotional scene—that wretched boy, Martin ! Perhaps you could find us some sherry, Jo, or some kind of cocktail, do you think ? "

" Good idea, Mother ! " said Jo.

But as she rose to carry it out, she was amused and surprised to see the door open, and Dotey enter with Mr. Hogan— Angèle's admirer of Sunday—at her side. As she saw him she remembered her own idle and half-mischievous invitation to him to come to supper one evening of the week. What an evening he chose ! And how lucky Mother is, in a way—she thought bitterly—if her idea is simply to confuse the issue. What better aid to mischief already done than such an anti-climax, absurdly imposing delay on explanation ?

" Here's a nice surprise for you, Hannah," Dotey was

saying. " Mr. Jeremiah Hogan to see us, no less ! I'm just
after telling him how delighted you'll be——"

" I trust I don't intrude inopportunely, Mrs. Kernahan,"
said Mr. Hogan, " but Miss Josephine was so very good as to
assure me——"

Hannah greeted the very boring man with much grace,
whilst wondering if from where she halted him in the outer
drawing-room he could see Angèle in tears, and Tom on his
knees beside her.

" Ah, I observe that the gifted Mademoiselle is still with
you," said Mr. Hogan eagerly. " Delightful, oh delightful,
Mrs. Kernahan ! "

The Thirteenth Chapter   THE BISHOP

ON Thursday, the day after she had cried and made a scene
in the drawing-room, Angèle drove with Tom to The Palace
at Mellick, waited for him in the car while he was interviewed
by the Bishop, and after fifteen minutes was summoned herself
to his Lordship's library.

The Bishop was an ageing, cautious man, who had come
to his office late in life. He was kindly, considerate, and just ;
he had known the Kernahan family always, and was fond of
Tom and willing to see him happy and settled in life. But he
also knew Dr. O'Byrne well, and regarded Norrie as an ideal
wife for a man in Tom's situation. It had sometimes struck
him as odd that so right a marriage as that of Tom and Norrie
should be did not take place. He did not easily concede marriage
dispensations of any kind ; he thought that the young should be
directed to seek their partners without impetuous breaking of the
rules ; and he was prejudiced against that Tom Kernahan of the
last generation who had been such a wild fellow, and had
apparently led a debauched and selfish life in foreign parts. So
he listened with disappointment to Tom's story and his appeal.

Hannah had agreed to the lifting of the secrecy ban to the extent of discussion with the Bishop, but Tom had had to promise her that he would impress on his Lordship that for the moment his news must go no further. He gave this message dutifully—and the Bishop thought he saw in it a sign of the secret disapproval of a mother too loving and indulgent to dispute her son's desire outright. As he admired Hannah very much, this indication made him still more grave. An actress, a French girl, a first cousin, the daughter of wild Uncle Tom. And now war starting, and all this sense of haste and heedlessness. Still, this Tom was a good boy, and had judgment and integrity of his own. His plea must be heard, obviously. So the Bishop asked to see Angèle.

At first sight he disapproved of her ; too pale, thin, and exotic, with far too much red on her mouth ; too delicate-looking, and—the old man thought—about her dark blue eyes and lofty brow, too like her father and this boy, her would-be husband, for good marriage. A preposterous wife, indeed, for a farmer.

But as he spoke and as he watched her, the Bishop's heart softened, and he grew worried. She has a gentle way, he thought ; she's very disarming and ladylike, and her eyes are innocent—childlike indeed. She's a good girl—and there is something very romantic about her, I can see that. And he loves her.

The Bishop felt unhappy. He could see no way, in any case, he told them, to dispense them and marry them at the speed they urged. Angèle explained their need to get to France at once, her desperate necessity. The Bishop suggested that she should go alone, and try to get back again, as she probably could. Her face, at this, lit up with a hope that astonished him. She's lonely already, he thought. That'll get much worse, maybe. He wondered if the young man saw the flash of vivid longing in her face.

The Bishop told them that he advised more thought, more patience, war or no war. For his own part, he would reflect and pray upon the matter, and to-morrow maybe would consult the Nuncio by telephone, and would also ring them up. But at best the matter would have to take ten days or so to settle, and by then he very much feared that Europe would be in a blaze. He begged them to have patience, but as he lectured them his eyes were kind and he made them feel his genuine sympathy with them as well as his formal disapproval of their request. There was nothing more that they could say, except to thank him.

Tom was dejected for the rest of the day, though he did his best to conceal this from Angèle.

He had seen the sudden lighting of her eyes and of all her features, it seemed, when the Bishop suggested she should make a dash for France alone. He read far more into it than the Bishop could.

Tom was not reassured about Angèle's tears and Martin's behaviour of the evening before. By the time he got her to himself—in the schoolroom for a little while on their way to bed—it was late and she was tired. Jeremiah Hogan's attentive admiration had been incessant through the evening, and she had tried to make him laugh about that a little, and when he asked her what was wrong with Martin and why she had cried, she assured him that it was all nonsense, and just anxiety about the war, and that he must forget it. She seemed only to want to rest in his arms and kiss him and be still. But Tom, to whom Martin had never, since nursery quarrels, spoken contemptuously or unkindly, kept hearing ever since : " What have I done ? Think again, you great complacent fool ! " Perhaps he was a fool, but not so great as not to know the meaning of the word " complacent " ; not so great as to think lightly of such distress and anger in the face of a brother never prone to anger against him.

Tom's heart was heavy, therefore, before he saw the Bishop. The interview in general did nothing to lift it ; and the longing, the light he saw, for one split second during it, on Angèle's face, laid a new weight, a wretched, vague anxiety upon him.

Angèle, on the contrary, was feeling happier and more courageous throughout this day than seemed entirely reasonable to her. She suspected that part of her cheerfulness arose from her having had the courage to make a scene, even an abortive, confused one, with Hannah. Deplorable as her emotional outburst might have appeared, it had established some naturalness, and made her feel less afraid of future encounters. It had helped her to feel more naturally towards Martin too, with whom perhaps she might now make some kind of way back to friendship. And it had brought out into the light, not again to be buried however Aunt Hannah manœuvred, the whole question of the marriage date, her personal problems and her anxiety for France and her own people.

Also, each day gave her new courage by revealing to her more surely than the last how much she loved Tom, and how greatly fit for love and in need of it he was. She had taken him blind, simply because he appealed to her and because she was ready at last for passionate love. She had taken him in gambler spirit, and without allowing herself to look too closely at the sacrifices he must ask of her. But now each day and often for long hours in bed she did look at them, and they frightened her and made her feel lonely and anxious very often —yet she knew that what she had felt at first was true, and more than true ; that she loved him enough. She was not yet ready to explain to herself why his appeal to her increased so much from day to day. She thought that the answer might be far back in some long-fixed ideal she could never trace. Certainly it touched and pleased her to realize that this marriage she was about to make would have pleased her mother. Establishment in country life, in a Catholic family of tradition and respectability ; neither grossly rich nor very poor, with a husband who was young, good-looking, and good ; and farewell, once and for all, to the insecurities, disappointments, and bitter triumphs of the theatre. Mother would have preferred a Frenchman, and country life in France—and she would not have smiled on Aunt Hannah. But having married an Irishman herself and loved him faithfully and kept his love, she could have raised no serious objection to her daughter's doing the same. And she was too French to view the marriage of cousins with great alarm. No, Mother would have been glad —though surprised, as Angèle herself was, at her deep and sudden change of heart.

One thing Angèle was already able to observe through the new bewilderment of loving—that, safe in her love, Tom was immensely companionable to her. They were at peace together in conversation and in all the small traffic of the day to a degree which she found delicious and surprising. He was unpretentious and simple, but without false modesty, and he made her talk to him of things and people hitherto outside his interest and experience. "I don't think it's too late for me to try to acquaint myself a bit with the things you like to read and talk about— do you, Angèle?" "Any more than it's too late for me to learn to ride Hippolyte," she said. "Oh, you love! You'll ride him all right. I'll teach you to ride him for Dublin Show, my girl!"

She knew he was sad on Thursday, but she felt that his sadness rose from Martin's anger and crudity, and that she had better not lay hands on anything so old and fixed as the feeling between these brothers. She knew too that the Bishop's pessimism about the dispensation depressed him, and she feared he had not liked the idea of her going to France alone. She would talk to him about that—but not yet awhile. She wanted to think it over—and perhaps he would mention it first. Let it wait a little.

"Oh Tom!" She slid against him in the car, and took his left hand into both of hers. "Oh Tom! I love you, I love you!"

He laid his mouth against her hair.

"I wish they hadn't made you cry," he said. "Oh, I wish to God there weren't so many bloody regulations in the world!"

When they reached Waterpark he had to drop her at the

gate and drive on to see about some crops of feeding he wanted to buy a couple of miles away.

Angèle found Jo doing some ironing in the schoolroom.

She sat on the edge of the big table and told her what the Bishop had said.

Jo wagged her head.

"It won't be an easy thing to rush through," she said. "Anyway, he'd be against the idea by nature, I think."

"He's a nice old chap, though."

"Oh yes—I believe he's a very holy old man—but you couldn't call him impetuous or romantic! Why should he be?"

Angèle laughed. They lighted cigarettes.

"I'll finish that ironing for you."

"No—thanks very much—it's just done."

"What are *you* going to do, Jo—if there's war?"

"Funny you should ask—because I've really made up my mind in the last two days, I think."

Angèle looked at her hopefully.

"I'm going to refuse the travelling studentship, and I'm going to take the veil *quam primum*," said Jo. She gave a quick little laugh, "or anyway as soon as I can gather ye olde trousseau together."

"Oh! Oh, Jo, I *wish* you wouldn't."

"In some ways I wish too. But all those wishes are nonsense, temptations—and it's what I really want to do. 'It is something to be sure of a desire,' " she quoted shyly.

"Yes," said Angèle. "Yes—I think so."

They looked at each other measuringly.

"All I hope is," said Jo presently, "that I manage to get to *Sainte Fontaine* before Europe is quite cut off. I'd hate to be fobbed off with some old *ex tempore* novitiate in Ireland."

"Oh Jo—let's make a dash for Europe, you and I!"

Jo looked at her kindly and laughed.

"If only we could!" she said. "But I *have* to proceed in orderly fashion, you see, and take my chance. I have to present myself as a postulant to the Reverend Mother at *Sainte Famille*—

206

my old school, you know, that I showed you from the car the other day."

" Ah yes !   And then what happens ? "

" Well—at their convenience I may be received as a novice there after a few weeks and then sent to *Sainte Fontaine*, or I may with luck be packed off to Bruges while I'm still a postulant."

" I see.   I hate it, Jo."

" So do the boys.   But honestly—I can't help it."

Angèle moved away to the window ; there were tears in her eyes with which she did not want to trouble Jo.

She turned back after a minute.

" Will you give me your advice ? " she asked.

Jo was putting the ironing things away in a cupboard.

" Wait a minute," she said.   And then : " Now—what is it ? "

" The Bishop suggested my making a dash for France now —before I'm married, and getting back as best I could.   Would you, if you were me ? "

" It's not a bad idea.   But of course it would drive Tom frantic with worry."

" He looked rather wretched when the Bishop said it. I—I suppose he'd never come with me, Jo—do you think ? "

" But—like a shot, of course, if he'd only himself to think about.   That'd be the thing for you both to do, in fact—while you're waiting on the Nuncio.   But——"

" But what ? "

" Well, Mother really would raise hell.   You can be sure of that.   It would be an awfully awkward situation for Tom, Angèle."

" I don't see why, exactly——"

" Mother would make awful trouble, (a) about your travelling together unmarried, and (b) about his being interned or imprisoned or bombed, or something——"

" Oh, nonsense——"

" Well, such things *might* happen, I suppose—if France is invaded at once."

"But whatever happens, the Germans won't be in Paris, child!"

"Of course they won't. And I agree it would be a good idea if Tom were to go with you, now, at once. But it'll be over Mother's dead body, I warn you. She's quite capable of giving him a small dose of poison or something, enough to make him unfit to travel——" Jo laughed.

"Then—I'd better not suggest it to him," said Angèle sadly. "It would make an issue—and make him miserable."

"That's what I think. And you see, if he were interned or delayed over there—he'd go clean mad worrying about Mother. You'd have hell, I warn you."

"He'd have hell, anyway. Oh, why is she so selfish with him, Jo ? "

Jo looked troubled.

"It isn't *all* selfishness," she said. "It's a sort of tangle of pride and love and various disappointments, I think. Still—I admit you have your work cut out."

Angèle was looking grave and absent-minded.

"What will it be like, Jo—this war ? "

"Ah—it'll be bad. For my part I haven't the courage to try to imagine it at all. I can see nothing to do, Angèle, except pray, and be as good as one can, and try to hold on to one's childhood faith in a merciful God."

"Yes. One can pray. Would you help in the war ? "

"Pacifically—yes. That's one reason why I wouldn't mind getting to Bruges in time. There might be something Christian one could do—for refugees or children or in air raids. Still, Eire will be right to be neutral, you know."

"I suppose so. I don't know enough to judge."

Silence fell. They sat on the window-seat and smoked. She's worrying, Jo thought ; she's sad. I wonder what on earth will be the end of this conflict ? I wonder what is its right end, what she should do ?

"Could I wash my hair, Jo ? "

"'Course."

"Is the water hot ? "

" It ought to be. You're always washing your hair, you lunatic ! "

During the evening Angèle left it to Tom to report their visit to the Bishop to his mother ; she saw the two walking together by the haha just before supper and presumed he told his news to Hannah then. She did not think he looked happy when they came up the iron steps to the drawing-room. Martin did not appear at supper, and Angèle thought Tom's face became very sad indeed when Hannah reported lightly that he had gone to Mellick to the pictures, " being, no doubt, ashamed of himself, poor boy." However, supper and the earlier part of the evening passed lightly enough, in jokes with Corney and in general easy talk.

Only once did Hannah seem to try a sword—when she observed to Angèle that surely it was rather dashing of the old Bishop to have suggested that she should try to get back to France alone, at this uneasy time.   Tom looked startled.

" But of course, Mother—it's a crazy idea, as I said."

" I agree, son. Inconsiderate of the poor old man, really."

She was watching Angèle, who decided not to play ; she was not going to distress Tom merely for the sake of giving Aunt Hannah the contradictory answer she desired.

" Oh, he didn't mean it that way," she replied in demure neutrality, and thought she noted a slight shadow of perplexity cross her aunt's pretty eyes. The subject fell away, and Tom looked happier. Angèle felt a pang at having cheated him thus a little—but she would speak to him of their concerns in private, not as pricked forward by his mother, she vowed.

When they did his rounds, as he called it, looking into loose-boxes, shutting gates, and kennelling dogs, he asked her suddenly if she thought him very selfish.

" Of course I know I am, a bit—but would you say I'm extra selfish, Angèle ? "

" You ?   You extra selfish ?   Oh Tom—don't be silly ! "

But he stuck to his point—moodily.

"I am, perhaps. From something Mother said to me—oh, she didn't say I was selfish, she wouldn't. But I've an idea—oh, about you, and Martin, and various things—she seemed worried about you, Angèle——"

"Love—she couldn't be!" She was not going to add to his anxiety now by making any rash comments on his mother. "Anyone might worry, of course, about the way I'm worrying you about the war, and France, and what to do—I know! But if I could I wouldn't, Tom! I swear. You see I just can't help what I feel about that—I'll be better, darling, and all this strain will pass."

"Oh, Angèle—I know. I know what you're going through. But we'll find a way out, love, we'll get this dispensation thing, we'll go to France together. I swear we will. Only—I don't know—Mother seemed a bit—well, she's awfully sensitive, and she may not have thought that I'm behaving very well—she's upset about Martin, perhaps——"

"Oh, love!"

"Blast this war! It's getting on all our nerves before it starts, even! Isn't it, darling?"

"Forget it, Tom. Forget it for just one minute."

She kissed him, and kissed him again.

"I adore you, love," he said.

"Sing 'The Low-Backed Car,'." she asked him.

He sang it, sweetly, lightly—smiling at her pleasure—as they strolled under the dark trees.

"'. . . but Peggy, peaceful goddess,
        Has darts in her bright eye
        That knock men down in the market town . . .'"

The Fourteenth Chapter   IN THE SNUG

"WELL, it's a relief," said Martin. "Drink up, girl."

Angèle drank up. It was a relief to her to be out of Water-park House for a while, and in Martin's company.

" What are you relieved about, Martin ? "

He stretched his legs out under the table and his arms across it, towards her. He spread out his hands in a gesture expressive of general goodwill.

" Being friends with you, being at war——"

" You aren't at war yet."

It was nine o'clock on the evening of Saturday, 2nd September.

Angèle was unhappy, tired, and bewildered. She realized that she could be, to-night, no more so than millions of other people, or, to bring it more home, than any of her friends wherever they were, whatever they were doing. There was no excuse, therefore, for making a great weight of personal feeling. Yet personal feeling persisted in the heart ; most ludicrously heavy.

She smiled at Martin, envious of him and admiring. He was no soldier, nor had he any great political passion, or high moral tone. All he had was a selfish easy liking for study and drink and women and the free movement of ideas. And all of that was over. And there was at least a fifty-fifty chance that in a year or less he would be dead—before he was twenty-six. And he was quite imaginative and still perfectly sober ; yet he looked happy, quite truly and simply. He looked younger than he had looked for days. As he smiled at her and lifted his glass, she was reminded of their swim at Carahone, six days ago, and how happy he had looked in the sea, with his wet hair plastered across his forehead where now it fell so softly.

" I envy you," she said. " I envy men their bravery."

He looked shocked.

" Oh God ! " he said. " Envy the brave ones if you like— but include me out ! No—we didn't come here to be literary, Angèle. We came here for a reconciliation. Oh, I've a thing or two to say to you ! "

Major Vandeleur paused by the table.

" Good-evening, Martin."

Martin stood up and introduced him to Angèle. He looked very desolate and thin and red-eyed.

"Have a drink with us, won't you ?" Martin said.

"That's very kind of you !" He sat down. "What do you feel about the situation, you young people ?" he asked with attempted brightness.

"Maggie May," said Mrs. Cusack, from her table near by, "the Major's usual—to Mr. Kernahan's table, if you please."

"Will you join us, ma'am ?" said Martin.

Mrs. Cusack inclined her head, and Martin nodded to Maggie May.

"You don't seem very gloomy, Kernahan ?" the Major said.

"What call would he have to be gloomy ?" said Mrs. Cusack. "There'll be no war, Major ; I go bail for that."

Everyone in the snug laughed.

"So you haven't changed your mind, ma'am ?" said a big, cheerful cattle-dealer in the corner.

"No war to be *so* called, Mr. Flanagan," she said, and composed herself to her glass of rum and lemon, lifting it politely towards Martin.

The Major drank his double whisky, half-closing his eyes and looking at Angèle.

"Will you be staying amongst us now, do you think, Miss—Mademoiselle—Maury ?"

Angèle did not know how to answer.

"I—I don't exactly know—the war is so bewildering," she temporized.

"It won't affect us here," the Major answered, but wearily, vaguely.

Angèle considered his wretched story, which local kindness had buried, but which Jo had told her once, reluctantly, as they watched him listlessly fishing near his shack. There had been some mystery about him, when he was invalided out of his Guards regiment in 1917, and came home to run his estate under the firm guidance of his mother. And during the troubles, he had first, in heat and folly, associated himself with the " Black and Tans " and then—for terror of his life, it was said—withdrawn from them and published abroad his kindly feelings towards the rebels. But still he was held suspect and absurd—and at last was believed to be an informer against *both* sides. In the bitter days of 1920, just before the Treaty Truce, he almost met his death at the hands of a Republican soldier in this very snug. The story ran that Helena Cusack stepped between him and the gun, and said to the young fellow : " It'd be no nobler handiwork than shooting a sick dog," and the young man had laughed and put up the gun. And that was all. He was the last of a proud " settler " family, and he was allowed to live in peace in a tin hut, his shame forgotten, but without a friend within or without his class, save Helena Cusack.

Angèle wondered what stirred in his dead frame to-night, what old fears and gestures troubled him, what names or faces the grave repetitive hour was bringing back. The sight of him deepened her sadness ; she wished he hadn't come to drink with them. He was a terrible effigy for a young man to meet on the threshold of a new war.

But Martin was talking to him contentedly, was quite used to him, of course.

" Oh yes—we all knew Dev. would declare neutrality," he was saying reassuringly. " It isn't Eire's trouble, for once."

" Hard lines on you though, Kernahan—interrupting your studies and all that. I don't know, indeed I believe Dev.'s right, as you say—but somehow I think that in my day, in my day the young chaps wouldn't have been defrauded—they'd have been off to it, Kernahan——"

" Perhaps," said Martin soothingly. " *Autres temps, autres mœurs*, old chap."

The Major looked vague and disappointed, as if he thought young Kernahan should be more soldierly.

" In my day, we knew what to do," he said wearily.

No doubt you did, Angèle thought—no doubt in 1914 you were a fine figure in the Brigade of Guards. The irony of him, the parable, made her feel desolate. She thought of all she knew in France ; thought of Tante Julie's tears falling, falling in the *salle à manger* in Rue d'Estrées, as they had fallen, wearily, ignobly almost, in the week of Munich ; she thought of Séraphine's village, Berneaux, beyond Dijon—geraniums foaming round the houses now, the vintage ready and the boys who had been babies there with her in many summers, departing all, departed. She thought of theatre dressing-rooms she knew in Paris, and of Rouart's studio, darkened and confused; she felt and heard the widespread grief of Paris. She saw the old roofs and the river, and the reflections of all the lights that must now go out. And then, irrelevantly, memory jumped two years, took her to her mother's bedroom in Rue Madame, on a day when sunlight streamed through shutters and lace, to fall in distorting lines upon the bed, upon Jeanne's dead face, the exuberant flowers which her theatrical friends had heaped about her.

Martin bent across and took her hands.

" Have a drink," he said. " What is it ? Tell me. Don't look like that."

He had brushed the Major aside, it seemed. Angèle saw the tall figure slouching back to Mrs. Cusack.

" I'm glad," she said, her eyes following him. " He makes me sick with sadness."

" Nonsense. He's a peaceful poor chap with nothing on his mind, and Helena gives him all the whisky he wants."

" I know. It's awful."

He looked at her affectionately.

" I wish you'd come clean," he said. " After all, you did ask me to be friends, and I thought you really meant it."

" Oh, Martin, I did—I do."

" Well, if I'm going at all, I'll go to-morrow."

" It still may not start to-morrow."

" Zero hour at 11. We kick off to-morrow, honestly."

She smiled at the sporting expression.

" You're going very British over it ! " she said.

"Maybe—but I'm making for Paris, all the same."

She raised her eyes to him in wonder.

"Yes. You see, although I think G.B. will be in on the right side this time, I'd feel funny in the King's uniform. I'd be afraid of being haunted by the benevolent shade of William Redmond—but you couldn't know what I mean by that, Angèle! Anyway—all I mean is, I'll march a bit more naturally for France. There's something I can join, I take it? Something not quite so written up as the Foreign Legion?"

"You're going to France—to the French Army?"

"That's what I thought. At least the hanging about won't be as boring there. And it might be fairly safe in the Maginot."

She stared at him.

"Thank God for the Maginot," she said mechanically.

"That's what they always say in Paris when you mention it. Have you noticed? It's like touching wood. That's a rotten drink you have—gin and tonic. Maggie May, have you got some decent brandy?"

"We have brandy in this house, for them that can pay for it," said Mrs. Cusack, "of a brand that His Majesty Edward VII saw fit to taste and enjoy."

"Good," said Martin. "We'll pay for the honour. If you please, Maggie May."

"Ought I to mix my drinks?" Angèle said.

"You can mix gin with anything."

Maggie May frowned on them as she laid down the new drinks.

"Let you be careful, young lady," she said. "God is not mocked."

"Attend to your duties, Maggie May," said Mrs. Cusack.

"She's very good-looking," said Angèle, looking after the tall barmaid as she withdrew.

"Yes—she'd have had a fine life in the convent. All the kids would have been cracked about her. It's a pity."

They laughed—and then stopped. Each had thought of Jo, and knew the other's thought.

"Jo has made up her mind," Angèle said.

"Ah, she might as well now," said Martin. "We're all grown-up anyway now. It's over here. She might as well do something totally different."

"You're sad now."

"You can always be sad when you think of family life, and the warm illusion it is, and the way it has to split up and leave its units to cool off as they can."

They sipped their brandy.

"Talk, Angèle. Talk French, or anything. Recite a poem. Let me see if you're a good actress."

"Here? In the snug?"

"Go on. Something I know. One day last winter I heard Cécile Sorel reciting Baudelaire, if you please! It was terrible!"

"The *Comédie* people can't recite—well, not anything later than de Vigny, anyway. Mother agreed with me about that— but then I don't think she thought there was anything very much worth reciting—after de Vigny!"

"Say something in French," he said, over the top of his brandy glass. "Just say the very first line of French verse that comes into your head. One, two, three!"

"'*Sois sage, ô ma douleur, et tiens-toi plus tranquille.*'"

"Go on."

"'*Tu réclamais le Soir; il descend; le voici . . .*'"

"You'd never go right through it, I suppose?"

She shook her head.

"Angèle—what are you going to do?"

She looked at him quite wildly.

"I don't know," she said. "Anyway, don't ask me to recite Baudelaire." She laughed, took too quick a drink of brandy and choked a little. "I envy you," she said. "Oh, not for the heroics or anything—I don't *want* to fight and die. But only because if I were you, if I were a man, there'd be no issue. I'd just be going back to France to-morrow, whether I liked it or not! Oh, Martin, the *relief* that would be!"

"What's the position?"

" God knows."

" It was very determined of him to dash off to Dublin this morning. Will he be allowed to see the Nuncio, do you think ? "

" I'm not sure. He didn't tell me about this plan until late last night—but it seems he rang the Bishop again yesterday and made this suggestion——"

" The poor old Bishop must think he's crazy ! "

" Well—I gather he was a bit cross with Tom, but told him to do as he pleased. I think Tom also wants to find out about what will happen to travelling once war is declared. But— he couldn't say much yesterday—indeed, I hardly saw him. And he left at eight this morning."

" I'm glad he didn't take you, anyway."

" He absolutely refused to. He said the drive both ways in one day would kill me ! " She laughed. " And something about getting on faster by himself. What time is it ? I expect he's home by now ? "

" Hardly. It isn't ten. Well, no-one can say he isn't dis- playing initiative."

" Have you made friends with him yet, Martin ? "

" Hasn't been a chance."

" You will—won't you ?—before you go ? "

" I will. I'm not going to die ' black out ' with Tom, as we used to say."

Not going to die. All their generation were bracing them- selves amiably to die, while she and Tom made this fuss about whether or not to marry.

Yesterday morning Germany had invaded Poland and taken possession of Danzig.

At breakfast Hannah had endeavoured to rally the white- faced young around the table.

" Why all this fuss about *Poland* ? " she asked.

Martin lost his temper.

" Great Christ Almighty ! For the last and lucky time I tell you, Mother—it *isn't* a fuss about Poland ! "

" But, my darling boy, it is."

217

Jo snapped, sarcastically.

"It's only just a point in human history, Mother. The most desperate ever—that's all."

"Thank you, Jo. I thought we were neutrals in this house. Angèle, of course—it's very different for her—if France really is going to be so rash——"

"Oh, please, Aunt Hannah!"

Tom stood up.

"Walk as far as the upper yard with me, Angèle?"

On the way through this sweet, bright morning, they held each other's hands and could find little to say. Tom looked about him at his smiling, innocent world, and his eyes were full of tears.

"I can't bear it," he said. "It's devilish, it's inconceivable. I can't bear it."

"Darling, it won't come here. Ireland will be all right."

"Oh that! I know. But think of all those other places, as quiet and harmless as this—this lovely morning—in Poland——" his voice broke.

"And thousands more of them to come. In France and England, and God knows where."

"You're torn to bits."

"I love you, Tom. That's certain anyway. And you'll be safe."

"Yes. I'll be safe. Isn't that grand?"

Angèle went back to the house. On the way she passed Bernard; he was standing on the edge of the path, and singing loudly in Gregorian chant; tears poured down his face; he gave her no sign of recognition.

"'*Recordare, Jesu pie* . . .'" he chanted harshly.

She ran from the awful words.

The whole day had been miserable and vague; everyone made spasmodic efforts at brightness, in an attempt to recover the ground lost to family accord at breakfast. Dotey talked in a pious stream about their blessed fortune in living in Eire, and acclaimed De Valera a saint, God bless him. Corney turned out a china cupboard, washed its treasures at the pantry sink, and stopped from time to time to dry his eyes. Tom was busy, and out of the house. Jo went to Mellick, and to Reverend Mother at *Sainte Famille*, she said. At one dead moment, standing near the radio, listening or not listening to some news, Angèle and Martin had turned to each other and smiled. She put out her hand.

" Be friends with me, Martin."

" Not that," he had said, taking her hand. " I'm wild about you."

The snug was quiet. The cattle men were gone ; Miss Toomey had slipped in and joined Mrs. Cusack in her corner. She drank gin and peppermint ; Major Vandeleur was stretched in his chair, his eyes half-shut, a double whisky in his hand.

" We want some more brandy, please, Maggie May," said Martin.

" I suppose 'tis the way Mademoiselle here is going to settle down amongst us, Mr. Martin ? " said Miss Toomey playfully.

Martin stared at her.

" Well—I mean—if she was meaning to get home now, she'd be wanting to be off at once, wouldn't you say ? "

The Major opened his eyes in faint amusement. This Miss Toomey never *had* known her place.

But Helena Cusack knew what's what.

" There's no occasion at all for a stampede, Miss Toomey," she said. " There will be no war—to *call* a war."

" I drink to your great judgment, ma'am," said Martin. He turned back to Angèle and dropped his voice.

" You won't talk ? You won't ask my advice ? "

" In a way, I'd like to. But I can't—behind his back. I'd say things I don't exactly mean."

" You're still of the opinion that you're in love with him ? "

" Yes. I'm in love with him."

" God ! You're crazy."

Angèle made no comment. She drank some brandy.

" The trouble's not the war," Martin said. " It's Mother."

" We could manage the war.   After all, we could go to Paris now, together, and see what the situation is, and settle things there—about whether or not to marry.   If he were free, Martin ! If he were just normally free ! "

" He never has been.   And the thing has weakened him a bit, you know—it's an obsession.   He can't see past it.   And by degrees his vanity has got mixed in with it—as well as hers."

Angèle considered that.

" It's a hard saying," she said with a laugh, " but it's shrewd. She's doing things to him in these last days," she went on, " that I can't get hold of.   She seems to say nothing definite, and yet—he's changed in a way I can't account for.   He's lost confidence, he's puzzled.   And I can't help him.   I can't get him to talk quite naturally about the difficulties.   Oh, at first —he was so natural, so clear and sure ! "   She paused.   " Of course, it may be only that he's upset about you——"

" I'm being used, I've no doubt——"

Angèle looked at him gravely.

" Ah !   I hadn't meant that."

Martin lit a cigarette.

" She'll be too much for you always.   You'll never make a go of it.   Funny, because you're quite subtle too—but you're honest.   She'd come easier to a simpler person.   It's no good, Angèle.   It's a miserable battle, and you'll lose it.   She doesn't want you.   She hates you—in a way."

" Why ? "

" She'd hate anyone Tom loved, I think.   She honestly can't help that.   But you—well, that's an old story, and we'll never hear the rights of it.   Only, once she was engaged to marry your father."

" Oh ! "

" Yes.   The whole three of them were mad about her.   Poor old Corney !   Can you imagine him ?   And she was engaged to Tom, and then she jilted him and married Ned.   And that's all I know.   But there's a catch in it somewhere—and that's why we were never told of your existencee, or your mother's."

"I see. Poor Father!" Angèle laughed outright. "What a very different wife he got." She mused. "Do you know, I believe he never told Mother that. Perhaps he did, though. Mother didn't tell me everything."

"The album episode seems to cheer you up," said Martin.

"Well, it *is* amusing, somehow! Father with his talent for self-preservation!"

Martin looked troubled.

"Mother is very beautiful, you know," he said. "And she has great qualities."

Angèle took his hand.

"I can see that. She keeps her children faithful."

"In their fashion." He laughed gratefully. "She was very sweet when we were kids."

"Tom is still back there."

"Can you possibly face it, Angèle?"

She paused, seemed as if about to answer, then smiled dismissingly, and drank some more brandy.

"I could only talk to Tom—if he'd let me."

"All right. Then I'll generalize, and you needn't say a word. You should come away with me to-morrow."

"Is that what you call generalizing?"

"Yes. You are urban. Fall in love right, left, and centre —all right. But come to no conclusions. You're only beginning. You're a slow thinker, and you're complicated. You're very French too—very accurate and real. You'd die here; long before they buried you. And you aren't a breeder. Every time you slept with Tom you'd have to chance another litter——"

"'Sh!"

"You're as bad as Mother."

"Well, she and I are civilized."

"Yes. That's the trouble for both of you. We haven't civilized human love yet in these parts."

"Ah—don't be glib."

"All right. But you belong to the town, and to yourself.

You'll fall in love a great many times, Angèle. You're not the least bit simple. You should have Tom, if you want him—certainly. But then you should have me too, and your film director chap, and his chauffeur, and old Stalin, if you like, and Vandeleur here——"

" Shut up ! Disgusting."

" Maybe. I only mean that if you do the other thing you'll make a hell of Waterpark House—you and my mother between you."

" That's a very loose argument."

" I'm a loose chap."

" Fast and loose."

" God ! You're almost witty, Angèle ! "

" We must go home. Tom will be back."

" I've done no good. I've got nowhere. And you're as sad as ever."

" What did you expect ? "

She stood up, and so, reluctantly, did he.

Miss Toomey was gone. The Major slept in his chair, and Mrs. Cusack read—the last few pages of *Gone With The Wind*. There was no sight of Maggie May.

" Good-night, ma'am," said Martin.

Mrs. Cusack laid down her book.

" Good-night, Martin," she said. " Come home to us safe. There aren't so many of the old stock left."

" Who said I was going anywhere ? "

" Helena Cusack needs no riff-raff coming round to tell her what she knows. Good-bye to you—you were ever a gentleman, I will admit—though in the literary style, of course."

" Thank you, ma'am."

" Good-bye to you, Mademoiselle. And *bon voyage* ! "

Her eyes returned, even as she spoke, to *Gone With The Wind*.

Martin and Angèle smiled at each other and left the snug.

They walked home slowly.

As they passed the low mossy wall below which the river moaned very loud and close, Angèle remembered leaning there on her way to find Waterpark House ten days before—and winced again at memory of the critical, sneering child she had encountered.

"You're cruel in Ireland," she said to Martin. "Indeed, you're downright rude."

She told him about "what happened your lips?"

"I've thought of it often since," she said. "The detachment, the bland intention to give offence——"

"Don't rub it in," he said. "We're neutrals—but honestly, we have good reason."

"I dare say."

He held her arm and stroked it shamelessly, and bent and kissed her hair.

"No, no."

"Damn it, yes. I'm your *poilu*. May I give your love to France?"

"Oh—give my love, indeed!"

They passed into the shadow of the high wall, where the road curved and the voice of the river was diminished. It was an exquisite night, full of fragrance and soft sound. In the drive the trees thinned, and they could see the sky and the panoply of stars.

"It can't be eleven yet," said Martin. "Come down to the river."

"Tom will be waiting for me."

"Ah! Well, remember me sometimes. I meant well."

She laughed.

"Yes—I meant everything."

At the last bend of the drive, as the house came into sight, formidable and respectable in the moonlight, he took her into his arms. Holding her he lifted his head and looked about him, and listened to the night.

"I won't be here again, for a long time," he said. "I love you—terribly. Will you give me a kiss?"

She kissed him.

"Martin, Martin," she said.

223

He let her go.

"Still," he said, "I'll be glad to be gone. I'm mad to see Paris again."

They walked very slowly to the house and up the steps. He looked around before they entered the hall.

"' *Entends, ma chère, entends la douce nuit qui marche . . .*' Say it you, Angèle—say the line, will you ? "

She said it.

"' . . . *la douce nuit qui marche,*' " he echoed gently as they went indoors.

The Fifteenth Chapter   VICTORY

TOM got back from Dublin earlier than he had hoped to. He drove very fast, sick of the futilities of his day and burning to see Angèle. He would talk to her to-night ; they would clear the air and make a plan.

He entered the drawing-room at half-past nine, and found only his mother there. She had switched on a reading-lamp and had *The Irish Press* in her hand. The vast double room was in shadow beyond the little circle of her lamp—but the curtains and the window were open to the deepening dusk.

"Welcome, son."

He glanced about into the shadows.

"Hello, Mother." He bent and kissed her. "Where's everyone ? "

"Well, I sent Dotey to bed—she had indigestion or something. And Corney's gone round to Bernard, I suppose. Jo said she wanted to do some work, in the schoolroom. I'll give you your supper—you must be dead tired."

She had risen, and was lighting the wick under a spirit-kettle. There was cold food on a little table with the tea equipment.

"Yes—but Angèle, I mean ? Where's she ? "

"Oh—I'm sorry. I thought you'd know about Angèle. Martin and she went off somewhere after supper. Somehow I supposed she'd have told you."

"No—or anyway I don't remember." He sat down as if very weary. "I didn't know she and Martin were on speaking terms, since that fuss the other day."

"Didn't you? Oh yes! They made it up—as I knew they would."

"I'm glad," said Tom.

The kettle began to sing.

"You must be dying for tea, son. How was the day?"

"Oh, so-so. These red-tape merchants!"

"Princes of the Church!" said Hannah gaily.

"Is there any whisky in the house, Mother?"

She looked at him uncertainly.

"I dare say there is. Are you as tired as that? I'll get you some."

"Don't bother. I'll go."

He rose and left the room with long, tired steps. Hannah looked after him and her eyes were shrewd and anxious.

He came back with what he wanted on a salver.

"I'll have this first," he said, lifting the decanter. "Tea later. You have some tea now. You must be bored, waiting for me."

He drank some whisky and soda and sat down again.

"I couldn't eat any of that stuff, Mother—this bread and butter is all I want."

"Oh Tom—just a little bit of chicken? After that long drive?"

He smiled at her.

"No, thank you—honestly. This is grand."

He ate some bread and butter, ate a great deal of it quickly, and finished his whisky and soda. He began to feel better.

"When will they be back, Angèle and Martin?"

"I don't know really; but they shouldn't be late. They went out after supper."

"They can't have gone far, without the car."

"That's true. They said something about wanting a walk. Perhaps they went to see the O'Byrnes."

"Oh no. They won't have done that."

There was a pause.

"It's a long time since we saw Norrie," Hannah said.

Tom was lighting a cigarette.

"Sunday last," he said.

"Yes. Sunday last. A long time."

He let the lighted match burn out between his fingers.

Neither spoke for a minute.

"What's the matter, Mother?" he said then, in a lowered tone, anxiously. "Why are you like this with me?"

"Like what, darling?"

"Oh, I don't know—disapproving or something. What have I done wrong?"

There was a long pause.

"My son—I don't know that you've done anything wrong, truly. In any case, you always seem almost perfect to me, I admit." She laughed at herself a little. "But—ah well, it's no good trying to conceal things from you—I'm worried."

He looked at her gravely, and then he said an uncharacteristic thing.

"So am I."

She was hurt—and he saw her wince.

"I know that. That's why I've tried to keep my worrying to myself. But you did ask. I'm sorry. Let's say no more."

"God!" he said. "I must be going mad!" He threw his cigarette out of the window and took her hands. "Forgive me, Mother! I'm lost if you don't! I simply can't stand it if there's going to be anything wrong between you and me!"

She pulled one hand from his grasp, and stroked his head and smiled at him. She looked lovely in the mixed light of dusk and lamp.

"How could there be, you foolish boy? Here, let me give you some tea now—or do you want more whisky?"

226

" No. I'd love tea. Thank you, Mother. Tell me—tell me what's bothering you."

She came to him with his teacup and set it near his hand ; then she went back to her chair.

" I wish I—didn't have to."

" Well, you have to."

" That's true really ; truer than you think. I'm the only one who could dare it, actually. And—if you misunderstand me— well, I suppose I'll have to put up with the consequences."

" I won't misunderstand you, Mother," he said humbly. " I promise. After all, I know you."

Hannah took a long breath.

" It must be a very long time now since I last scolded you," she said.

Tom smiled at her tenderly.

" I don't remember any scoldings, ever," he said.

" Oh yes, indeed—you must ! There were a good few when you were a baby. You were terribly obstinate—and you used to stand and roar, just *roar*, for what you wanted ! "

" I'm glad you broke me of that," he said. He looked pleased and touched, as people often do when their baby prowess is recalled.

" It's a very long time since you last roared at me," Hannah said. " And you've been a most extraordinarily good boy ever since."

" And now ? "

" Oh Tom—how *can* I say it ? I've never called you selfish, have I, or heedless, or cruel—or—complacent ? "

He started.

" Complacent ? That's what Martin said ! "

" Did he ? When did he say that to you ? "

" Here in this room, Mother—when Angèle was crying ! "

" Did he indeed ? I can't remember. I was so distressed at the time."

" Oh, it doesn't matter ! But now, you're saying it too ! You, Mother ! Why ? "

227

"It's complicated." She paused. "I wish you hadn't gone chasing after the Nuncio to-day," she said thoughtfully. "But you're so simple, Tom, that sometimes I'm half-afraid that people will mistake you for obtuse." He moved uneasily, but she went on. "You didn't do much good by the trip, did you?"

"I believe not," he said wearily. "They want all sorts of documents. Even if they could agree to grant a dispensation, the formalities will be endless. And we haven't *started* arguing yet!"

"I see."

"I inquired about travel to the Continent too. It seems that for the present, so far as they know, it'll be all right for getting there, if your papers are in order. But of course no one knows anything about getting back."

"Naturally."

"To hear some of these know-alls in Dublin you'd imagine the Germans were going to be in Paris next week!"

"Well—they might be."

"Good God, Mother! France has an army!"

She laughed.

"Don't talk to me as if you were Martin, son. To be sure France has an army—of some sort." A shadow crossed her face, and he saw it.

"What is it? Come on!"

"It's Angèle. I'm—I'm worried for the poor child."

He was immensely touched.

"Oh Mother! Mother darling!"

"She isn't happy, Tom."

"I know. But——"

"Son—here goes—the point is that you *don't* know. Let me go on now. Let me say this dreadful thing I must say— and *nunc dimittis* then perhaps. Angèle is unhappy about the war and France and being caught so far away from all her people at such a tragic time—of course! That's clear, and anyone can understand it. It's circumstantial, it's ABC. But— have you no other fears about her, Tom?"

228

He stared at his mother blankly. He opened his mouth as if to speak, then shook his head.

"It's all my fault in a way," Hannah said. "I brought you up here at my side, and was only too content to have you stay here. I never encouraged you to roam and sow wild oats, as I suppose a mother should."

"You were perfect to me. I've always been perfectly free."

"Of course you have. Still, I liked you innocent and good, and I thought that that was how your wife would like you too, if she was a good girl. Angèle is very good, very dear. At first I didn't pay much attention to her really—because, well, she was just your cousin, and I—well, I thought in any case that you were thinking a bit of Norrie. But when I saw how the wind blew, I was glad, in a way—in spite of the difficulties, and in spite of some quite selfish sadness."

He patted her hand.

"Oh Mother, Mother!"

"No, I'm not crying. Let me go on. You *know* that when you told me you were engaged to her I was happy—we all were! She is so distinguished and lovely! She almost seemed good enough for you, darling! And I was so much moved by your great happiness that—well, I wasn't very intelligent, that's all. I didn't think! I just looked on at the romantic picture you made, the two of you—and dreamt my dreams. And that is what you did too! Neither of us *thought* quick enough, my darling. I mean, of all that had gone to make Angèle just what she is, of all the complications behind that very light and fair façade. Neither of us thought of the absurd price we were asking her to pay, for falling in love with you."

"But, Mother——"

"Wait a minute. I saw it all when she cried here in this room on Wednesday evening. Martin—poor Martin, he behaved very badly, but then he is in love with her, Tom——"

Tom stood up.

"In love with her?"

"Oh darling, don't! Don't be so *simple*, son! She comes

from Martin's world, she speaks his language, she's used to the way he goes on, the kind of ideas he has, and so on. Why should he *not* fall in love with her? To tell you the truth, I thought up to last Sunday that she was also falling in love with him. But I was wrong in that—as in so much! She fell for you, as Martin would say—and how could she fail to?"

Hannah smiled at him, but he did not look at her. He was standing against the window-sash, a tall, great shadow, and his eyes were on the river.

"When she was crying the other day, I saw it all. She fell in love with you, romantically and hastily—thinking perhaps that you were like Martin, or that anyhow by declaring your feelings you might both find out what in fact they meant to you. But then she found out what you were like, how simple you are, how forthright, how good. And she saw—you made her see—that she had your whole future happiness in her hands. Well—she's a Kernahan, after all, Tom. That means she has a sense of obligation. And she loves you, and she is gentle and would hate to give you pain. But, in spite of herself, when you started rushing the marriage preparations, and when on top of that she saw war coming, and exile, total exile, perhaps for many, many years for her—oh my dear! She was so loyal to you in her distress the other day! But anyone could see that she felt—well, *trapped*, my son."

"Trapped? Oh, Mother! Trapped?"

"You've rushed her too much. You've been too sure, I think. Too innocent, really." She paused. "Tom, it's all my fault. I do know life, after all, and I should have been watchful, and guided you. But one thing I always vowed, that when you fell in love I'd stand well back, and interfere in nothing. And I kept to that. Now didn't I?"

He made no answer. He stood very still against the window-sash.

"You see, son—she's an artist. Artists are creatures of quick, warm feelings and sudden dreams. But they are not to be held to their dreams. And we shouldn't, we just shouldn't

230

ask them to shoulder the whole of life with us, no matter how they seem to want it. We only lay up to-morrow's tears for them if we take to-day too much for granted."

" Too much for granted. I see."

" I'm saying terrible things, Tom. I'm breaking your heart. But I have been so proud of you for all these years—and, over Angèle—my son, over Angèle I've seen you drive too hard a bargain. For the only time in your life."

There was silence. The river roared, increasing it.

" Angèle or no Angèle—I couldn't bear that. I—I had to speak. I'll never be forgiven, perhaps. But still—I cannot have you less than perfect, son. I had to say what I have said."

" I know. I see."

" I'd better leave you now, I think. To think it over. I've talked too much, and perhaps I've exaggerated. But you'll allow for that."

She stood up, and came near him.

" You'll be very unhappy for a bit—and I've made you so. But better that than misery for good—the awful misery of making her unhappy."

" But—I love her. She loves me."

" I know. That's the trouble ; that's the trouble, darling. But there are many kinds of love ; the kind *you* mustn't fall into, my son, is the greedy kind."

She took his hand.

" Will you say good-night ? Will you kiss me—after this terrible scolding ? "

" Oh, Mother, yes. Of course."

He kissed her. His face was drenched with tears and he was shaking. She pressed his hand against her lips.

" You are so good and honest. It will be all right, son."

She left him, crossed the two drawing-rooms, and went upstairs to bed.

He stood a long time leaning against the window-sash. All that his mother had said was whirling about in him, but louder, newer than it, as if she had made it her refrain, rose Martin's words that had been hurting him for days. "Think again, you great, complacent fool."

Think again. There was no need to; he was no good at thinking anyhow—and the thinking had been done for him. Clearly, clearly he had been driving too hard a bargain. Clearly he was mad, with love and self-love.

Mother had done her best to spare him. She always would. But there it was. He was a great, complacent fool. Oh Mother, Mother!

He moved away from the window-sash and fidgeted across the room. Without noticing what he did he poured another whisky and soda. But he forgot to drink it. He left it on the salver, and walked on. He went into the outer drawing-room and out on to the iron steps.

The air fell kindly on his head.

He went down into the garden.

He walked along beside the haha as far as the plank bridge. He paused there, because people always did, for the expanse of view on every side. He leant against the trunk of an ilex tree and lighted a cigarette.

The river ran westward of him, and from here he had a fine, wide view of its arrogant sweep to the south. It roared at him consolingly, deadening pain, awaking long, safe memories. In front his house stood, square and cold in moonlight, very deep-set in its place, familiar as the river's voice, and as indifferent to the momentary grief. To his right a shaggy stretch of lawn and the gravel sweep lay white and open before the contrasting blue mass of the great yew tree, and the deep cavern of the timbered drive.

He looked about him at the place he loved, and wondered how he was going to bear the weight of it henceforward, without her beauty, without her grace and love.

He heard steps eastward, slow, strolling steps in the dark drive. Voices too. Martin's deep voice and quick speech, and Angèle's light answering tone. He moved to go in their direction, and then he saw them. On the edge of the cavern of trees, where the moonlight could just meet them, he saw them stand and kiss each other. He saw Angèle's white dress drift cloudily against the shadowy grey of Martin's clothes. He saw them stand and cling together.

He went back by the haha to the drawing-room side of the house, a path on which they could not see him. You great, complacent fool, he thought. He went up the iron steps again, into the drawing-room. He dawdled there a bit, pulling himself together and lighted a cigarette. Then he went out into the hall.

" Hello, Angèle," he said, as he switched on a light.

" Oh Tom—hello ! Have you been back long ? I'm sorry. Martin and I went to the snug, to celebrate our making friends again. Are you tired, Tom ? Did you have an awful day ? "

" No, I'm not tired. I'm glad you're not very late—could we talk a minute ? "

" I'd love to."

Martin came nearer.

" Tom," he said. " I'm sorry for what I said—I didn't mean a word of it. Will you shake hands, and forgive me ? "

They shood hands.

" That's all right," said Tom.

Martin stared into his face.

" Are you sure ? Are you all right ? "

" I'm perfectly all right. Honestly."

" I'm glad. You look a bit shaky somehow. Oh well—I'm not feeling so grand myself ! Good-night to you, boss. Good-night, Angèle. God bless you."

He waved to them and vanished through the heavy door that led to the staircase lobby.

Tom opened the drawing-room door, and followed Angèle through it. They went to the inner room, where the reading-lamp still burned, surrounded by moths, and where the supper tray lay.

Angèle put her arms round him and tried to kiss him, but

he pressed her gently down into the little Victorian chair that faced his mother's empty one.

"What is it, love?" she said anxiously. "You look terribly unhappy. Have you had supper?" She indicated the food on the tray. "Have you been lonely?"

"No—I'm all right. I had food. Mother's been with me until a minute ago—I was talking to her."

"Ah!"

"Did you have a good time—with Martin?"

"Yes. We went to the snug and had a lot of brandy. How was the Nuncio, Tom?"

"Depressing."

"Oh! Oh, I'm sorry."

"It doesn't matter."

She looked at him sharply.

"What *is* it? Who's been hurting you? Come here to me!"

"No. Let me stand here."

"All right—but speak to me. Oh, don't be cruel, Tom!"

"Cruel? That's what Mother says I am—one of the things."

"What did you say, darling?"

"Nothing, really."

"Oh love, please! Come nearer! Give me a cigarette!"

He came and gave her a cigarette and lighted it.

"Angèle," he said, "I—I want you to go back to France— at once, love, to your own people. When I asked you to marry me—I didn't see all these difficulties—the war and the dispensation and all the misery for you—and I didn't think about your being an actress, and French, and lonely here, and everything! Angèle! I'm sorry! I'm sorry! I was an ass! I didn't know!"

He dropped on his knees; he was crying. His head fell into her lap and she took it in her hands. She stared beyond him, out into the night to the river.

"Your mother's been talking to you, you say?"

234

" Oh yes ! She explained it all. She made me see what a conceited ass I've been. Angèle, I loved you ! I didn't mean it that way ! But now I see—of course ! Oh please, Angèle— I swear I didn't mean to be a fool ! "

" Stop ! Stop ! "

There was a sudden silence. He knelt quite still.

" What else did your mother say ? " Angèle asked.

" Oh—I can't remember. She made it clear anyway. She's been worried to death about you, Angèle. About your being an artist—and being *trapped*. I see. I understand, Angèle ! I see."

He was crying again.

Angèle caressed his hair and stared in front of her. It is hopeless, she thought. A fighter would stay and fight. So would I—if it weren't for the war, if it weren't for wanting to be at home for the war. It's hopeless anyway, against her. Better let it all go. It's too much. I haven't the courage, I haven't the brains.

" As if I'd want to trap you, love ! " he was crying. " Oh God, oh God ! "

She rocked his head against her breast.

" Sh—be quiet. Tom, I know, I know."

I love you, I love you, my gentle lamb, her heart was saying. I love you, and I hate the fighting, filthy world. And I hate your mother. All right—it's best this way.

" She explained about Martin too, Angèle——"

" What did she explain about Martin ? "

" Oh, about his being in love with you, and your liking him, and being his sort, of course, and speaking his language——"

" I see."

Silence came again. Tom stopped crying, and lifted his head.

" Don't mind what I'm going to say, love," he said. " I'm only saying it so that there'll be no—no awkwardness between us. But I saw you just now—I saw you kissing Martin, in the drive."

"Did you? I'm sorry. Oh, it must have disgusted you. I'm sorry, Tom."

"That's all right. I couldn't spy on you and not let you know. It was an accident."

"I know. I kissed him because—just then—I wanted to."

"Yes. Like an artist feels. I know. Mother explained."

Angèle almost flung him away.

"Oh no! She didn't! She didn't!"

He stared at her in wonder and she pulled herself together.

"I kissed him because I wanted to," she said. "I might have wanted to anyway—but I kissed him to-night chiefly because he's going away to-morrow, to enlist in the French Army."

"To enlist?"

"Yes. He's going to Paris—to fight for France."

"Ah! Ah, God!"

"Does your mother know that?"

"No. Martin! Martin in the French Army!"

"My father—your uncle—was a *poilu* in the last war."

"I know."

His head dropped back on her lap.

"I'm sorry, Angèle. Forgive me. Go home, love, and forgive me. It'll be all right."

She took his head in her hands again.

"I'll go home," she said. "Only because I'm beaten, though. Not because I'm an 'artist,' and not because you're selfish. I love you. But I'll go home all right. After all, I love France too."

She stroked his hair, and stared out at the river. It roared like a god at her. Moths beat feebly round Hannah's reading-lamp.

All right, Angèle thought wearily. All right. There's a war on, and I'm lonely. I'll go home. You win, Aunt Hannah.

ANGÈLE stood alone in the drawing-room at midday on Sunday, and listened to a recorded repetition of the speech which Mr. Chamberlain had delivered to Britain at a quarter-past eleven.

Delia had told her about it.

" It's war, Miss. War to the knife, God spare us all ! And France will be in it from minit to minit, God save us ! "

She had stayed in her room all the morning. Jo had brought her some tea and toast there, and she had talked to Jo while she packed her things, and explained that she was going that day.

" The four o'clock will be running—to catch the mailboat," said Jo. " Martin is going too. He told us at breakfast that he's going to try and join the French Army. I expect you know."

Angèle nodded.

She told Jo as much as she could of what had happened the night before.

Jo nodded her head.

" Tom looked like death at breakfast. Ah, breakfast was dramatic, one way and another ! Here, eat yours."

" Jo—shall we meet again ? "

Jo looked at her gravely.

" It's unlikely," she said. " I wish it weren't. Perhaps after the war you'll make inquiries about me at Place des Ormes, in Brussels. The headquarters of the Order. God knows where I'll be—but write to me, if they give you an address. We're all over the world."

" You talk in a very committed way."

" I am committed. I settled it with Reverend Mother on Friday."

" Oh, Jo."

" Don't—please ! "

" I know. I'm sorry. Poor old Red Hugh ! What'll he do with all his chocolates ? "

" God knows ! He proposed to me for the last and lucky

237

time on Monday night, when we went up to the lake—and I told him then that this was a certainty."

" What did he do ? "

" He cried a bit."

They smiled at each other.

" Chamberlain is going to declare war for England some time this morning," Jo said.

" And France ? "

" France is declaring too. I don't know when though. But it'll be to-day. I'm sorry you're going. But you're right, really. You made a mistake. I want to get in a second Mass to-day—— Do you mind if I fly ? "

" No, off with you. Sometimes I think you're the nicest person I've ever known, Jo—except Mother."

Jo laughed.

" Funny how you and Tom *both* have the Œdipus complex," she said.

" What an odd thing for you to say ! " said Angèle in feminine astonishment.

" Old-fashioned, at that. Anyway, I don't believe a word of it. I only said it for fun."

" Ah Jo—you're awfully nice ! "

" So are you. You're lovely as well."

She dashed away to second Mass. And then Delia came in with news of " war to the knife."

Angèle packed the little shell box that Martin had given her ; she held Tom's shell to her ear, and listened to the sea, and packed that too. She put her room in order and closed her suitcase. And when she went downstairs to hear what Mr. Chamberlain had said the house seemed empty.

She switched off at the end of the record of his speech, and, turning, found Aunt Hannah in the room.

" Good-morning, Angèle."

" Good-morning, Aunt Hannah. Forgive me for not having come down to breakfast. Have they told you that I'm leaving to-day ? "

" Yes. Jo said you were. It's sudden, child—but I suppose, in the circumstances, you must. There's a good train, for the mailboat, at four. You'll come back, Angèle ? "

" No, Aunt Hannah. I won't. Tom knows I won't. Don't worry."

" But—my dear child——"

" You have won, Aunt Hannah. If I were braver, or older, or if this war wasn't on, I'd stay. I'm not going because I don't love Tom, or for any of the reasons you gave him about me."

" Reasons I gave him ? But what on earth could you mean, Angèle ? "

" Oh, stop it. You're my elder, and my hostess. Anyway, you're too clever for me. But don't imagine I'm fooled."

" My dear, dear girl—— ? "

" I'm not. Stop it."

" How very rude you are ! "

" Yes. And I'm a coward too. That's why I'm ratting. If I had any guts I'd try to set up my illusion for him against yours. But I haven't. Anyway, I couldn't concentrate, with France at war. So you win—hands down."

" I can only repeat that you're very rude."

" I hope so. You've been rude to me. But that's no matter. What matters is the grief and misery you left him in last night. I love him, Aunt Hannah. For what it's worth, remember that—and be good to him. I'm going away simply because I funk you and I hate you. But I know I ought to stay."

" Does Tom know that you're going ? "

" Yes. He's resigned, because of what you told him about his character. Aunt Hannah — did you know, could you possibly know, how you cut pieces out of his courage and his goodness last night—so that I'd go ? "

" You're talking like a lunatic, Angèle."

" So well I might. I love him, and yet, like a cad and a skunk, I hand him over to you. Oh well—I'll be gone at four o'clock."

239

Corney came into the drawing-room. He was dragging a heavy picture under his arm. His eyes were red.

"Angèle ! They tell me you're going ! "

"Well, I must, Uncle Corney. I'm French, you see, and after all——"

He looked at her blankly and then at Hannah, whose colour was high and angry. He was quick about some things. He sighed.

"Will you take The White Horse, Angèle ? Oh please ! Will you take it, just as a little souvenir ? In case the war is long. In case I don't see you again ? "

She bent over the heavily-framed picture with him.

"I'd love to," she said.

She held it up and fixed it on a chair so that the light caught it correctly.

"It's lovely," she said sadly. "Oh Uncle Corney, I *can't* take it right into the war."

"That's what I was afraid of," said Corney. "I wish I could know you had it with you, Angèle."

"I'd love to have it. It's a lovely picture."

"The poor old White Elephant," said Hannah coldly.

Martin came into the room with Hugh Delaney.

"Good-day, Mrs. Kernahan. I gave Martin a lift back from eleven o'clock Mass. This is terrible news of war, isn't it ? Where is Jo, do you know, Mrs. Kernahan ? "

"I believe she went to second Mass, Hugh. You must have missed her. Yes, it's terrible. *And* very foolish. It could all have been avoided, obviously."

"Bernard says it couldn't," said Corney. "Bernard says it's anti-Christ, and the wages of sin."

"Poor old Bernard ! No doubt he's right," said Martin.

Jo came into the room and smiled at Hugh, and explained that she had left the chapel during the Last Gospel and cycled home.

"Is there anything to drink ? " said Martin.

Jo went to look for drinks.

Angèle looked at Martin.

" Has France declared war yet ? " she asked.

" No. She's due to any minute," said Hugh. " Martin tells me he's off to enlist to-day, Mrs. Kernahan ? "

Hannah smiled.

" That's right, Hugh. He doesn't seem to understand that the Irish are neutral. I hope you do."

" Oh, I'm not so sure ! What do you think, Jo ? Should I join the R.A.F., do you think ? "

Jo laid down a tray of bottles and glasses.

" I'd try being a doctor first, if I were you," she said.

" Oh—that's hopeless ! "

Everyone laughed.

" Twenty-two Misfortunes," said Martin.

" For the last and lucky time, Martin, why Twenty-two ? "

Angèle stood as if in the centre of a dream. In four hours they would be a dream, they would be imaginary. In four hours these ten days of fantasy would have slid into the formal shapes of memory, and she would be on her way to war.

Tom came up the iron steps and crossed the outer room towards the group. He looked dead tired. With a strange, grave kindness in his eyes he came and stood beside her.

" How are you, Angèle ? "

" I'm all right. Oh thank you, Jo——" she took a glass of sherry. " Tom, Uncle Corney wants me to have The White Horse—to take it with me. But I can't take it into the war with me. Will you keep it here *for* me—in memory of me ? "

Tom looked very sadly at her.

" In memory of you, love," he said softly. " Oh Angèle ! "

Martin came to him with a glass of sherry.

" Drink up, Tom," he said.

" Jo," said Hugh, " Jo, don't you think I'd better join the R.A.F. ? "

Dr. O'Byrne swept into the room, with Norrie in his wake.

" We thought we'd look in on our way from Mass, ma'am," he said, " seeing the black day it is. Even for us poor neutrals ! "

"We're very glad to see you, Dr. O'Byrne," said Hannah. "And how are you, Norrie dear? You'll both have a glass of sherry? Yes—it's a day for counting friends, and visiting them!"

"Is it true what I heard at the chapel, Martin," said the Doctor, "that you're off for the French Army?"

"True enough," said Martin.

"Good God!" said Dr. O'Byrne. "Well, I suppose you're right, if you feel it—but I always thought you were a man of books, not of the sword."

"I don't expect to use a sword much," said Martin.

"He'll be useful to me on the journey anyway," said Angèle, who felt a bitter desire to clear all clouds from Norrie's mind.

The Doctor turned to her attentively.

"Yes, isn't it dreadful?" said Hannah. "All this upheaval! Martin set on chivalry towards France, and poor Angèle, naturally, compelled by all the tragedy to break her holiday and dash for home."

"Indeed? Of course!" said the Doctor. "It seems we'll be lonely here in our neutrality!"

"It's been a lovely holiday," said Angèle politely.

"Perhaps you'll come back soon," said Norrie.

Angèle shook her head.

"I don't expect to come back ever," she said softly.

Tom stood beside her, not far from Norrie, and looked from one to the other as they spoke.

Dotey came wheezing in with a message for Hannah. Brother Nicodemus had called to say that Father Gregory was back from Cork, and would be calling on Mrs. Kernahan at four o'clock.

"That will be very nice," said Hannah.

"Have a glass of sherry, Dotey," said Jo.

"And Lady McNamara is dead," said Dr. O'Byrne, "and it won't surprise me if the Trinitarians of Drumaninch are the better of that to the tune of twenty thousand pounds."

"As much as that?" Hannah queried.

"More sherry, sir?" Martin asked the Doctor.

"I will, faith. It's very good."

Glasses were filled again.

"God knows where we're going," said the Doctor.

"There's no knowing," said Corney. "Bernard says it's anti-Christ, and Bernard's no more mad than you or I. Not mad at all, poor fellow."

Norrie smiled at Martin.

"Are you really going, you silly?" she asked.

He nodded.

"On the four o'clock, for the mailboat."

"So am I," said Angèle. "Do you think we'll get to France, Dr. O'Byrne?"

He smiled at her.

"Oh yes, you'll get there all right. We'll all be praying for you."

"To be sure we will," said Dotey. "God bless and preserve you both."

Silence fell, rather sadly, about Dotey's words. Martin smiled at Angèle. I'll be with her all the way, he was thinking. We'll be in Paris together.

Dr. O'Byrne lifted his glass.

"It's a sad day," he said. "But we must hope for better. *Vive la France éternelle!*"

"*Vive! Vive!*" said Martin.

They all lifted their glasses. Angèle tipped hers with Tom's, and saw that tears were pouring down his cheeks.

Croyle, Cullompton
  September, 1942

THE END

243

VIRAGO MODERN CLASSICS
&
CLASSIC NON-FICTION

The first Virago Modern Classic, *Frost in May* by Antonia White, was published in 1978. It launched a list dedicated to the celebration of women writers and to the rediscovery and reprinting of their works. Its aim was, and is, to demonstrate the existence of a female tradition in fiction, and to broaden the sometimes narrow definition of a 'classic' which has often led to the neglect of interesting novels and short stories. Published with new introductions by some of today's best writers, the books are chosen for many reasons: they may be great works of fiction; they may be wonderful period pieces; they may reveal particular aspects of women's lives; they may be classics of comedy or storytelling.

The companion series, Virago Classic Non-Fiction, includes diaries, letters, literary criticism, and biographies – often by and about authors published in the Virago Modern Classics.

'Good news for everyone writing and reading today' – *Hilary Mantel*

'A continuingly magnificent imprint' – *Joanna Trollope*

'The Virago Modern Classics have reshaped literary history and enriched the reading of us all. No library is complete without them' – *Margaret Drabble*

VIRAGO MODERN CLASSICS
&
CLASSIC NON-FICTION

Some of the authors included in these two series –

Elizabeth von Arnim, Dorothy Baker, Pat Barker, Nina Bawden,
Nicola Beauman, Sybille Bedford, Jane Bowles, Kay Boyle,
Vera Brittain, Leonora Carrington, Angela Carter, Willa Cather,
Colette, Ivy Compton-Burnett, E.M. Delafield, Maureen Duffy,
Elaine Dundy, Nell Dunn, Emily Eden, George Egerton,
George Eliot, Miles Franklin, Mrs Gaskell,
Charlotte Perkins Gilman, George Gissing,
Victoria Glendinning, Radclyffe Hall, Shirley Hazzard,
Dorothy Hewett, Mary Hocking, Alice Hoffman,
Winifred Holtby, Janette Turner Hospital, Zora Neale Hurston,
Elizabeth Jenkins, F. Tennyson Jesse, Molly Keane,
Margaret Laurence, Maura Laverty, Rosamond Lehmann,
Rose Macaulay, Shena Mackay, Olivia Manning, Paule Marshall,
F.M. Mayor, Anaïs Nin, Kate O'Brien, Olivia, Grace Paley,
Mollie Panter-Downes, Dawn Powell, Dorothy Richardson,
E. Arnot Robertson, Jacqueline Rose, Vita Sackville-West,
Elaine Showalter, May Sinclair, Agnes Smedley, Dodie Smith,
Stevie Smith, Nancy Spain, Christina Stead, Carolyn Steedman,
Gertrude Stein, Jan Struther, Han Suyin, Elizabeth Taylor,
Sylvia Townsend Warner, Mary Webb, Eudora Welty,
Mae West, Rebecca West, Edith Wharton, Antonia White,
Christa Wolf, Virginia Woolf, E.H. Young

Also by Kate O'Brien

THE LAND OF SPICES

Bright, sensitive Anna Murphy is the youngest-ever boarder at the Compagnie de la Sainte Famille and her poetic nature captivates Helen, the Mother Superior. No longer content with convent life, Helen recalls her happy childhood, her brilliant agnostic father – and the betrayal she met with a different, subtler treachery. She watches her young charge suffer her own family dramas, and her heart softens as Anna tastes the first fruits of experience. *The Land of Spices* is a luminous novel which explores the nature of love, forgiveness and destiny within the discipline and haunting beauty of an Irish convent.

'If novels can be music, then this is a novel with perfect pitch' *Clare Boylan*

Now you can order superb titles directly from Virago

☐	The Land of Spices	Kate O'Brien	£6.99
☐	The Ante-Room	Kate O'Brien	£6.99
☐	Mary Lavelle	Kate O'Brien	£6.99
☐	I Capture the Castle	Dodie Smith	£6.99
☐	Love	Elizabeth von Arnim	£6.99
☐	Kinflicks	Lisa Alther	£6.99
☐	The Bread and Butter Stories	Mary Norton	£6.99
☐	Novel on Yellow Paper	Stevie Smith	£6.99

Please allow for postage and packing: **Free UK delivery.**
Europe; add 25% of retail price; Rest of World; 45% of retail price.

To order any of the above or any other Virago titles, please call our
credit card orderline or fill in this coupon and send/fax it to:

Virago, 250 Western Avenue, London, W3 6XZ, UK.
Fax 0181 324 5678   Telephone 0181 324 5516

☐ I enclose a UK bank cheque made payable to Virago for £ ....
☐ Please charge £.............. to my Access, Visa, Delta, Switch Card No.

☐☐☐☐☐☐☐☐☐☐☐☐☐☐☐☐☐☐☐

Expiry Date ☐☐☐☐   Switch Issue No. ☐☐

NAME (Block letters please) ....

ADDRESS ....

....

....

Postcode ....Telephone ....

Signature ....

Please allow 28 days for delivery within the UK. Offer subject to price and availability.

Please do not send any further mailings from companies carefully selected by Virago ☐